THE GIRLS
IN THE
FIRE

BOOKS BY DEA POIRIER

DETECTIVE HARLOW DURANT SERIES

Find Me in the Dark

The Girls in the Fire

DEA POIRIER

THE GIRLS IN THE FIRE

bookouture

Published by Bookouture in 2022

An imprint of Storyfire Ltd.
Carmelite House
50 Victoria Embankment
London EC4Y 0DZ

www.bookouture.com

ISBN: 978-1-80314-237-1
eBook ISBN: 978-1-80314-236-4

This book is a work of fiction. Names, characters, businesses, organizations, places and events other than those clearly in the public domain, are either the product of the author's imagination or are used fictitiously. Any resemblance to actual persons, living or dead, events or locales is entirely coincidental.

For the light that finds us, even when we don't want to be found.

How do you convince someone you're not a killer? Even when there's evidence and motive, and all the signs point to no one but you? My last day in Plattsburgh, there was a lump in my throat and a tightening around my stomach. In front of me, the yellow tape shuddered in the wind, the markers of the crime scene creating a barrier outside of the station. The yellow cut across the parking lot and I questioned what side I should be on —across the tape, that's where law enforcement belonged, but did I belong there? Especially now. My eyes lost focus on the blood-red gash cutting through the snow. I forced myself to focus again on the boot prints marking the paths the team took as they surrounded the body, cataloging the evidence.

It took me too long to sift through it all in my mind, to try to answer questions I didn't have answers to. I left. He died after I'd already left the station—didn't he? I sat for an interview, talked about my last night in the station—everyone who'd been in the station that day had to. And somehow, Sergeant Dirby believed me. Everyone believed me.

In the early hours, when the world is quiet, I hear my father's voice. The echo of his past, the stories of his crimes, the things he's done call out to me. I've tried to leave them behind, his trail of destruction, the victims, the bones. But this trail of blood follows me wherever I go.

Yesterday my team all came back to the station in Monroe. It's been a week since Green died. And while I'd like to say that it feels good to be home, it doesn't feel like home yet.

When the sun burns on the horizon, the fiery glow coaxes me out into the world, though I haven't slept. Most of my team likes to rise later, to slip into the office after morning traffic has died down. I prefer the cold mornings, when the birds first awaken and the silence is thick. Before the press has emailed me, before the roads clog downtown, before the darkened gazes can follow me as I walk into the office. I'll take this solitude, the tranquility of this, anytime.

As I shuffle to the front door of the station, I've got my coffee tucked between my arm and my stomach, along with my jacket. My bag is slung awkwardly over my right shoulder as I struggle with the keys. In the state office, we don't have a receptionist or officers on duty twenty-four/seven, so when the last of us leave for the night this place is sealed up like a tomb. I'm usually the first one in, and it's comforting finding it like this. My shoulders are relaxed, there's no prickle of anxiety in the pit of my stomach. Here, alone, I can actually breathe.

Since we caught the Plattsburgh killer, I thought my standing within the team might improve, that maybe after what I did, the risks I took, I'd earn some respect from the other guys; but that hasn't happened. They still look away when I walk by, avoid speaking to me. But at the very least, I'm thankful I have my partner, Lucas. And even though Sergeant Dirby questioned whether or not I should have stayed on my last case, for now at least, he remains thoroughly on my side. Something tells me, though, my time may be limited; his kindness will only go so far, especially now that Officer Green is dead. It's only a matter of time until I'm a suspect in his death—given my father's history.

As I walk through the empty bullpen, the chill in the air nags at me. Though spring—or as much spring as you can call it in upstate New York—has hit, in the early mornings, it still manages to be cold enough for a jacket.

My phone dings with an email, and I check it out of habit. A new message waits for me, a familiar name flashing on the screen that cuts straight through me. Deirdre. My mother. I don't want to read the email, but I'm not strong enough to delete it and pretend I never saw it. Instead, I unlock my phone and scroll down the message, skimming it, as if the words will have less of an impact that way. It takes me a few seconds to piece it all together and get to the point of the long-winded text. She and my father are *worried* about me because of all the news coverage of my case in Plattsburgh. Apparently, they both saw me on the news, and she was able to find out my new name.

Frustration ripples through me. This isn't the first time that my mother has tracked me down. For the most part, I've been able to keep thousands of miles and many years between us. But every few years, she's able to finally close the distance. Now that she's found my name, I know it's only a matter of time before she shows up.

I throw my things on the back of my chair at my sparse desk. Everyone else has pictures, knickknacks on their desks, something that gives it a little personality. When I first started, I decided to get a couple succulents for my desk, hoping it'd add a little flair. But within three weeks, they were all dead. So, for now, my workspace is about as barren as my life; easy enough to pack everything up and run again—the thing I'm the most skilled at. Lucas has pictures of his dad, mother, and grandmother on his desk, along with a ridiculous portrait of his cat that someone painted to look like George Washington.

You're already in the office, aren't you? My phone dings with a text message from Lucas. A smile creeps across my lips as I scan the words, but I'd never admit to him that they made me grin. Somehow, this little text helps me shake off the frustration that had been building inside me after reading my mother's email.

You know it. I fire right back.

You need help. A LOT of it. His next text makes my phone vibrate against my fingertips.

Are you even out of bed? I ask as I take a sip of my coffee and laugh to myself.

The door to the bullpen flies open, and Lucas strolls in. He looks from his phone to me and flashes me a wicked grin. His dark brown hair is a little shaggy. He's letting it grow out. His grin tells me that he must have seen me pull into the station. "Ta-da, look who's up early today." He gestures to himself. He's got on an outfit that's a little too polished, which will make him stick out when the rest of the team is here. His button-up shirt is crisp, recently ironed, and his skinny jeans fit him in a way that makes me jealous to my absolute core. I'll never find jeans that fit me like that—the curse of being a tall woman.

I offer him exaggerated applause. It's not as if Lucas is typically late. He's actually annoyingly punctual. He, however, just doesn't get in as early as I do most days. So, he's turned it into somewhat of a competition between the two of us.

"Good for you," I say with a little laugh.

He throws his jacket down on the desk next to mine. Thankfully, we've got our stations side by side, so most of the time I can pretend that the rest of the officers on the New York State Crime Bureau team don't exist. It's an unhealthy coping mechanism, as my father would say. But he's not here, he's in prison, so I'll cling to whatever helps me get through the day.

"What have we got this morning?" he asks.

"I finished up getting the files over to the DA last night for the Plattsburgh case." There will be lingering things they'll need from us for months as they prep for trial. The case in Plattsburgh was my first serial killer, and Lucas's first homicide. Prior to that case, Lucas worked in missing persons.

He nods. "Did you check the tip line yet?"

I shake my head. The tip line is usually filled with idiots panicking that cars backfiring or fireworks are automatic gunfire, as if shootings are so common in these small towns. At this point, I let Lucas handle the tip line and I avoid it at all costs. But he doesn't seem to have noticed yet.

"Yesterday, there was another missing persons case that came in from Plattsburgh," he says.

I raise a brow to that. "Another one?" When we started the case in Plattsburgh, we got called out because a body had been found in the snow. It wasn't long before we found three bodies, and the hunt for the Plattsburgh Slayer began. While we were working the case though, it became quite clear that there was a problem with missing persons cases there, but Plattsburgh PD didn't take them seriously. Several of the missing women were connected to the serial killer we eventually caught, but there were at least five still open when we left.

Now, those cases have fallen on the missing persons department in the New York State Crime Bureau, and Lucas isn't happy. That was his old team, and it's driving him crazy that he can't be involved. He's stuck firmly in homicide with me. I'm not letting him go back.

"Any chance we're going to get dragged into the mess in McKenzie?" I ask. In the past few weeks, several bodies have been found by hikers in McKenzie Wilderness, a state park not far from Saranac Lake. All of the homicide team, save for Lucas and me, since we were working on another case, are on that case trying to track down the killer. I don't want to be involved because of the guy leading that team, but every time another body is found, I feel we're one step closer to being dragged into it.

He shakes his head. "As the black sheep of the team, I don't think they have any interest in pulling us into that investigation. Chad already has his claws in so deep, his DNA is all over that scene. There's no way he'd give our new *hotshot* homicide detective a chance to steal his spotlight."

I know that Lucas is talking about me, but I couldn't feel like any less of a *hotshot*. Most of the time I feel like I got lucky with my first serial killer case. Every single step of the way I was terrified I'd end up with more blood on my hands, that another woman would die because of me. The last thing that I want is to jump into that again right now. Who would have thought that blood would end up on my hands in a different way?

"If anyone tries to give me that spotlight, I'll leave town," I tell Lucas. And he of all people knows I'm not kidding. Not long ago, he learned about the darkest parts of my past, and he didn't flinch at any of them. Something I will never forget or stop feeling grateful for. He's the first person in my life who has truly stood beside me when they learned about my past.

"Don't you dare," he says, his words nearly a threat. "Could you make some coffee while I dig in to all of these calls?" He motions toward the phone, the light flashing rapidly, indicating how many messages have been piling up on the tip line.

I nod and shove up from the desk. I'd love nothing more than to make coffee to atone for my lack of attention toward the tip line. Now at least I can shrug off any of the guilt I've been feeling by offloading that work onto Lucas. The phone rings, the shrill sound cutting through the office. I hear the mumbling of Lucas answering the call.

As the pot gurgles, I fill two cups and head back to our desks with the dark liquid swirling. Lucas looks pale as I approach, his face wan in a way I don't normally see it. The phone is cradled between his shoulder and his ear as he listens to a someone on the other end. His eyes are far off, downcast toward the desk, but I know he's not seeing any of it. His expression looks far too haunted. I appraise him as I set the cup down gently, trying to catch his eye to glean some idea of what's happened. My heart pounds as I wait, the anticipation needling the back of my neck. Finally he looks up to me. He swallows hard, his gaze meeting mine after a moment that seems to stretch on for far too long.

"Yeah, we'll be there shortly," he says before hanging up the phone.

"What's wrong?" I finally ask when he doesn't speak.

"We just got a call from Saranac Lake PD. Someone found a body on fire on the outskirts of Saranac Lake," he says.

My mouth goes bone dry as I consider the implications. They could be wrong, it's possible. Maybe it's not a body, but some detritus that someone was trying to get rid of. But then again... with the things I've seen here, it's not impossible. If the last year taught me anything, it's that nothing is impossible.

"That's south of us, right?" I ask. The name of the city triggers something in the back of my mind. I'm not as a familiar with the state as Lucas since I grew up in Washington. I've heard the name of that city before, but where? That's when I realize Saranac Lake is where the rest of the team is.

He nods. "Yeah, about an hour depending on traffic," he explains.

"I'll call the sergeant to see who he wants to send out," I say. Because it's so close to Chad's case it may get added to his team. But something tells me they're too inundated. There aren't any other homicide detectives currently available. I grab my cellphone as my neck prickles. I wonder what we'll find beneath the flames.

2

TWENTY YEARS AGO

The thing about seeing your father murder someone is, it doesn't seem real. My brain feels like it left my body and someone stuck it inside a Jell-O mold. My thoughts are far away, like they're trapped inside some kind of sludge. I can't look away from the body, the woman slumped on the floor, the purple gash cutting across her windpipe. Her red satin robe flared around her on the floor, the fabric soft, delicate, forming a halo that looks like petals that have been plucked from a rose.

I could have stopped him. Or screamed. Or told someone. But I didn't. I let her die.

My feet are frozen as I stand among dying flowers in the flowerbed. Right outside the window. If a neighbor looked out to see me, I'd probably look like a peeping Tom. I could have been standing here for minutes, or hours, or days. Everything is so close and yet so far, like I'm viewing my life through a keyhole.

My mind is desperate to make sense of it all. To understand how or why my father could have done this. But he couldn't have. No. My father would never be able to kill anyone. I must have imagined it, maybe I'm dreaming. I look down at my feet, the tears pooling in my eyes making my vision fuzzy. I need to wake up. I have to wake up.

Suddenly, my thoughts collapse, and all at once it hits me. I look up again. My dad... where is he? Where did he go?

In my ears, my pulse rushes, warning me, tempting me to run. To get far away from here. This is dangerous, deadly. What am I risking by being here?

But my father would never hurt me—would he?

My throat is bone dry as I finally peel my gaze from the woman's body. The rest of the room is still dim, the soft glow of the orange bulb casting long shadows against the striped wallpaper. It's too dark for me to make out the colors, but I think it's gray or maybe blue.

The crunch of a boot on dead grass behind me makes my stomach clench and my guts turn to water. I'm going to vomit all over the window in front of me, the plants, my shoes. A hand brushes against my shoulder and I hiccup a sob. The tears come so fast and furious that I have no control over them whatsoever. My whole body shakes. I should have run; I should have gotten away from him while I had the chance. And now, he's going to kill me next. I know it.

He tugs at my shoulder, and I don't move because my body has turned into a statue, as if I just stared into Medusa's eyes, not my father's. He picks me up and pulls me into him. The warmth from his body bleeds into mine, and I realize for the first time how cold I am.

"You're shaking," he says, and he rocks me from side to side as he hugs me.

I try to say something, anything. But a strangled sob is all that squeaks out of me. My father holds me tighter, closer, squeezes me so hard that I feel like I could just dissolve. And after what I've seen, maybe that would be better. Because how do I go on after this? With this secret bottled up inside me. My father killed a woman. He *killed* her.

"Harley Jane, it's okay," he says, his words and his breath hitting my ear.

The weight of it all threatens to make me collapse, and I go limp in my father's arms. Just like that woman did. Another sob hits me. I've never felt like this, so completely out of control, not even when they fight and hit the walls so hard that I think they'll tear the whole house down. At least then, I know how it'll end—someone will storm off, someone will give in. Silence will follow. The calm after the storm.

He scoops me up and carries me like a baby to the van. With one hand, he manages to open the passenger side and slip me into the seat before carefully closing the door. I try to watch him walk in front of the van, toward the other side of the vehicle, but my eyes are so filled with tears it's like trying to make out shapes when I open my eyes underwater. His muddled form seems to shimmer in the night as he walks. He's a little more hunched than usual, his shoulders sagging. Does he feel the same weight on him that I do?

When he climbs in, he doesn't turn to me, he doesn't say anything. Instead, he starts the van, throws it into drive, and continues down the street like nothing happened. Once we're two blocks away, he turns on his lights, and the heat. This is one of the few times I don't mind the suffocating roar of the heating system in this shitbox. It's as if someone froze my bones. My teeth chatter, even after the prickle of cold is long gone.

My breaths are rapid, my heart still pounding, as we leave Tacoma proper. In the dark, I can't see the evergreens that I know should be streaming past us on the highway. The sky above us is inky black. The only thing I can see is the ten feet in front of us that the headlights illuminate, the yellow line splitting the lanes that get gobbled up by the darkness as we drive.

"Are you okay?" he finally asks as he turns off of the road and into the woods.

I only know the change because we're on a dirt road, a

logging path that probably extends far into the mountains. The van sways as he drives too quickly over divots and pot holes. Rocks skitter through the night all around us. This is the kind of road where you could kill someone and leave their body, and they'd probably never be found. A lump swells in my throat, and I try to talk, but I can't form words around it. Suddenly the chill is back, and my body shakes again.

You're next. He's going to kill you next, the rapid beats of my heart seem to say. The whole world narrows to this point, to the minutes I probably have left to live. All the things I'll never be able to do, all the things I'll never see flash before my eyes. Time slows, and I look to my dad, my eyes pleading. I don't want to die. But more than that, I don't want my dad to be a killer. Every second with him, every moment that I know what he's done, it breaks a splinter off of my heart. Even if he doesn't kill me, this knowledge will. The weight of it presses down on me. How did I not know?

"Are you... scared of me?" he finally asks, as he appraises me. His brows are low over his dark eyes as they flit across my face, searching for something, but I don't know what.

"You just killed someone," I finally manage to say. The words weren't easy to find, to bring to the surface. And I can't even imagine how I'll find more.

"No," he says, his words as sharp as a knife. They're so harsh they nearly slash at the air between us. His gaze is dangerous when it meets mine again. "I *saved* her, Harley Jane. I don't kill people. I save them."

My thoughts skid to a halt and I want nothing more than to slip out the window, out of the car, to vanish into the woods and never be seen again. Because *this*, this is not a safe place to be. My father, he's not in his right mind. I have never been more certain of anything in my entire life. There is something seriously wrong with him.

"You... saved her," I say, my words punctuated with my

disbelief. I'm careful with them though, because I know the danger inside the man next to me. I know what he's capable of.

"Yes," he says simply. And a strange smile slips across his lips, as if he is so happy that I've figured it all out. That I finally know his secret.

My mind reels. "Are you... going to save me?" I ask, my question catching on my fear. Tears burn my cheeks and I wedge my hands beneath my thighs to keep them from trembling.

His cheeks flash red and his eyes change, they're venomous. My body presses backward automatically, the curvature of the door slicing into my spine. But I don't flinch against it. I lean into the pain. Because for every inch, every millimeter that I'm closer to this door, the farther I am from him—and only a thin piece of metal away from freedom.

"I would *never* hurt you," he says.

His words confuse me. Because on some level he knows that he hurt that woman, that he killed her. Obviously. Since the idea of *saving* me makes him so angry. But how can he stay in denial of what he's doing? How can he kill people?

"You can't tell *anyone*," he says, his eyes meeting mine again. The anger is gone now, diffused like it was never there at all, as if I imagined it. His words, the way he says them, this is the way my father usually speaks to me, the voice that resonates in my mind when I think of him.

"And what if I do?" I say, my words almost taunting, though I don't mean for them to be. The way he's looking at me now, it helps unwind my fear.

"Then I'd go to prison and you'd never see me again. Is that what you want?" His words are so simple, so smooth, that the impact of them doesn't hit me until I dissect the words, pick them all apart one by one. Prison. Prison would mean that I'd be alone with my mother, forever. What would she do to me then?

A sickness spreads inside me along with guilt. I watched a

woman die today. Someone I didn't know. What if she had children, a family? What if she was actually a good mother with kids that will miss her? The world has one less life in it because of my father. And my mind whirs on that fact, churning with knowledge of all the other stories he's told me over the years. He's killed before. He has to have. As long as I can remember, he's told me about the women he's *saved*. I want to vomit, but I swallow it down.

I have two options here. I can be a good person; I can turn him in. I can save lives. Or, I can have my dad back. I can forget, pretend. Because if I don't, I'll be stuck with her. And her anger. It'll only grow if he's in prison.

"I won't tell anyone if you come back to live with us," I say.

I'll keep his secrets. For now.

3

After calling Sergeant Dirby, and telling him about info we've received from Saranac Lake, I've got twenty minutes to pack a bag and leave with Lucas for the scene. Well, technically there's no need to pack a bag at all. I can take the one I just brought back from Plattsburgh. Though most of the team is already there, they're so deep in an investigation that they're stretched thin. So, the sergeant wants us to work this new homicide.

Because I've fled so many times, moved with no warning, I can pack for extended periods on no notice. It may be my super-power. Twenty minutes is actually a luxury. I once left with a bag and moved out of state in five minutes. After I'm sure that I've got three weeks' worth of clothing packed up, and have shed some of the items I've worn too frequently in the past few weeks, I climb into my Jeep and text Lucas. His small bungalow is a five-minute drive from my place, and by the time I pull up, he's waiting outside for me, a bag hiked high on his shoulder, his posture askew to accommodate the weight. He's tapping on the window, saying goodbye to his cat.

The deep indigo bungalow looms behind him, the white trim really makes the shade pop. A maple stands in the center of the front yard, the leaves a deep green. His flowerbeds are currently barren, but even without them, the house is well kept and adorable. It amazes me when someone my age owns a home, because I cannot imagine putting down roots like that. To be tied down some place *forever*, I'm not sure I could do it.

He jogs down his front path toward my Jeep, flings his bag into the back, then climbs in. A quick swipe of his hand through his hair fixes the few strands that came out of place during his jog. He looks up, then back to me.

"Top off for the whole drive?" he asks, almost grimacing, as he motions toward the sky.

"You can brush your hair when we get there. I'm going to savor every minute of warmth before we get another cold front. Let me get in my fix," I say, my words a little harsher than they need to be. Today is warmer than it's been since I moved here, and I want to take advantage of it. The weather as the tail end of winter seeps into spring is so fickle here, or so I've heard.

"Fine," he says as he clicks his seat belt. "You don't have to be so bitchy about it."

"And you'll survive if your hair doesn't look perfect for an hour drive," I snap right back at him.

He rolls his eyes, but turns his head, as if I won't notice. I crank the stereo and drive down the street. In a few minutes, we turn onto the highway, well, what they like to call a highway in upstate New York, anyway. In reality, this road is two lanes with nothing but evergreen and pine trees, creating a barrier between the cars and the wilderness beyond. On either side of us, the trees climb up small hills, and sheer rock cliffs climb toward the sky. The longer we drive, the more the view of the road starts to hypnotize me. It reminds me of Washington, the paths I'd drive with my father next to him in his van, long before I knew he was a killer, long before he ruined everything.

When a large lake opens up to our right, Lucas warns me that we're nearly there. Cars are pulled off to the side, families splashing in the water. Though I'm sure it's still a bit chilly, this is the first bit of warmth we'll get for the year, so I understand why they're savoring it.

As we veer off the logging road toward the McKenzie Wilderness, I realize how close we must be to Chad and the rest of the team. At the end of the long dirt road, we find the forensics vans and Saranac Lake PD cars parked in a circle around the scene, yellow tape spiderwebbed between vehicles. A lone news van stands on the outskirts, two reporters chitchatting with one another, no longer filming. It's nearly noon, so they've likely already done their morning coverage and won't be on again until the afternoon. I point them out to Lucas and he nods.

Gravel crunches beneath my tires as I pull in alongside one of the forensics team vehicles. When I climb out, I squint against the high afternoon sun. I throw on my sunglasses and scan the faces of the officers who are swarming around the scene. Racquel is the only one I recognize, so I set my sights on her with Lucas at my side. As we approach, she offers us a wide smile.

"Hey, Durant," she says as she offers Lucas a little wave. "Lucas." Her black curly hair is shiny and flows past her shoulders. She's got a fine bone structure, sharp cheekbones, and warm brown skin.

"Afternoon. You got down here fast," I say.

"I was already in the area. There was another body found by a hiker this morning in the wilderness, so we came over from there. It's been a long day and it's only noon," she says as she sighs and wipes some sweat from her brow.

"What's the deal with those bodies? The MOs aren't similar?" I ask. I've wanted to get more details on the McKenzie Mauler while I've been in the office, but Chad is so damn territorial about the case that he won't talk about it. I'd swear that he pisses on all his crime scenes so that no one can steal them from him.

Her eyes darken for a moment. "No, they're not similar at all. Those bodies... they're incredibly mutilated. Someone has taken a knife to them so many times, it looks like an animal mauled them to death. The faces look like they're chewed off, the bodies so badly maimed that I'm not sure how they'll even identify these victims," she explains. "Some have their jaws destroyed and teeth removed, so DNA will likely be the only evidence." It's clear she's trying to remain composed; she grimaces slightly.

Though I know Racquel is an absolute professional who's been doing this for years, it's clear in her tone that seeing these scenes has gotten to her.

Homicide gets the best of us sometimes. There will always be some cases that manage to worm their way under our skin. At the end of the day, I think that's a good thing though. It shows that we're still human, that seeing all this carnage, the depravity, hasn't stolen that spark of humanity from us. The day I become numb to the death, that's the day I walk away.

"Are the victims male or female?" I ask.

"All have been female thus far," she explains.

That, unfortunately, isn't unusual when it comes to serial killers.

"Can we get into what we've found here... now?" she asks, and though she's being respectful, it's clear that she wants to move on from the topic of the McKenzie Mauler.

"Sure," I say.

Lucas glances to me and pulls a face. There's warning in it. He's a bit protective over Racquel. Clearly he's never seen Racquel react quite like this either. We follow her closer to the scene, dodging other forensics team members as they place markers and take pictures of the body.

"How long have you been processing this scene?" I ask.

"A couple hours," she says. "We're nearly done. The coroner is coming to retrieve the body to deliver it to Dr. Pagan pretty soon. They'll likely be pulling up any minute. You got here just in time."

As we walk closer to the body, the greasy smell of charred fat and meat fills the air. There's something acrid to it, like burned hair and chemicals. It's not something I've ever smelled before, and I can't say that I ever want to smell it again. Surrounded by the caution tape and markers, the vague shape of a human body remains. Blackened, scorched flesh twists atop the pockmarked dirt. Pieces of the body are so burned, they look like they're going to flake off; the darkest ashen bits threaten to be carried away by the wind. No humanity remains here. There's no hair, no unsinged flesh.

The scene chills me. This was a person. A woman, most likely. And someone burned her to death. A part of me hopes that she was already dead when the fire was set, that this was just an attempt to destroy evidence. And unfortunately, it will likely work. Once all the DNA is burned up like this, it'll be hard for us to identify who did this to her, or any evidence that lingered on her skin. What we need is evidence from other parts of the scene. Some may remain, but it'll be difficult for the team. This is where real police work comes in.

"Jesus, I've never seen anything like this," Lucas says as he crosses his arms and glances down at the body.

I nod. "Neither have I. There haven't been any other scenes like this around here, have there?" I ask Racquel. This seems a bit too ritualistic to be a first kill.

She shakes her head. "Like this? No. I don't think I've ever seen a body left in this condition before."

"Is there any reason to believe that this is linked to the other homicides in McKenzie?" I don't think it'd be too far of a leap to go from maiming bodies to burning them. But typically, killers change their MO for a reason. It's not random. And if they just found a body today in McKenzie with the usual MO, I don't see why this body would be connected. Why would this one be burned while the others were not?

"We don't have any reason to believe so. On this scene, we've got a boot print. We haven't found anything like that at other scenes."

"Any tire tracks?" I ask, looking down the dirt road. The ground here is loose, the type of material that would be great for holding on to tire tracks.

"There are a lot. This is a heavily used turnaround. It's unclear if they're related to the homicide. There are two sets of footprints that lead out here, and only one heading out. So they walked here together before our victim died," she explains.

"At any point did the footprints change?" I'm curious if the victim was dragged or forced here, or if they walked on their own.

She shakes her head. "Not that we've seen, no. It's pretty much the same all the way from the start of the logging road."

"Were the footprints side by side, or did it look like the killer was walking behind the victim?" Lucas asks.

"Side by side, that remained unchanged."

Our victim had to be comfortable with their killer, because otherwise they would not have walked all the way out here. There's nothing out here, no other destination they could have had. And if they were walking side by side, that also lends credibility to that theory. If the victim was forced to come out here at gunpoint, the killer would have likely been walking behind the victim, urging them forward the entire way.

"Any bullet casings?" This scene looks like the staging would have taken a while. There are no real signs of a struggle, so it seems like our perp had to take his victim down fast. That says gun to me.

"Not that we've found."

That's not to say there couldn't have been a casing picked

up by the killer. But again, meticulous, that speaks to experience. Not a first timer.

"Do we know if the victim was male or female?" I ask.

She shakes her head. "Not yet, no. We suspect the victim
was female based on the size of the footprints leading out here.
The other shoe prints were large enough that we suspect it was
a male and female walking out here," she explains as she pulls
up pictures of the shoeprints on her phone and shows them to
me. The larger prints are at least three to four inches longer
than the smaller prints. The toe of the print is the darkest,
which is odd. Typically, footprints are deepest on the heel and
they look as if the larger feet dragged a bit as they walked;
maybe our perp is older, or walks with a limp.

Behind us, two vehicles pull up, the coroner's van and a
squad car from my team. I glance at it, wondering if Sergeant
Dirby has decided to head out here to check out the scene. But
when I see ear-length dirty-blond hair, I clench my jaw and the
nerves in my neck tighten. It's not Dirby, it's fucking Chad. His
ice-blue eyes scan the scene, then come to rest on me and Lucas.
I sigh. I was really hoping that I could avoid running into him,
but that was obviously naive.

We finish up with Racquel after she promises to send the
boot prints off to the lab—maybe they're unique enough that we
can track them down. I cross the scene back to Chad, cutting
him off before he can storm over to us. He's fired up already, the
heat in his cheeks obvious against his normally pale skin. Even
with the scant light pouring down from the cloudy sky above us,
Chad's sharp cheekbones cast deep shadows across his face. His
mouth is a bit too wide for his face, and when he frowns at me—
like he's doing right now—it looks even bigger somehow.

"What the fuck are you doing here?" he snaps as he
approaches. His words don't surprise me. He's never shown me
even an iota of respect. In the office, I'm not a fellow officer. I
get treated worse than an intern.

"Investigating a homicide," I say as I motion toward the body. "Need me to explain better than that? I can go grab a crayon."

"Yeah, *my* homicide," he says as he stalks a little closer to me.

Lucas shifts, moving closer to my side, as if he will get between Chad and me if it comes down to it. I wonder if Lucas thinks I'll throw the first punch, because if that's what he thinks, he's absolutely correct.

"Your homicide? I didn't see your name on it. We took the call. Your team is busy with something else," I say, motioning to the forest that stretches on behind us, the tall pines swaying in a breeze that I can't feel. That's where he's been working his homicide case. He doesn't need another. "How many bodies do you have now?"

"This is my jurisdiction." He grinds the words out through gritted teeth. But he ignores my question.

"Fuck off, man," Lucas grumbles. "You have your own toys to play with."

"Actually, everything in this state is *our* jurisdiction. It's not all your sandbox, Chad. You can't stick your flag in it and claim it as yours. We're all here to help these victims," I say, a bit more barb to my words than there needs to be. But goddammit, I need to put this guy in his place or he's never going to get off my back.

"Bullshit, Durant, and you know it." He glances to Lucas, his finger jabbing the air. "Stay out of it, Lucas." His attention snaps back to me, and I have half a mind to punch him. "You're just trying to get more time in the spotlight. You want to swoop in and take all these cases from me so you can get more requests for interviews." The jealousy comes off of him in waves. I could bottle it.

"Yes, Chad. You've figured out my master plan. I'm hoping to help all of these homicide victims so I can get an interview with Oprah, so step aside and let me get to it." I roll my eyes.

He steps forward, his index finger extended. It hovers high, nearly in my face. I half expect him to poke me in the chest.

"You're going to regret getting in my way, Durant. I will end you," he says, the threat dripping on every single word.

But this guy doesn't scare me. I see worse people than him every goddamn day. Chad is probably just pissed off that his favorite polo had a wrinkle in it this morning.

"You can try, Chad. You can try," I say as I turn. "Oh, and Chad, get the fuck off of my crime scene." I wave him away with dismissal.

His face flushes even redder, even though I didn't think it was possible. A vein in his neck throbs as he surveys me, his fists clenching at his sides. But as quickly as his rage rises, it fizzles, and he turns and stalks back to his car.

Lucas glances to me. "Are you going to let me help with that situation?" he asks as he motions toward Chad's car.

I cross my arms, and clench my jaw. "No, I'm not. I can fight my own battles."

"You know, every battle is fought by an army. Not by one person. You *could* ask for help."

I know that he's trying to help me. That he has good intentions. But I don't know how to ask for help. More importantly, I don't know how to let someone help me. Because it might destroy me if I let someone in, and then they disappear too. I've lost every person I've loved. They've all let me down. They all abandoned me. And since then, since I was thirteen years old, I've been on my own. It's been so long that I'm not sure that I can change, or that I even want to.

"I appreciate the offer," I manage to say, which is still a big step for me. Most of the time, I'd tell anyone that offered to help me to fuck off. I've always had walls up, and the second that anyone tries to break them down, I scare them off. Because that's easier. Hurting myself is better than letting someone else hurt me. I'm content to make my own scars.

We leave the scene as the coroner hauls up the body of the victim into the transport. There's nothing else to be done here by us. The forensics team will be wrapping up shortly and moving on, so it's time for us to go. I load Lucas up in my Jeep and head into town. We grab some coffee, go to our motel rooms, and drop off our stuff. The room is small, but I like it better than the one that I was stuck in in Plattsburgh. Saranac Lake is more of a tourist town, and what I've seen so far reflects that. The downtown is quaint, with cute storefronts meant to lure people in. Several motels stand throughout the city. A few of them have been here since the 1800s when this was a haven for tuberculosis patients and socialites looking to escape Manhattan.

I leave Lucas, and wander the street outside of our motel, checking out a small coffee shop, a diner, and a bookstore. There are several restaurants in walking distance, along with a small family-owned pharmacy. As I walk toward the coffee shop, I notice a newspaper bin standing outside. The face of a man stares back at me beneath a headline, CROSWELL FORTUNE IN JEOPARDY. It's a local paper, with local problems, I guess, because I have no idea who the man is. Underneath, another headline catches my attention—LOCAL COP DEAD, POLICE INVESTIGATING POSSIBLE HOMICIDE. Though the heat presses against me, it's like ice has settled in my stomach.

It's only a matter of time until they knock on my door with more questions about Officer Green's death.

4

The afternoon sun is trying desperately to claw through the clouds as we pull into the parking lot of the ME's office, scant rays streaking through the slashes, casting glowing pods on the hills. It drizzled a few hours ago, leaving the air thick and the roads shiny. With our last case, each time we arrived here, the lot was nearly empty, the two-story brick building looking abandoned, forgotten; but now, we actually have to hunt for a free spot, like at a mall at Christmas. The number of killings in McKenzie must really be stretching the team thin. When I finally shut off my Jeep, Lucas surveys all the vehicles around us.

"Did they have to call in reinforcements or something?" he asks.

"They've had over ten bodies in McKenzie now. I'm sure they have. I can't imagine the amount of heat there must be on that case right now," I say. Not that I feel bad for Chad. Actually, I hope he gets nailed to a fucking wall because of this case. I know it's only a matter of time before the FBI ends up in town, trying to take this case from our department. I'm going to stay the hell out of all of it and hope that it doesn't bring any attention my way. I'm already getting emails with requests that I talk about my last case, but all of those get swiped straight into the trash.

We climb out of my car, and the wind whips at us as we walk toward the door. The way the air is shifting, I half expect that we'll end up with thunderstorms by the evening. There's static in the air, something wild. I throw the door open and nod to the receptionist, and though I show my badge out of habit, I don't need to. She remembers us. After all, we just saw her a week ago.

"Dr. Pagan will come grab you in a few minutes," she says.

The reception area is hospital white, the tiles too. It's so bright in here, it's like staring straight at the snow as the sun reflects off it. Around the edges of the room, long forgotten plastic chairs sit, their seats freckled with dust. I don't think anyone has actually sat in them in years. Law enforcement doesn't typically make it a habit to spend much time here. A strange scent lingers in the air, the acridity from the smoke this morning, I think. My nostrils curl each time I smell it in the air. It's like a BBQ gone bad.

The clicking of heels on the tile floor alerts me to Dr. Pagan's approach. She makes it to the doorway separating the hall from the reception area, and waves us back. She's got on her usual crisp white lab coat, a slim smile, and a few new highlights in her dark curly hair.

"Good to see you again," she says as we walk back to the morgue together.

"You too," I say.

"How's everything going here?" Lucas asks as we approach the door to the morgue.

She shoves the door open and waves us inside, the chill in the air hitting us immediately. "It has been so busy lately. With the serial killer in McKenzie Wilderness, I'm not sure I'm ever going to be able to get any sleep again. We've been poring over what's left of these victims, and they're in such bad shape, DNA is really our only option. And you know how that goes," she says as she shakes her head.

While DNA is one of those things that's incredibly helpful in law enforcement, the key to it is having something to match against. DNA on its own isn't of any use if there's no comparative sample. We may be able to get some details on someone's ancestral background or general details, but we won't get their identity without matching it to someone. Online ancestry DNA databases are helping, giving us something to go on, finding some familial matches. But unless those continue to expand steadily, some victims may never be identified.

"Have you been able to take a look at this new victim yet? I know how busy you must be," I say.

"Unfortunately, not me personally, no. I have had some of the junior examiners go over the body to get us some initial details. But it will be a few days before I have the time to dig in myself. I'm sorry I don't have the body out on the table," she says, motioning to the empty metal table. "But the remains have quite the stench, and for now, I prefer to keep them sealed up unless it's absolutely necessary."

"I understand." Honestly, I don't have any desire to look at the remains again right now.

She grabs a clipboard that has several sheets of paper on it. On the top sheet, there's a diagram of the human body, front and back, with notes indicating wounds, concerns, and overall condition. She glances over the first sheet, then flips to the next two pages before looking back to us.

"Some initial points from my team: This victim was female. Though we will not be able to determine age without much further analysis. Dental records will show the victim was over the age of eighteen, we suspect, given the back teeth present. But all of her front teeth had been removed, so we will not be able to match dental records," she explains.

"Removed?" I ask. "Are you sure they weren't burned up?" This is the first time I've encountered this in a case.

She shakes her head. "No, bone and teeth do not burn. Those will always remain. There's no way all of the teeth would be destroyed during the process." She motions toward her mouth as she speaks. "Even in cremation, while tissue is destroyed, the bones will remain. Here, we have a partial cremation, essentially. A lot of the body was damaged by fire, however, it was not enough to completely irradicate all the tissue. We can still pull DNA from the remaining tissue."

"Were the teeth pulled or broken?" This could go one of two ways. If a killer broke the victim's teeth as the result of blunt force trauma, that wouldn't surprise me. But if this perp extracted the teeth—maybe to have a trophy—that makes this killing incredibly ritualistic.

"They were removed. If the teeth had broken, fragments or pieces of the root structure would remain. That's not the case. They were not broken at all, which leads me to believe the teeth were extracted after her death."

So our suspect is an arsonist and a freelance dentist. A sick feeling swims in my belly, but I push past it.

"Was she set on fire prior to her death?" Lucas asks, as he makes notes on his phone.

"We will need to open her up and look at her lungs to determine that. Also, based on what we see from the fat distribution on this body, we believe that either this victim had a mastectomy or that the killer removed her breasts before her death," she explains.

My mouth goes dry. I hope she was already dead before she was mutilated. The perp possibly removed this woman's breasts? But I can't let this trip me up. The fact that the other bodies in McKenzie were also mutilated to some degree makes me wonder about our killer or killers. Could this be an extension of the homicides happening in the wilderness? A copycat maybe? Not all the details of the brutality of the crimes in McKenzie have been released to the press. Typically, in law enforcement, we have holdback information that we keep from the media. This helps us identify the real perps from someone just coming in off the street trying to get attention or information out of us. It also helps in these cases of possible copycats. I don't want to draw attention to that fact yet and force our way into Chad's investigation. I want to be absolutely sure before I mention this to the sergeant.

"Was there any other damage to the body?" Lucas asks.

"There are acute fractures to the face, the skull, and the ribs. It looks like the victim was badly beaten before their death. Most of the trauma was focused on the face and the chest."

"Are you certain that the teeth were removed, then she was beaten, killed, and mutilated—in that order?" I ask. I'm trying to piece together the timeline before death. There's no way that our suspect would have had time to extract teeth, remove breasts, mutilate, beat, and torture this victim on a busy logging road without being spotted. So how did this all play out? How were there two sets of footprints leading out there? Are we looking for two suspects?

"For now, that is where the evidence is pointing, yes."

"In your opinion, does it appear that the same killer acting in McKenzie Wilderness could be responsible for this victim as well?" The other bodies were maimed, their faces destroyed, that's what Racquel said.

"There is a lot of knife work, stabbing, puncture wounds on the bodies in McKenzie. In many cases it looks like an animal mauled the victim. That's what we thought at first, that they were victims of a bear attack, maybe a wolf. Then we found puncture wounds that had to be from a knife." She's quiet for a moment, contemplative. "There's more blunt force trauma on this victim, no knife wounds thus far. I'd say this victim was struck repeatedly with a hammer, possibly a rock. The only knife work I see is the possibility of the breasts being removed. To me, it seems like different methods of killing."

Her expertise makes me feel better about this case falling on Lucas and me. It seems less likely this'll end up in the hands of Chad. Or that we'll end up having to work together.

"You've already collected the DNA and submitted it to the database?" Lucas asks as he tucks his hands in his pockets.

"We're getting it submitted this afternoon. If we get any hits, we'll be in touch. But it usually takes at least forty-eight hours to see any results," she explains. "It could be longer though since we're a bit behind right now."

"Thank you," I say.

We finish up with Dr. Pagan and head out of the ME's office. I wish that we had more to go on, more details about this body, the crime scene. We've got a good start with the boot and shoe prints, but we need more. And whatever it takes, I'll find it.

5

Lucas and I drive lazy loops through Saranac Lake trying to familiarize ourselves with our surroundings. The town isn't much different than Plattsburgh, Morrisonville, and Malone. As if all the small towns follow the same blueprints. The main streets of downtown are lined with small shops, bars, restaurants. Some fast-food restaurants have infiltrated the outskirts, a chicken place that always has a line, a Starbucks, Burger King. They're the kind of businesses that I wouldn't expect to flourish here, but they're still standing, fighting for business. The houses are quaint, some Victorians, Dutch colonials, farmhouses, bungalows. Most are at least a hundred years old.

On the outskirts, about ten minutes from the town center, that's where the affluent in Saranac Lake live. They've all got views of the water, because obviously, that's what the rich are after. Their boats bob in a small marina, all spotless, looking as if they've never left the dock. Log cabins, modern homes, and sprawling Victorians spread all around it, creating a cloistered circle of wealth.

We pull into a diner, the parking lot filled with older cars. Mag's Diner is a small blue building with a white roof and trim.

The front has a large porch, making it clear that the building used to be a home that was converted into a restaurant. The porch groans as we approach the front door, its age showing with every step that we take.

Inside, we find more tables than I'd expect for them to be able to fit into the space. They've clearly knocked down walls, opened the space up. A brick bar stretches along the right-hand side, with rough pine barstools lining up like soldiers along it. An older woman with a poof of white hair stands behind the bar and waves to us as we enter.

"Hey, y'all," she says with a deep southern drawl. My time in Texas tells me it's her real accent, not something she's putting on for show.

"Afternoon," I say. "Can we sit anywhere?" I motion to all the empty tables, each stacked with sugar packets, ketchup, and syrup.

"Yup, anywhere you like. There's seating on the porch too, if you'd like to enjoy the weather," she offers.

I turn to Lucas. "Want to sit at the bar?" I ask.

He shakes his head. "Nope, there's an upstairs porch that faces the lake. Let's sit there." He points toward the stairs.

"Upstairs it is," I say.

She grabs a couple menus and hands them over. "Go find any table that you like. I'll send my granddaughter up to you."

"Thank you," I say as I grab the menus and head toward the stairs.

Lucas and I climb up and follow signs through the old house to the porch. On the porch, we find several other patrons sitting, drinking coffee, and eating a late breakfast. They're all chatting as we walk out, but the moment they see us, their voices fall to hushed whispers. We're new in town, clearly, and that's drawn all their attention. In a town this small, no one misses out on details like that.

At the far end of the porch, we find an empty table and take a seat. Once we've plopped down, the conversations start again, their attention turning back to their food. I look over the menu, surveying my options, until a teenage girl approaches our table to take our orders.

"What can I get you?" She glances between the two of us as she holds a little notebook.

"I'll take the pancakes with extra bacon." I point to the menu as I speak.

She nods. "Good choice. And you?" she asks as she looks to Lucas.

"Turkey club sandwich with fries, please," he says.

Her brow furrows, and she steps closer. "You sure? The fried egg sandwich is much better," she offers with a wink.

He appraises the menu again. "Okay, fine. You talked me into it." He laughs.

She smiles, apparently pleased, and disappears with our menus. A few minutes later she reappears with drinks for us, and I look out over the lake. Behind us, several older women are gossiping about the town, and I can't help but listen.

"I don't know, Veronica. I heard that Jacob Croswell has been trying for years to put Baron Fowler out of business. He stole his contracts in China, and then he stole his wife. We saw them together last week! Jacob just cannot leave the Fowlers alone."

"Oh come on, Ruth, you don't believe that. They might have been out talking business. Just because we saw Jacob and Vivica together for ten minutes does not mean they're up to something. You can't assume that."

"You know as well as I do that Vivica has no business talking business, if you know what I mean," Veronica says, a bit of disdain in her voice.

"Okay, you have a point. She may not be able to run a business, but we'll see if she can make another husband disappear. I bet you that within a month, Baron Fowler will be gone, and no one will have the slightest idea where he might have gotten off to."

Both of the women cackle together. I might have to keep an eye on the local gossip while I'm here. It sounds like there are some interesting things going on in this town.

"Did you see that new cop skulking around town, the one with the blond hair?" she asks.

"The pretty boy that looks like he's from California?"

From the conversation, I know they're talking about Chad, but Lucas scoffs.

"Chad, a pretty boy?" he grumbles.

"Are you mad that you're not the pretty boy?" I tease him.

He rolls his eyes but doesn't answer. I reach across the table to pat his hand.

"He may be pretty," the woman says, "but I'll tell you, he's up to something."

6

TWENTY YEARS AGO

In the passenger seat, I've got my arms crossed firmly over my chest. My father is driving through the thickening night, his swollen hands gripping the steering wheel too tight. The headlights make the evergreen trees on either side of the car flicker as the light hits them, and then in only a second they're devoured again by the night. It reminds me of an old movie, the way the picture would cut in and out, so unstable you weren't sure if it'd shut off completely, if it'd stop.

"Are you still mad?" my father asks, his voice low, but I can still hear it over the roar of the wind against the car.

"I'm not going to not be mad until you make good on our deal," I say, my words sharp. I told him very clearly that I would keep his secrets, that I wouldn't tell anyone what I saw him do, that I saw him kill—but only if he moves back in with me and my mother.

"Harley Jane, it's going to take time. Your mother didn't want me in that house anymore. I'm going to have to convince her to let me come back. I can't do that overnight," he says. There's an edge to his voice. He doesn't want to do this. He doesn't want to live in a house again with my mother and me. A knife twists in my heart, as if it wasn't damaged enough already when he left the first time. Neither of them want me.

He doesn't want me. He would have been happy to abandon me and slip into his new life like I never existed. But I tell myself I don't care. I just want my dad back, even if he doesn't want me back.

"Well, then you better get started now. If you aren't back in the house with me and Mom within a week, I'm going to the cops." My voice is surprisingly firm, holding a threat I'm not sure I can actually bring myself to follow through with. Because I know what'll happen if I turn him in. Then I'll be stuck with my mom, forever. There's a huge risk to me too if I turn him in.

"A week? I need at least a month. Probably more like three." His voice is unsteady, tenuous in a way that I'm not sure I've heard before. My dad has always been strong, sure of himself, sure of what he's saying. Seeing this side takes me aback.

"Three months? No way. One month max," I snap right back.

"Two," he fires back at me.

"Fine, deal," I say. I hold my hand out to shake his.

My dad's large hand wraps around mine and he shakes it. When we pull back up to my mother's house, my heart sinks. It was so easy to promise two months when this seemed far away. But now that I think about possibly having to spend sixty days alone with her, a sickness spreads through me.

"Can I please just stay with you?" I ask as I look at the house.

He squeezes my shoulder gently. "I have a studio apartment, kiddo. There isn't anywhere for you to sleep."

"Not even on the couch?" I'm nearly pleading. I don't want to go back in there with my mother. I think I'd rather die right here in this van.

"I don't have a couch," he says uneasily.

"Then what do you have?" I pry. I can't imagine my dad living in an empty apartment. He must have done something.

"An air mattress. That's what I've been sleeping on since I started sleeping near the office. For a while, I just slept in my office on the couch. Then when I realized the situation was going to be more permanent, I got the apartment."

"Why don't you have a real bed?" I ask.

He sighs. "It's hard to explain."

"Then try," I demand. He doesn't get to psychoanalyze me all the time and then not give me the barest details of his other life.

"I guess all this time I was hoping that your mother would want me around. That she'd want me to come back, but it became clear that it wasn't the case." He sighs. "So, I kept putting off buying real furniture."

"But she's constantly yelling that she's mad that you're never home, that you abandoned us..."

"That's what she says in the house. But when I'm gone, she calls to tell me that she's happier when I'm not there. That you both are better off without me." He doesn't look at me while he speaks, instead his eyes are on the house. The lights are all off, and I wonder if my mother has even noticed my absence—I doubt it. I've only been gone about five hours. She probably went to bed after my dad left and didn't even bother to check my room.

"Come on, let's get you back in there," he says as he pops his door open.

I nod, though my body is paralyzed, practically frozen to the seat. My dad grabs my backpack from the back of the van and then opens the door for me. I force myself out of the car, my legs unsteady, my body too rigid. His hand meets the small of my back and he urges me forward. It's the only thing that keeps me moving.

Finally, he slips the key into the front door and opens it

slowly. He ushers me inside and follows closely behind me. We shuffle silently through the foyer, toward the hallway. As we pass the living room, the light clicks on, bathing my mother in an orange glow where she sits in an armchair. Beside her, on an ornately carved wooden table, she's got a bottle of whiskey in a crystal decanter and a glass that's half empty. Her eyes are dark, venomous, as she glowers at the two of us, her gaze narrowing on the backpack slung over his shoulder.

"What the fuck are you two doing?" she asks, her words rounded in a way I never hear them. I wish I could slip away without her seeing me, that I could collapse in on myself right here and disappear completely.

"I just... took the kid to get some ice cream," my dad stammers behind me. He inches closer to me, as if he expects my mother to lunge at me or maybe both of us.

"You took her to get ice cream at one in the morning? Do you think I'm an idiot?" She hurls the words at him like daggers. Beside me, I see him flinch.

"Well, we got ice cream and then we got to talking. She was telling me about school, you know. We had a lot to catch up on."

"You never were a good liar," she says smoothly, her eyes falling on me, as if she expects me to back up his story. But I stay silent. If I say a single word, she will smell the lie on me before the words even leave my mouth.

"I just want to go to bed," I say as I stalk toward my room. But my dad grabs me, and hands me the backpack. I want to run to my room, so I can unpack it and hide the evidence before my mom can figure anything out.

"Good night, kiddo," he says as he offers me one last hug.

"Two months," I warn him as I look up to him, and squirm out of the hug. Hugs aren't what I need. Closeness isn't what I need. I need him to protect me from *her*.

"I know," he says smoothly.

As I escape down the hall, I see my dad disappear into the

living room. Their voices are low, but I think I hear him ask my mom if they can talk. I slip into my room, pull the clothes out of my backpack and shove them back into my dresser, then I hide the backpack, hoping that my mother is too drunk to remember that she ever saw it at all.

I climb into bed, the covers feeling too cold against my flesh. Something about it feels off, wrong. Like it's not the bed that I left here. But nothing changed in the few hours I was gone. I know it's all in my head. I squish my pillow, hoping to find a comfortable position. The darkness thickens around me as I wait for it to take me, for me to slip into sleep. But instead, I listen to the echo of my heartbeat, my reminder that one day, it'll stop. Panic grips me, and I think of the woman, who only hours ago I watched die.

My door cracks open, and I look up, hoping to see my father. But it's not his face I find. It's my mother. She shuts the door behind her and takes a step closer to the bed.

"You think that you're just so smart," she says as she stalks toward my bed.

I sit up, and scoot backward on my bed until my back hits the wall. Though there's no space, I'd squeeze myself between the wall and the bed if I could, to hide from her. But even with her as drunk as she is, she wouldn't forget that she saw me here.

"No, I don't," I stammer. Even though I'm nearly thirteen, when she talks to me like this, I feel like I'm still five years old, helpless. As if I can't fight for myself. Something about my mother does that to me, it unhinges me. Maybe because she's never done anything but make me feel helpless.

"Yes, clearly you do. You and your father think that you're so smart and I am so stupid. Because you both think you can lie to me all you want and I'll never figure it out." She lets out a sad little laugh, one that sounds too sharp. "You tried to run away." Her voice is deadpan, flat. Even in the darkness, I can feel her staring through me, not at me.

"No..." I start, but my words fall flat. Is there even any point in lying to her? She's not going to hate me any more than she already does. It's not as if this is going to be the nail in the coffin of our relationship.

"Yes, you did. You tried to run away. You thought that your father wanted you. But I think that you learned a valuable lesson today. That your father doesn't want you. No one wants you. You are lucky that I let you live here and take up space." A sick smile slithers across her lips and she takes another step closer to me. "You should be grateful that I feed you, and clothe you, that I let you have a bedroom, that I let you do anything."

"I didn't—" I start to say. And though I don't want them to, her words cut deep. Because she's right. My father didn't want me either. At least she let me stay. He turned me away the second that he saw me there. He brought me right back *to her*, knowing that he was sending me into a lion's den.

"Stop lying to me, Harley."

"I'm sorry," I manage to say. It's all I can say. There aren't any other words. Or if there are, I can't find them. I can't sift through all of the thoughts in my head to pull out the words that are necessary.

"Of course you are. And you should be. You are ungrateful. But you'll learn. I'll teach you." Her words scare me. They make me want to melt into the wall, to run away and try to live in the woods. I'm not sure I can make it two months alone with this woman. She may actually kill me.

7

It's been four days since we found the charred remains at the end of the logging road. Since then, the whispers in the town about the possible victim, the circumstances surrounding her death, and who could have killed her have grown to a roar. Eyes watch us as we move through the town, and I can feel them waiting for us to find the killer. Tension fills the streets, as if we're reaching a tipping point. Lucas and I have canvassed the town, searching, listening. But thus far, nothing has helped us track down who this woman might have been. My gut tells me that maybe she isn't a resident of this town—because by now, surely someone would have noticed that she was missing.

We pull into the small police station, a three-story stone building overlooking the river. The station is in the middle of the town, on the main thoroughfare, so every car must pass by it at least four times a day. I've been surprised that the team in Saranac Lake is rather large for the population, with a chief, three sergeants, and ten officers. For a town of this size, I'd expect half that or a little less. Maybe it's because this is more of a tourist town. However, they have been a bit more welcoming than Plattsburgh was during our last case, but it's not as if they've rolled out the red carpet. There is one thing that seems to be pervasive across law enforcement, and that's being incredibly territorial. Teams don't like working with one another, they don't like sharing information, and they don't want their cases taken.

On the first floor of the police station when we walk in, we find a waiting room and the receptionist. I nod to her as we head back to the staircase. On the second floor is where the main offices for the sergeants and chief, the bullpen, and the interrogation rooms are. The basement houses the cells, and the third floor, that's where they keep a few conference rooms and a few extra offices that haven't been housed yet. If you ask me, it looks more like storage, packed with stacked desks, chairs, and boxes of files. I'm surprised that Chad's team has been using it in this state. He's a bit of a diva about absolutely everything, so I'm shocked he hasn't demanded better. Lucas and I stalk to the back of the room, a bit winded from climbing the stairs all the way up here—that's the one shitty thing about some of these old buildings, no elevators. I throw my things on my desk, and plop down in my chair before taking a swig of my coffee.

"We still don't have anything new from the ME," I say as I open up my laptop and start to scan over the case notes. I've got at least fifteen contacts in here, people I've talked to in the town, asking if they've noticed anyone missing, anything strange going on. All I ever get is gossip about the Fowler and Croswell families. Someone is cheating on someone else, someone is after nothing but money, someone got cut out of the will. I can't keep up with it all. There was one mention of a creepy new guy who had been lurking around town, but thus far I haven't heard that corroborated and I haven't seen him anywhere.

"So far, the boot print isn't giving us much to go on. It appears to be a men's steel-toe work boot that's very common for loggers out here to have, a men's size ten," I say. These details also don't give us much to go on; it's not as if I can look up all the men in this town who wear a size ten work boot. And that'd be assuming our killer is from Saranac Lake—he may not be. Many killers, especially ones this ritualistic, can hunt in places miles from home, making them harder to catch. As it is, thirty percent of homicides go unsolved and if our killer didn't know his victim, the statistics get much worse.

"What about the woman's shoe size?" he asks.

"Size seven. She was also wearing boots. Though, the smooth sole tells us they were more for fashion than for function," I explain.

My phone vibrates with an incoming call. It's not a number that I recognize, but I pick it up anyway.

"Durant?" the unsteady voice asks as soon as I answer.

"Yes," I say simply.

"This is Officer Moody, from Saranac Lake PD. We had a missing persons report come in this morning. Since it could be related to the body that was found, I wanted to go ahead and let you know about it. Ashley Gordon called and reported her daughter Ellie missing," he says.

I'd asked that they call me should an MP report come in, but after some of the bad experiences I've had with other departments, I can't say that I actually expected them to contact me. I figured I'd have to slog through the database myself, so this is a pleasant surprise.

"Can you email the report over to me? I'd like to talk to the family to see if it lines up with what we have on this victim. We have little to go on, but at least this is a lead to match DNA against," I explain.

"Of course, I'll email that to you right now," he says. He sounds a little bit excited that he gets to be involved in this process.

"Thanks, Moody," I say before ending the call.

I turn to Lucas and let him know about what Moody told me on the call. This could be our first real lead in this case. And even if it doesn't pan out, at least it feels like we've got a little movement so far. Days of *nothing* really makes you feel like you're losing what it takes to be a homicide detective, like maybe the last case was a fluke or I got lucky.

"Where are we headed?" he asks, as I pull up the missing persons report on my phone.

"Looks like they live on the north side of town. We should head over there. Apparently, the mother was very panicked when she called this morning. She said this is completely out of character for her daughter. So even if there isn't foul play, there must be something going on," I explain.

He nods and pulls on his jacket. "Let's go."

After we climb back into my Jeep, we drive through the city, over the cracked streets, past the small businesses downtown, and head north, where the hills start to swell. Though I expect the streets to be filled with more trees here, like they were up in Plattsburgh, most of the neighborhoods are pretty sparse, with green lawns and only squat trees. I wonder if it's purposeful, or if they have a hard time growing large trees in town.

On the corner of Elm Street, we find a red-brick ranch with green shutters and a yellow picket fence. A large black pickup truck sits in the driveway, and an American flag flaps in the wind next to the garage. I pull my Jeep up along front of the house and climb out. A few streets away a dog barks over and over. The neighborhood is eerily still, no wind, no movement. We walk toward the front door and, when we reach it, Lucas knocks. It takes only seconds for a woman to open the door. Her eyes are raw, wild, as she opens it and surveys us.

"You the cops?" she asks.

I nod. "Yes, you spoke to Officer Moody, I believe," I say.

She opens her screen door and waves us inside the house. The front foyer is filled with family pictures. A shoe-covered bench sits beside a staircase. Several coats are thrown over the banister. The woman leads us into the kitchen, and gestures for us to take a seat at a round dining table. She plops down in front of us, as I grab my notebook from my jacket and lay it on the table in front of me.

"How are you holding up, Ms. Gordon?" I ask.

"Well, my daughter is missing. So, I would say that I've been better," she snaps at me. But I don't hold it against her. I can't imagine what it must feel like to have a child go missing. "I've been over to her apartment at least twelve times, and she's not answering."

"I'm so sorry about that, but I'm hoping that we can help you track her down."

"You both investigate missing persons?" she asks as she glances between the two of us. "I've never seen either of you in town."

"That's been my focus for years, actually," Lucas says. And I'm glad that he jumped in, because it wouldn't be best for us to let her know that we mainly work homicides. If we brought that up right now, I can only imagine how that would go over. "We're both from the state team. The local team lacks expertise in missing persons, so we can offer more help there."

"So, let's get to it. The sooner that we get these details, the sooner we can help you find Ellie. When is the last time that you saw her?" I ask.

"Six days ago," she says. "Maybe seven."

"How old is Ellie?" Lucas asks.

Ashley wrinkles her nose in frustration. I'm sure she didn't have to give this kind of information to the Saranac Lake team because they know who her daughter is. "She's twenty-six." Her words are laced with venom.

"Does she live here with you?" I ask.

"No, she has her own apartment downtown. She lives over the bookstore," she says, and then gives us the address. We note it down. "I was actually hoping that you could go to her apartment to check on her. I've tried, but she doesn't answer. And I don't have a key."

That seems odd to me that her mother wouldn't have a key to her place. I write that down as well. Usually in homicide investigations, family members and people close to the victim are investigated first, because most victims know their killers. It's incredibly rare to be murdered by a complete stranger, especially in a town like this. "We'll check her apartment to do a wellness check."

"So, do you normally go stretches of six to seven days without hearing from your daughter?" Lucas asks. He's got his notebook out in front of him as well, and he's taking detailed notes. I can see his stick-straight handwriting on the paper.

She shakes her head. "No, that was unusual for her. But we'd had a fight before she disappeared, so I assumed that she was mad at me. That she was giving me the silent treatment, it wouldn't be the first time. But I've called probably four hundred times, and at this point, she would have normally at least answered to tell me to leave her alone." She sniffles and wipes her nose as she speaks.

They had a fight before her disappearance? That's a bit of a red flag. "What was your fight about?" I ask.

"I think that it's time that she gets married. She's in her mid-twenties. She can't keep dating around forever. She needs to settle down and get started on having babies or she'll never do it. She's too focused on her career, on what she could do with her life rather than building a family. It makes me so sad to see her live so selfishly," she says as she crosses her arms.

I raise my brow to that. If she thinks that Ellie is too old because she hasn't had children in her mid-twenties, then I must have a uterus that's made of dust. I'm well past my prime according to women like this. I'm nearly in my mid-thirties and never wanted to keep anyone around for longer than a few months at a time. In her eyes, I'm a waste of space, I guess. But I wouldn't have it any other way. I hate the viewpoint that women are only valuable for what comes out of their body. If you don't breed, your life is worthless. What a crock of shit.

"Did Ellie have a boyfriend or was she dating?" I ask, not wanting to get into an argument with this woman over her incredibly antiquated views.

"She dated on and off, all the time, actually. But I think she was more interested in sleeping around then she was actually making a man stick." There's a disgust to her words that nags at me. This woman clearly did not like her daughter's choices. And this level of disdain makes me wonder what a woman like this is capable of, what lengths she would have gone to to change the way her daughter lived. I'm going to dig into her background.

"Do you have any names of the men that she was dating?" Lucas asks.

"You could throw a handful of pennies from a roof downtown and hit at least one man she dated. You could ask them all. I'm sure they've spent some time with my daughter." She sneers as she speaks.

"Did Ellie have any bad breakups or trouble with any of these men?" I try to glaze over her comments, but they each stick out to me and make my blood boil. I tighten my fist around my pen as I try to swallow down my frustration.

She offers a little shrug. "There were so many it was difficult to keep track of them. It's not like I could keep them straight. I'm sure there were at least a few that she had problems with."

This woman is so flippant, it absolutely enrages me. I don't understand how she can dismiss her daughter so entirely like this. Even if she disagrees with Ellie's choices, that's still her daughter.

"Did she ever mention to you that she was concerned about anyone or that she was scared?" Lucas picks up the questioning, as I'm sure I have an edge to my voice. I want to rip into this woman, to tell her to stop judging her daughter. She's missing, she's not on trial for how she lived before all this. I hate when victims are put on trial, as if living your life is a crime. Nothing Ellie did means she earned her fate.

"No, not really. Not that I remember." She shakes her head. "If something happened to her, I know that it's all her fault because of how she was living. It just makes me sick that if she was being a good girl, if she had gotten married and settled down, she wouldn't be missing right now."

"It's a little early to jump to conclusions. As you said, you two had an argument. Maybe she's not missing at all but she's still avoiding you because she's harboring some resentment from the argument that you two had," Lucas offers. He's so much better at this than I am. If I keep going, I'll end up giving this woman a piece of my mind. I won't get anywhere or help solve anything. I know I'll end up with Sergeant Dirby breathing down my neck because I let my temper get the best of me. It wouldn't be the first time.

She nods tersely.

"What was Ellie's typical schedule like?" Lucas asks.

"She worked at the bookstore that she lived above. She and the woman who owns it are best friends. So most of the time—unless she was on a date—she was there," she says pointedly.

I grind my teeth at her dig about Ellie dating.

"Do you have any good pictures of Ellie that we can use for social media posts or media outreach to let people know that she's missing?" Lucas follows up as he takes notes. "Have you posted anything online about her disappearance?"

"No, I haven't." She gives Lucas the information for Ellie's social media where the images can be found. I bring up the accounts on my phone so that I can save them for later. When I glance at the first account, it's clear why Ms. Gordon is so on edge about her daughter. Ellie was incredibly attractive, with bright green eyes, and long black hair. She was thin, with ample curves that she shows off on her social media pages. I can only imagine Ashley's reaction to seeing these images that her daughter posted. We'll have to crop a few of them, but they should help with media outreach. The news loves nothing more than to plaster a pretty face all over their airtime.

We collect DNA from Ms. Gordon to put into the database, just in case, though she seems very cagey about the entire ordeal.

"Did your daughter ever mention any stalking from social media?" I ask as I scroll through the accounts. She had lots of followers, and given what we just went through with social media stalking leading to murder in Plattsburgh, it's fresh in my mind.

"She never talked to me about her social media. So, I don't know. I'd suggest that you ask Raven, the owner of the bookstore. She would know more about my daughter than I do," she explains.

"Did your daughter have any identifying marks? Scars, tattoos, birthmarks?"

She sighs. "They already asked me all this. It's in the report. Did you read it?"

"Yes, ma'am, we did," Lucas says coolly, even though we haven't received it.

"We read the report, but we want to ensure that no information was missed. No matter how small it is, sometimes those little details help," I explain. Last year I dealt with a lot of details going missing in missing persons cases, and I want to be sure none of that is going on here.

"Oh!" she says, like she missed something. "She always wore a gold crucifix, if that helps. It had blue sapphires in it and silver ivy that curved around it."

I nod. "We'll look for the necklace. If you can think of anything else though that might help our investigation, please give us a call. We'll let you know how it goes looking through her apartment later today," I explain.

"Thank you, officers," she says, though her words don't hold an ounce of sincerity. I don't know if this woman is just on edge because her daughter is missing or if this is her usual demeanor.

Lucas and I finish up with Ms. Gordon, get her permission to enter Ellie's apartment if necessary and grab evidence there, then climb into my Jeep. We need to talk to Ellie's best friend and see if we can find anything else out about Ashley and her daughter.

8

We drive across town to the small bookstore. On the main street, sandwiched between a pharmacy and an antique store, we find the shop where Ellie lived and worked. It's a three-story building, like many of the others on the street. The ground floor has a brick façade, while the two upper stories have buttery yellow siding. White frame windows with maroon shutters overlook the busy street. As we approach, through the plate glass windows, I can see shelves stacked with books running all the way to the back of the shop. The name is etched on a wooden sign hanging over the door: A PARLOR OF PAGES.

The door chimes as we walk inside. The air is thick with the fragrance of books, coffee, and chocolate. Along the back wall of the bookshop, they've got a little coffee area and a pastry case filled with what look like French pastries and cupcakes. A short woman with a blue pixie cut, light brown skin, and a rockabilly dress waves at us as we come through the front door. She's got tattooed sleeves up and down her arms and across the parts of her chest I can see from the cut of the dress.

"Good morning," she calls as she approaches. "You two are new in town," she says, her words almost a question. I wonder if she greets everyone who comes into the shop this way, or if we are getting special treatment because we're outsiders.

I nod, and explain that we're detectives working with Saranac Lake PD. Her eyes go wide, and she glances between us, disbelief swimming in her large eyes.

"You're Raven?" Lucas asks, and she nods in response.

"We were actually hoping that we could speak with you about Ellie," I say.

Her narrow brows furrow as she takes a step closer. There are a few patrons at the back of the store, sipping coffee and chatting. I'm sure she doesn't want them overhearing our conversation as she lowers her voice. "Ellie?"

"Is there somewhere a little more quiet that we could talk?" I ask.

She nods. "Of course, my office is back here," she says as she leads us through the shop, down a narrow hall, and to the left into a small room.

The walls in here are bathed in a rich royal purple. Along the back wall she's got several bookshelves that are painted gold, stacked with books of all shapes and sizes. Some look more modern, while others have soft leather bindings and embossed gold letters along the spines. She offers us both a seat in velvet claw-foot chairs that sit in front of her antique desk. Everything in this room, from the peacock drapes to the taxidermy butterflies on the walls, has the same eccentricity that this woman does.

"Okay, so what about Ellie?" she asks, nearly breathless.

"Ashley, Ellie's mother, called us and placed a missing persons report for Ellie. She said that no one has seen her in a week. So, we are here to ask if you've heard from her and to do a wellness check on her apartment. We understand that she lives upstairs?"

Raven's mouth hangs open with surprise as she glances between the two of us with disbelief.

"She's missing?"

"When is the last time that you heard from Ellie?" I ask.

"A little over a week ago." She grabs her phone and glances at the screen. "She last texted me on April 8th. She and her mom got into a fight and she asked if she could take a little time off. I told her that was no problem at all and I could handle things here," she says.

I note down the date. That means Ellie's been missing nine days. "Is it unusual for you two not to talk for this length of time?" Lucas asks as he pulls out his notebook.

She nods. "A bit, yes. But it was a pretty bad fight, and she told me that she needed a little time to think about everything that happened. I sent her a text yesterday to check in, but she didn't answer. It concerned me a little, but it wasn't something that I thought would end with the police showing up here, to be perfectly honest."

"So you don't have any reason to believe that she's missing?" I ask.

She shakes her head. "No, not at all. I mean, I don't really watch her apartment to see if she's coming and going. But I assume that she's up there right now."

"Do you mind if we go check on her? We may have a few more questions for you after," I explain. Our next steps will depend on what, exactly, we find in that apartment and whether or not she's in there.

"No, of course, go check."

"Do you have a key to the apartment?" I ask.

"Yes, I have a backup key," she says as she opens her desk drawer and begins to rummage around inside.

"If she doesn't answer, as the owner of this building, do you give us permission to enter the premises to check on her?" I ask. It's very important that we get permission from the owner of the property, otherwise, if in a worst-case scenario there's evidence in there, it could be thrown out in a trial. We can't afford for something like that to happen, so we've got to do this by the book. We already got permission from her mother, which should cover us—but I want to be sure that there's no doubt left here, especially since it seems that Ellie and her mother didn't have the best relationship.

"Absolutely." She hands over the key. She's tense, obviously nervous. But that doesn't stick out to me. If they were friends or even work acquaintances, she should be at least a little concerned, nervous about whether or not we would find her friend.

She shows us the staircase that leads up from the back of the store to the apartments. It's not accessible from inside the store. We have to step outside to get into it. There are two apartments above the bookstore, each with its own floor. Ellie's apartment is at the very top. We climb the worn wooden stairs until we reach Ellie's apartment. Lucas knocks on the door, and we wait, listening intently for movement inside. Nothing.

Lucas tries again, and again. We spend nearly ten minutes outside of the apartment trying to get Ellie's attention. But to no avail. We try her cellphone number next, but it goes to voicemail.

"Ellie, this is the police. If you don't answer, we're going to enter the premises to ensure that you're okay," I warn loudly through the door as I fish the key from my pocket. We give her two more minutes of repeated warnings before I slip the key into the lock and turn it. The door slides open easily, and I step inside. The air smells clean, though slightly stale. At least I know there's no dead body waiting for us inside. If she'd been dead for a week, it'd already stink to high heaven in here. We'd probably be able to smell it through the door. That, at least, is a relief. The last thing that I wanted to find here was a dead body.

All of the lights in the apartment are off, but light still streams in from the windows, illuminating the open space that the kitchen and the living room share. The living room is filled with bookshelves. They're all white, and the books inside are arranged in alphabetical order. A large blue rug covers most of the wood floor in the living room. A white couch and silver coffee table adorn the room. To the left, there's a large bedroom and bathroom. A queen-sized bed stretches across the bedroom, a few pieces of clothes strewn atop it. Inside the apartment, at a surface level, there are no signs of struggle. I check her jewelry box for the cross necklace that her mother mentioned, and don't find it hanging inside with all of the others. If Ellie always wore it, like her mother indicated, then she's likely wearing it right now.

"No body at least," Lucas says as he walks into the bathroom and peeks inside.

I stalk through the bedroom, check the closet. She's got luggage that's stashed in the back corner. No large clumps of clothes are missing from the racks. It doesn't look like she left, or that she went anywhere. So, if she's not dead, there was no struggle, and she didn't leave—then where is Ellie?

From the desk in her bedroom, I grab her laptop. It occurs to me to check the closet for Ellie's shoe size. I look over several pairs before I find one that doesn't have the size rubbed off.

"Her shoe size was ten," I shout to Lucas.

"So, she wasn't on the logging road."

"Doesn't seem so," I say.

But that brings the question back around. If Ellie isn't our victim, then who is?

9

When we make it back into the bookshop, Raven is waiting for us, her arms crossed, jaw locked. Her eyes go wide when she sees us, and she walks quickly over to me. Sweat beads on her brow and her upper lip, and she looks like she's close to tears.

"So?" she asks as she approaches, her voice higher than it was before.

I shake my head. "She wasn't up there. We grabbed her laptop so that we can take a look and see if there are any clues there. Can we go back into your office?" I ask, motioning toward the hallway.

"Of course," she says as she starts walking toward the room, and we trail after her.

Once inside, I shut the door, take out my notebook, and take a seat.

"So, we didn't find her or any signs of a struggle," I say, and Raven lets out an immediate sigh of relief. "And there wasn't any evidence that she left town either. Her luggage is still there, her clothes, toothbrush. It doesn't look like she went anywhere in a hurry. She left her computer behind—so that leaves us with a couple scenarios. Ellie is staying somewhere else, she skipped

town without her things, or... something happened to her." I
don't elaborate on what the *something* could be. While the body
we found doesn't seem to be Ellie, there are all the other deaths
in McKenzie. "Is there anywhere that you know of where Ellie
might be staying, somewhere she might go to decompress after
the fight with her mother? Is her father around, maybe other
family members?"

"Her father died a few years ago from a heart attack. If it
wasn't for the fight, in a situation like this I'd always assume
she'd stay with her mother—or me. But I don't know why she'd
stay somewhere else in town. No one bothers her in her apartment or anything. That should be seclusion enough," she
explains.

"Well, her mother did say that she stopped by a few times to
knock on the door to try to talk with Ellie. Would that have
scared her off?" Lucas asks.

"I don't think so. She had no problems at all ignoring her
mother when she needed to," she explains, folding her arms
atop her desk. Her fingers are knotted together tightly, before
she unwinds them to pick at her nail polish.

"What kind of relationship did Ellie have with her mother?"
I ask, as I take down a couple notes. I already have an idea, but I
want more details to flesh out my view.

"Um, not great," she says, before swallowing hard. "Her
mom was always on her case about something. She wouldn't
back off and let Ellie live her life. No job she took was good
enough, because she didn't have a man. No one she dated was
good enough, because she hadn't married them yet. It was like
no matter what she did, she couldn't win. It was really exhausting; I don't know how Ellie put up with it." There's frustration
hanging on her words, like it really bothers her that she
witnessed all this from Ashley or heard about it from Ellie
firsthand.

"Do you think her mother would ever be capable of hurting

her?" I ask, paying close attention to Raven's body language. Family and significant others are always where we start our searches, and when a relationship is contentious like this, we have to take a closer look.

She gives me a one-shouldered shrug. "Honestly, I don't know. There is something about her that's... off. So maybe? But I've never witnessed anything personally that makes me think that she'd hurt Ellie."

"Do you know anyone that might have wanted to hurt Ellie?" I jot down a few notes about the mother. I'm definitely going to take a hard look at her.

"No," she says a little too quickly, then crosses her arms. Her brow furrows. "Actually, we did have another employee, Grover—I had to fire him. He was following Ellie around while she was in the store, making comments to her that were absolutely not work appropriate. Then he started doing the same to other women shopping in the store." She shakes her head as she sighs.

"Did his contact with Ellie cease after he was fired?" I ask.

She sits a little straighter in her chair. "Unfortunately, no. There were a few times that he was waiting outside, staring through the door. Then a few times I had to warn him off when he came inside and was lurking, watching her and other customers."

"How often did this happen?" I write down Grover's name and a few notes about why we need to speak with him.

"It happened pretty frequently right after he was fired in February, then it got less frequent," she explains.

That timeline concerns me. "When in February was this?"

"Mid-month? Around the fifteenth or so I think," she says.

"Ellie's mother mentioned that Ellie dated quite a bit. Is that true?" Lucas asks, as he crosses his legs and props his notebook atop them.

"I mean, I'd say she dated a normal amount. She used to

date more, but she'd stopped recently since her mother had
become so obsessive about it. Anytime her mother saw her out
in the town with a man, she'd start asking questions about when
they were getting married, even if it was only their first date,"
she explains as she rolls her eyes.

"Do you remember anyone in particular who she'd seen
recently?" I ask.

She shakes her head. "No one that comes to mind, no."

"When did you see her last?" I ask.

Her nose wrinkles as she looks off into the distance. "About
a week ago? I can't remember the exact day."

"Did Ellie do any drugs?" Lucas asks.

She coughs out a laugh. "Oh God no."

"Had she changed her routine recently or mentioned any
concerns to you other than the fight with her mother?" Lucas
continues.

"No, I don't think so. She had mentioned a couple times
that she was thinking about finally moving on from the town.
She wanted to get away from her mother, stretch her legs a little
bit. But she wouldn't just pick up and leave without telling
anyone, especially not without taking any of her things or her
car. That's not like her at all. If nothing else, Ellie was a plan-
ner. She was one of those, like, annoyingly organized list people.
If she had really been planning on this, she would have talked
my ear off about it for months."

"So you don't think she was serious about moving on? You
think she was just talking about it?"

She nods. "That's the thing. If it were something that she
had really set out to do, something that she was really
committed to, she would have made one of her pro-con lists and
brought it to me to take a look at. She hadn't gotten to that
phase, so I don't think it was a serious plan."

"What kind of car did Ellie drive?" I ask.

"She had a Jeep Cherokee. It's parked out back. That's one

of the other reasons I wasn't very concerned about her silence. Her car is still there."

"Do you have a key to that?" I ask, though I know it's unlikely.

"No, I'm sorry. I don't."

"Is there anything else you can think of that might be of help to our investigation?" Lucas asks.

"I don't think so. There's nothing else I can think of. I'm just really worried about her. Especially after that body was found last week. You don't think that was her, do you?" she asks.

"We don't have any reason to believe that was her yet," I say. Though the timelines do match, thus far, I can't connect Ellie to that location, or even piece together how she would have gotten out there or why someone would have set her on fire. And then there's the matter of the shoe size.

She nods. "Okay, well at least that's good to hear. Can I keep trying to call her?" she asks.

"Of course, and obviously if you hear anything back from her, please let us know as soon as possible. Hopefully this is all one big misunderstanding and we'll track her down soon," Lucas says. His words are so smooth it's clear that he's probably said this exact phrase at least a thousand times. The ease at which he works on these missing persons cases makes me a bit envious. None of this has ever come easy to me. I still feel like an imposter, like any second someone is going to figure out that I have no idea what I'm doing.

We wrap up with Raven and pass along our business cards to her before walking toward the back door.

"Oh, detectives, one more thing," she says poking her head out of her office door.

I turn back to see her. "While you were up in Ellie's apartment, I saw a news van circling the street. They might be looking for you if you want to go ahead and talk to them about

Ellie's going missing," she says as she points toward the front windows.

"Thank you," I say. I have no plans whatsoever to reach out to the media here, not yet. The sergeant will likely put out a press release and a short video for the media to circulate about Ellie Gordon's disappearance. I will be staying firmly out of the spotlight on this if I can. If the sergeant doesn't do it, then the Saranac Lake PD will.

We head through the back door to the parking lot where Ellie's vehicle is parked. It stands at the back of the lot, clearly unmoved in a while. A thick coat of pollen has formed a film over the windshield and the hood of the car. A New York plate is bolted to the front of the car, and I glance at it as we approach. I check the front windshield and find nothing in the car but dust. No parking tickets, no notes, no signs that anyone has been near this vehicle in a while. Next, I check the handles, each of them covered in the film of pollen as well. No one has even tried to enter it.

"Can we dust off the windows and peek inside, or is this part of the crime scene?" Lucas asks me.

I shrug. "That's weird territory, because technically there's no crime yet. She's just missing. So I think we can dust it off without worrying." The only way this would become part of a crime scene is if we find her body in the back.

I haul up my sleeve, wipe the window off, and glance into the passenger seat. She's got a few pieces of discarded mail, sunglasses, and some hand sanitizer in her passenger seat. Several cellphone chargers snake their way across the console and tangle themselves on the floor. From where I stand, there's nothing on the floor that I can see. I try the handle, but it's sealed up tight and won't open. Locked. I move to the back seat, wiping the window off there as well, all the while Lucas does the same on his side.

A news van pulls up to the far edge of the parking lot. The

screeching of the tires warns me of the approach. Have they already found my car and used that to follow us here? I can't figure out any other way they could have tracked us. Do they know Officer Green is dead? Have they connected it to me?

"Let's get moving," I say, not wanting them to link us to Ellie's car quite yet; for them to try and connect the dots when it's released that she's missing. Lucas nods and follows me back to my Jeep. As we climb in, my cellphone rings. Sergeant Dirby's name flashes on the screen and I accept the call. The sergeant has stayed back in Malone while we work on the case here. He needs to be available to the entire team. But I can't imagine he'll stick there for long with all the homicides that are happening in Saranac Lake. I'm surprised that with Chad having a serial killer with such a high body count he wasn't here weeks ago. But that's not my call or my business.

"Hey, Sergeant," I say as I accept the call.

"Where are we with this missing woman? And that body?" he asks.

I give him the updates—or I guess lack of updates—on both. I hate not being able to give him better news. In fact, it makes a pit of discomfort swell inside me. But at the end of the day, I can't change reality, and I won't lie to him. So all I can do is stand behind the police work that we've done so far, and hope that it's good enough for him. Of all the bosses I've had, Sergeant Dirby is one of the better ones. I've had some superiors before who were like working with loaded weapons. They'd go off all the time, unexpectedly. Hair triggers, most of them. Dirby is a bit more rational and even tempered.

"We need more on both fronts. Ellie's mother has the ear of the mayor and she's already firing him up about all this. She's pissed that we don't know where her daughter is," he explains.

"She just reported her missing *this morning*," I emphasize. "Less than two hours ago. What exactly does she think we can accomplish in two hours?" My words are a little harsher than I mean for them to be, but this is ridiculous. Involving the mayor after less than twenty-four hours? She can't be serious.

"She was going off about how her daughter has been missing for a week—"

"Because she didn't report her missing for a week," I fire back at him.

"Look, I know, I know," he says, clearly trying to diffuse me. "It's a tough spot to be in. She made her choices. But we've got to do whatever we can."

"We are doing whatever we can. Right now, it looks like her daughter might be avoiding her, hiding from her. There's no evidence that anything happened to her. She didn't skip town. We've got to follow up on a few more things and check her computer, but this might just be a mother-daughter spat," I explain. There's no reason for me to connect the dots to homicide quite yet.

"Let's wrap it up quickly. There's enough heat on Saranac as it is. The mayor is going crazy with everything that's going on. We need to get out of his town and seal this all up tight. He's afraid that this is going to affect the tourist season for the winter months if we don't close these cases," he explains.

"We've got images of Ellie for social media. Can you start circulating some posts that she's missing?"

He clears his throat. "Yeah, I'll get someone on it."

It's always about the economy, hurting the image of the town. It's never about saving more lives or protecting citizens. It's interesting what politicians prioritize over human life. But I don't say any of that to Sergeant Dirby. He knows as well as I do. He's been doing this for a very long time.

"Are you alone?" he asks.

I glance to Lucas and he raises a brow in response from my passenger seat. "Should I be?"

"No, I guess it's fine. I just wanted to let you know that Sheriff Crowley reviewed security footage from the night of

Officer Green's death and saw you leave very close to Green's estimated time of death."

My heart pounds. "Are you asking if—"

"No." He cuts me off. "Just giving you a heads-up. Take care of yourself, Durant," he says before ending the call.

I look up. Beside my Jeep several media vans have pulled in. Two women stalk closer, microphones in their hands. They're comically large, like cartoon drawings. One of the women slams her palm on my driver's-side window.

"Harlow Durant, can we please ask you a few questions about your investigation here? Are you working on the case in McKenzie Wilderness?" she asks, shouting through the glass.

"Just drive. We need to get the hell away from them before more of them show up," Lucas says.

I'm surprised there are already so many reporters in Saranac Lake. The media doesn't usually have much coverage in small towns like this, but I guess they were already lingering because of the McKenzie Mauler, as they've begun calling the killer. Right now, the killer in McKenzie is the most active serial killer in the entire nation, and we're knocking on his doorstep investigating this new crime. In the shadow of this tragedy, I want nothing more than to move unseen, but as I glance to the hungry eyes of the reporter outside my car, I know that'll be impossible.

10

HIM

There was a comfort to being in the woods. Something that made him feel at home. As if he slipped off his human skin entirely and became the predator he truly was inside. The night and the trees enveloped him, a cool breeze rustling the leaves. Though his footsteps cut through the night, the buzzing of insects and the pulse of the night covered his tracks.

He liked being out here, the challenge of remaining hidden. Though there were many reasons to come to Saranac Lake, one in particular was what drew him in.

His path through the woods was long. At the very edge, still concealed by the spindly branches of the evergreens, he waited in the shadows. The excitement of it all made his heart pound. He loved this chase, the challenge, anticipating where she'd be.

A Jeep pulled into the parking lot a few minutes later. He knew the vehicle well, and seeing it here made his heart hiccup. The door opened, and a woman slid out. She was tall, curvy, with long chestnut hair. In the dark her locks looked almost black, but he knew in the light, when the sun caught it just right, the strands sparkled with hints of copper and gold. She glanced up at the motel. It had too much of a lodge vibe for him. But instead of walking toward it, she turned, her eyes sweeping the trees as if she could see him.

"Harlow," he whispered under his breath.

11

Even though I'm carving my way through the city a little too quickly in my Jeep, my focus on the road, I can see Lucas looking at me out of the corner of my eye. I glance at him several times, but he says nothing. Beneath the surface, I can see all the words he wants to say simmering. I wish he'd just get it over with.

"What?" I finally snap.

"We should get some coffee," he says, his gaze cutting away from me as he scans the businesses for a coffee shop. "How about that one?" He points to a small coffee shop off of Elm Street.

That's not what I expected him to say. I wonder if he over-heard Sergeant Dirby. I shake it off. I'm probably reading too much into things. I pull into a lot a block away, scanning the parking lot and the street behind us for the media vans before I climb out. I'm sure they'll follow us. They'll find us eventually, but hopefully we can have a few minutes of peace before they figure out where we've gone.

It surprises me how many residents are always on the streets downtown in Saranac Lake. Shoppers stroll up and down the main streets, ducking into the small businesses. If this isn't tourist time, I'm curious how busy it gets when they roll into town.

The bell on the wooden door dings as we walk inside the coffee shop. Though I expect the inside to be a bit dated or old world, that's not what we find. Instead, the inside is modern, sleek. The back wall is painted with chalkboard paint, an intricate menu hand drawn on it. The counter is covered in contemporary tile work that's white, black, and teal. A sparkly teal countertop stretches the full width of the back of the room, marking the separation of the territory for the baristas from the areas for the patrons.

Around us, small tables with ornately tiled tops are scattered. There's lots of space in between each table, and I can imagine it filled with patrons clicking away on their laptops. But for now, the shop is empty except for a teenage barista smacking her gums behind the counter. We approach, and she looks between the two of us, her arms crossed.

"Can we get two lattes, please?" I ask.

"What kind?" she asks sarcastically, as she raises an eyebrow, her eyes sweeping over me from head to toe.

"What options do you have?" I ask. The menu isn't specific.

She points to a pyramid of bottles with many different flavors written on the labels. "Those over there."

So customer service is not the strong suit of this place. I lean over the counter a little to get a better look at the bottles. Then finally I see the flavor that I want.

I glance to Lucas. "Caramel?" That's typically his favorite.

He nods.

"Two caramel lattes," I say.

She rolls her eyes and begins to make us the lattes. Lucas pushes me out of the way with his credit card brandished and pays, then waves me over to a table close to the front window. I don't like the seat, as I feel like a fish in an aquarium. Anyone on the street can look in and see us. But I'm not going to argue with him about it. For now, at least, no one has followed us.

"Don't worry, this will let us see if the media tries to sneak up on us again," he says as he motions toward the windows and the door. To his credit, he's right. We do have a great view of the street and we'd see them roll up.

I nod. "Good thinking."

The barista comes over, drops off the two coffee cups for us, and then pops her AirPods back in her ears before disappearing to the back of the counter again. That's the last time we'll see her, I'm sure.

"So, now that you have your coffee," he says, motioning for me to take a drink, which I do. "What the hell is wrong with you? You're moodier than a bear with a mouthful of bees."

I want to roll my eyes at him, but he's right. Though I don't mean to be, I'm still prickly about this case, the media, Green's body being found, everything, I guess. It's all getting to me. Maybe I didn't have enough time to recover after the last case. Usually I'm not the type to be so affected by things. Typically I can let this stuff all roll off my back and keep going like it's nothing. But this time, it seems everything is getting its claws into me and there's not much that I can do about it.

"I'm sorry," I say. Another rarity for me. That's one thing I've learned in law enforcement that's become a bad habit: no apologies. If you fuck up, you keep moving, you don't look back, you don't dwell. But with a partner, I've got to do things a little differently. "The media focus is getting to me. It's hard for me being in the spotlight because I know it's only a matter of time before they blow my cover, before my whole life collapses again." I keep my voice low as I explain.

"I know. But you can't let it affect you so much. You'll end up becoming one of those neurotic cops that has high blood pressure and ends up croaking by forty."

I take a sip of my coffee and I have to admit that it helps.

Instead of amping me up, it helps calm me, helps me regain my focus.

A couple locals file in, the bell jingling, warning us of their arrival. Behind them, the breeze slips in, bringing in the scent of rain and car exhaust. The two women are deep in conversation and don't even look in our direction.

"The search party is meeting up this afternoon at two," one of the women says.

"I still can't believe Ellie's missing, and with all that mess in McKenzie... What the hell is happening to our town? You don't think that she—"

The women approach the counter and their convo dies down. I turn my attention back to Lucas.

"But I can't really help how it gets to me. It just... happens. This isn't normal for me. Maybe it's Chad getting to me because he's so protective of his case and I'm afraid he's going to try to take this one from us," I say.

"Chad has too much on his plate already. Dirby won't let him take this case. He can't even solve the one that he's got. He has zero leads. He's literally waiting it out until his killer goes berserker mode and ends up making a mistake so big that he's caught. There's no real police work or strategy there. Don't get concerned about what he's doing until he does it," he says. He's right. That's how most serial killers end up getting caught. But it could be years before this killer slips up enough.

I nod, though that's much easier said than done. I can't take a step back, and not prepare for what could happen.

"What will you do if the media starts asking you questions about my father?" I ask, because that's my next biggest concern. And chances are, that's what will happen. It's only a matter of time before the media gets on both of our cases about my father. I've learned every time that I can only hide for so long, eventually my past always catches up with me—it's like trying to run from my shadow.

"I'll tell them that I think he's a great guy, but things just didn't work out between us," he says with a little smirk. "No matter how hard he tried, he just wasn't my type."

I smack him in the arm. "Be serious."

He wipes the smile off his face in half a second. "Honestly, I'll tell them that your family history is none of my business and not something that I concern myself with. You're a good detective. You help people. That's what matters, not your past."

That's easy for him to say. But I've been told my whole life that my father's legacy will be woven into the fabric of my life no matter what I do. And so far, that's been right. I can't get away from his history, I can't separate myself from it. Because no matter what he did, it is a part of me. A thread of his choices is braided into everything I do, and every choice that I make. In Plattsburgh, I thought I was capable of becoming him. It would have been so easy to kill the suspect who was in my custody, to get justice for the victims with my own hands, and I contemplated it. I could have done it and saved everyone so much trouble, a trial. But I didn't do it.

Now, I ask myself if I didn't do it because I knew better, or because I didn't have enough opportunity. If I were alone, if I'd had enough time—I would have done it. I would have killed him. I'm pretty sure about that. Guilt nags at me, and my blood boils, as if my father's tainted blood is rising to the surface. His voice whispers in my mind, how many I could save with one simple act. It would be so easy. I grit my teeth. No, I'm better than that. If I killed, that wouldn't make me any better than those I bring in. I'm not Dexter.

"You should go to therapy," Lucas says when I've been quiet for too long. Then he winces. I guess he's connected the dots between what he said and my life.

My father was a psychiatrist, and that's how he picked his victims. If he'd worked in a hospital, he'd have been called an angel of mercy killer. He thought that he was putting his victims out of their misery because there was no mental health treatment for them. He saw these patients as beyond help and didn't think there was anything else to be done. This was how he could save them. From themselves or from the world, I'm still not sure. But that's how he rationalized the killings to himself anyway. That's what he told the court, the jury.

I wanted to believe him. From what I saw as a child, I do think that he believed this—or that he talked himself into believing it at some point. But though he told the court that he didn't see it as killing—he saw it as saving—there were signs to me that he knew exactly what he was doing. My father was one of the most prolific serial killers of the '90s. He was able to get away with what he was doing because he changed his MO constantly. How he killed his victims was based on their circumstances, not on a ritual like most other killers. It's a topic that's been studied for years. It's constantly popping up in the media again and again. And that's why no matter how many times I run, or change my name, his dark legacy will follow me.

"I've tried therapy. To say that it didn't work for me is an understatement," I say, looking down at my coffee cup. Most of my twenties consisted of me balancing a perilous schedule of working full-time, taking classes, and going in and out of therapy. It was so hard to manage it all, and to be honest, I let therapy slide a lot because of the cost and time. Most of the doctors I spoke to were little help, saying I needed to let go of my guilt. To imagine it floating away, as if it were really that easy. It's so hard to find someone who understands what I went through, who can really talk through it with me—instead of just telling me to *release my guilt into the universe*. Sorry, it just doesn't work that way. My guilt has claws, roots. It's braided into my sinew.

"Oh right," he says as he chews the inside of his cheek.

Lucas and I head back to the station just as everyone is streaming out for the search party. I get a text from Raven: after we left, Grover Stark showed back up at the bookstore and started harassing Chloe Williams—another previous employee —and she had to kick him out. I make a note of that. We need to talk to Grover. Upstairs in the station, I find Chad looming, staring out the window. He glances at us as I go to drop my bag on the desk.

"Got the whole town to do your job now, Durant? Must be nice."

"Hey, Chad, have you ever thought about fucking off?" Lucas snaps and I glare at him. I don't need Lucas fighting my battles for me.

"I don't know if you know this, but I'm a homicide detective. I'm doing them a favor." I grind the words out through my clenched jaw.

"Yeah, a favor." He turns to make sure I can see him roll his eyes. "I'm sure they'll feel great about that detail when she's never found."

Never found? Why would Chad assume she'll never be found? While I don't quip back to his comment, something about it rubs me the wrong way. And I won't forget it.

12

After Raven's text about Grover Stark, I know we can't put off talking to him. It takes me a few minutes on the phone with Matthew Chen of the Saranac Lake PD to get Grover's information so we can head over to question him. He lives in an apartment above the pawnshop right down the street from where Ellie lived. As we walk down the street, I realize that his apartment would give him the perfect vantage point to watch Ellie leave the bookstore each day.

We slip down a small alley that carves a path between the pawnshop and another store. As we turn toward the metal stairs that rise toward the second- and third-floor apartments, I notice a cellphone that's abandoned on the ground near a garbage can. I grab an evidence bag, carefully place the phone inside, and pocket it. Though there's likely nothing on the phone, and it's just lost, at the very least it doesn't hurt to grab it.

Lucas and I chat a bit about the possibilities for the phone as we walk up the metal stairs toward the third-floor apartment. Our feet thud hollowly on the metal, and I curse it giving away our element of surprise. No matter how quiet I try to walk, the metal rattles like I'm stomping. When we finally make it to the door, I spot a face glancing out at us from the window. Within seconds, the door is open, a short man with shaggy brown hair and dark eyes looking us over. His skin is ghostly pale, as if he never leaves his house. He's got on an oversized Def Leppard T-shirt and acid-washed jeans.

"What do you want?" he asks, his attention on Lucas.

"We were hoping to talk to you for a few minutes about Ellie Gordon," I say. "Can we come in?"

He leans against the doorframe and crosses his arms. "No." He lets out a gruff laugh. "I'm not letting cops in my house. Do you think I'm stupid?"

"Okay, well we can chat out here then. When is the last time that you saw Ellie?" Lucas asks without skipping a beat. I grab my notebook to take a few notes.

He shrugs, then pulls a vape out of his pocket. He takes a drag off it, and lemon cupcake–scented smoke curls in the wind. "I don't know, probably a few weeks ago."

"And what happened during that last interaction?" I ask.

"I went into the bookstore to look for a new book, and I'd asked Ellie for help—before I could even get the title of the book I wanted out of my mouth, Raven kicked me out of the store and told me not to come back." He rolls his eyes.

"We heard that you were asked to leave because you were harassing the employees, and that you've been kicked out because you were also harassing patrons," I explain.

"That's bullshit. None of that happened. Raven just hates me because I quit working there and now she doesn't want me in the bookstore."

"So, you weren't fired?" Lucas asks as he cocks his head.

"No," he scoffs. "Raven is so dramatic and she's such a liar." He grabs his phone, taps on the screen a few times and shows me a text thread of him quitting the job. Raven was clearly not happy about it in the exchange. Now this calls into question everything else that she told us.

"Where do you work now?"

"Downstairs, at the pawnshop with Max," he explains.

I note down the new job. "Do you have any texts that you sent to Ellie?" I ask.

He shakes his head. "I didn't have her number."

"We'll verify that with the phone company. What's your phone number?" Lucas asks.

Grover sighs before handing over his number to Lucas. But the action of handing it over tells me it's likely that he's telling the truth. Liars are more evasive. We finish up with Grover without many leads, then head back to the station to give the cellphone that we found to the tech team.

13

TWENTY YEARS AGO

The ringing of the bell for home room carries across the campus of my middle school. It's much louder inside. The way that it resonates through the halls, from out here on the outskirts I can barely hear it. The shrill sound warns me that I should be in class, but I'm not. And I won't be, not today. My dad still hasn't come back, and the last thing I can stand right now is being trapped anywhere else.

So, like most days, I'm lingering out back behind the school, counting down the hours. Burning my day away. Several of the girls with me are smoking, a habit that I cannot pick up because of my mother. The smell of it makes me think she's here, watching, waiting to yell at me about not being in class. My whole body is tense as my eyes dart toward the school. In the shade of the auditorium, with trees and a building shielding us from the rest of the school, I know that no one can see us. But it's still hard not to be on edge.

"Want a sip?" Stacey says to me as she offers me a small bottle of liquor. I look at the label, like I might recognize the brand—but I don't.

I've never drank before. But something about it calls to me. I wrap my fingers around the bottle and take it from her. The liquid inside swirls as I appraise it, the amber color catching in the light. I twist the lid off, the pungent smell making my nose curl. I raise it to my lips, knowing from the scent alone that it's going to taste awful. Before it even hits my lips, I wince. The liquid burns as it hits my tongue and throat. And though my body aches to cough, I suppress it and force it down. I've watched my friends make fun of another girl for coughing after taking a swig. So I force myself to keep a straight face and swallow it down like I've done it a thousand times.

"She likes whiskey, girls!" she whoops to our group, and I force a smile before taking another swig.

Warmth spreads through my belly as I hand the bottle back to her. Heat floods my cheeks, and the tightness in my chest eases. I can see why they do this, why every day they're out here choking down mouthfuls of this burning liquid. I could see how easy it would be to do this, to let it burn away all the pain and guilt swirling inside me.

I know later, this will catch up to me. My mother will hear about how I missed class—again. She'll yell at me, threaten me, like she always does. But for now, I'm going to drink and pretend that my life isn't in ruins.

14

My phone vibrates, cutting the night in two. The fragments of it claw at me, the sleep still fraying my thoughts, slowing my body. My eyes burn as I drag them open. The new part of the night, the one when I have to wake up, it comes so slow, like I'm swimming through mud. It feels like it takes hours for me to slam my palm against the nightstand as I search in the dark for my phone, but in reality it only takes seconds.

I glance at the screen, but my eyes are so fuzzy, I can barely make out the words. I blink furiously, clearing away the fog, and finally see Sergeant Dirby's name on the screen. A call now, at 2 a.m., that's never good news. My stomach twists as I press the phone to my ear.

"Hey, Durant, sorry to wake you, but I just got a call from dispatch that a body was spotted near one of the logging roads," he explains.

"On fire?" I guess, since he's calling me and not Chad.

"Yeah, unfortunately," he says gruffly. He gives me the address and I crawl out of bed. As soon as I hang up with Sergeant Dirby, I call Lucas and wake him up. We agree to meet downstairs in ten minutes and drive to the scene together.

I yawn and walk with stiff legs to the bathroom, make myself look semi-human, then pull on jeans and a jacket. Being this early in the morning, it'll still be on the cool side, so I've got to factor that into my outfit. I'm not sure how long we'll be out there with the forensics team as they investigate.

My mind is already alive, the adrenaline making me turn the thoughts over and over. This could be a serial killer, though we don't have enough bodies to fit the dictionary definition yet—we'd need three. Killings this ritualistic, I know what it could mean. I slow my mind. I'm jumping to conclusions; I don't have all the details yet. I need to get to the scene first.

In a few minutes, I bound down the stairs and find Lucas already waiting beside my Jeep. He's bright-eyed, as if he wasn't awoken in the middle of the night. Lucas is one of those morning people who is never groggy or tired. The moment he wakes up he's ready to go. I wish I had that kind of energy; every morning I feel like I've been dragged directly from the grave.

"Want me to drive?" he offers.

"Yes, yes, I do," I say as I toss him the keys. I walk to the passenger side and wait for him to unlock the door.

Lucas climbs inside and starts the engine, and I follow. I lean into the seat, and press my head against the cool window. By the time we get to the scene, I'll be awake and ready to go. I just need a few minutes. Lucas throws the car into drive and presses the gas.

It takes us a few minutes because of a quick pit stop to get coffee for us and Racquel before we pull up beside a row of vehicles parked at the end of the logging road. When we climb out, the scene is already swarming, spotlights set up, the air filled with acrid smoke. In the cool air, steam still curls off the body. They must have just recently put the fire out. As we approach, Racquel spots us and strides over, greeting us both. I pass her the coffee we grabbed for her before asking her what she's got for us.

"Thanks for this." She holds the coffee up for a moment. "Similar to the last scene," she says as she glances back. "Identical to it, actually." She's got a clipboard in her hands as she takes notes on the scene.

"Female victim again?" I ask.

"Not sure so far. This body is a little bit more burned than the last one, but the ME should be able to give you more details when she takes a look at the body."

"Do we have more boot prints this time?" I ask. The last time we had some footprints, so I'm curious if this scene has anything like that again.

"We've got boot prints and drag marks; it looks like this time the victim did not come willingly. The perp had to drag them for part of it." There are a lot of tire marks through here, hard to pin any down.

"Were they dead or alive while they were being dragged?" Lucas asks.

I'm not so sure our victim came willingly last time, based on the amount of damage to the body. How could our killer have done that out in the open? They were so exposed for what must have taken hours. It just doesn't add up.

"It looks like alive, because there are indications of an intermittent struggle," she explains.

"Did someone hear the struggle?" I ask.

"Not that we're aware of. The Saranac Lake team is still combing through the tip line to see if there were any calls," Lucas says, noting it on his notepad. If someone heard a scream, I'm sure it was called into the tip line. In a town this small, someone must have heard it.

"Who reported the body?" I ask.

"A trucker who was in the area picking up a shipment. He thought that it was burning garbage and called in the fire department, but when the fire department got here, they realized it was a body. So, they called us in and had us take over."

"Where's the trucker?" Lucas asks.

"Probably in Canada by now," she says with dismissal, as she looks toward the road, her dark eyes flashing.

No one questioned the trucker? "Did we get his info?" I ask. Racquel shakes her head.

We finish up with Racquel and walk toward the congregation of the guys from Saranac Lake PD and the fire department, Lucas trailing behind me.

"Think our guy is a trucker?" Lucas asks.

"Possibly, and that's what I intend to find out."

The guys fall quiet as we approach the team. I feel all their eyes on us, especially the guys from the fire department. We're outsiders, I get it.

"Who took the call about the body?" I ask, glancing at the men.

One of the guys, I think his name is Evan, steps forward. "I did."

"What details do you have on the caller?" I ask, as I take out my notepad.

He raises a brow, his head cocking to the side. "Details?"

"Yeah, name, phone number, was the guy local, things like that." I fire it off at him, frustration needling me. I know that these guys are local, small-town firefighters, but I know the training they get. They should know how these things work.

He shakes his head. "I don't collect info like that for fires," he says with a shrug, like it doesn't matter at all. "Why would I? It's just a fire, or so we thought."

I sigh. "If you get any other calls like this, please take down some details," I say. Evan nods with acknowledgement, but I'm not sure he'll actually do it.

. . .

It's late afternoon when we make it to the ME's office. Dark clouds have settled over upstate New York. Thunder crackles on the horizon, and arcs of lightning curve over the mountain tops. I've got on my leather motorcycle jacket, shielding me against the wind. I only hope we don't get caught in too much of a downpour as I appraise the sky on the way inside.

The receptionist waves us back as soon as we walk inside the building; clearly Dr. Pagan was awaiting our arrival, which probably signals bad news for us. Dr. Pagan has on a light blue lab coat when we stroll in. Her normally curly black hair is straightened and falls down her back. She's got on soft blue heels that make her a couple inches taller than me.

"Afternoon detectives," she says as she nods at both of us. She taps her long nails on her clipboard as she picks it up and appraises the notes. Again I notice that she doesn't have the body under a sheet waiting for us, a rarity. But it's likely because of the acrid smell these burned bodies give off. It'd stink up the entire room, maybe the entire building. I'm not sure how they handle it when they get a really old body in here that's badly decayed.

We make a little small talk and catch up with the ME. She tells us about her new puppy before she lowers her brow and makes it clear that she wants to get back to business.

"All right, so according to the notes the junior examiner made, we're looking at a nearly identical scene to the first victim from about a week ago. This body was badly maimed before the fire was started. The breasts were removed. Unlike the first victim there was enough breast tissue remaining this time to determine that this was not a medical mastectomy prior to death. This damage was caused to her body. It also appears that she was beaten badly prior to death, the bones in her face were broken, her nose and eye sockets in particular. The flames hadn't yet consumed that tissue."

"Were the wounds on the breast tissue there prior to her death?"

"Yes, I believe so," she says before clearing her throat. "However, it's impossible to be certain with the amount of damage we're looking at."

"Do you think someone damaged the face with their fists or..." I ask.

She shakes her head. "It's incredibly unlikely that this amount of damage could have been done with someone's hands. I would guess that an instrument like a hammer or another blunt object was used. The impact radius suggests a smaller tool. There was a lot of rage behind this attack. That's pretty clear," she says. "Like the last scene, this victim had all of her teeth except for the front ones pulled."

"Do you have any indication of whether or not either victim was sexually assaulted?" I ask as I look through my notebook.

"There really isn't any way for me to be sure with all the damage we're looking at. It's rather difficult right now to piece together what exactly happened to this victim before her death. Unfortunately, that's pretty typical in a case with this much ferocity behind it," she explains, her eyes darkening as she looks toward the drawer where I'd guess the body is kept.

"Were you able to extract DNA?"

She nods. "It has been extracted from the tissue and put into the database. Hopefully we'll get some results within a week if there are any to be found. As you know, it takes a bit of time," she explains.

I nod. "Is your thinking still that this is a different killer than the McKenzie Mauler?"

"So far, there doesn't seem to be any crossover in the MOs or victim profiles here. I don't believe so."

"Have we gotten anything back on the first victim yet from the database?" I ask.

She shakes her head. "I checked this morning and so far

there aren't any hits. I'm not sure that there's a match in the database for that victim, unfortunately. Have any other missing persons reports come in?" she asks.

"Just the one, but we've already submitted her mother's DNA to the database and we didn't get a hit yet."

"It could be a Jane Doe from another town. I think if anyone had gone missing in Saranac Lake recently that would have stuck out. It's a very small community," she says.

I nod. That I know.

We finish up with Dr. Pagan, and I take a copy of the notes on both bodies. It may not help right now, but maybe if I review all this information again, something will stick out.

It's been two days since we found our new victim, and we've got nada. We still have no leads on Ellie Gordon, despite reaching out to the media and thousands of shares on social media posts and two coordinated searches of the nearby wilderness. We've gotten a bunch of trash leads, things that are not helping our case at all, but nothing of substance has come through the tip line. The longer this goes on, the less likely I know that it is that we'll find Ellie. With no matches on the DNA of the first victim, I'm wondering if she has no family out there. That's always a possibility in cases like this. If the killer is hunting for a specific type of victim, maybe he's gone after women who have no family. No one to miss them, no one to match them either. Perfect strangers with hollow lives, like me. I needed a little time to myself to think over the details again.

I walk through downtown, going over everything from the case again in my mind. All the details filter together and swirl there, but none of them settle to the bottom with the weight that I need. We need substance, we need real evidence in this case. Right now, I've got two bodies and boot prints. No one has come forward saying they saw anything that night. But I have one last idea, something that might be able to help us. At the end of the short stretch of downtown, before anyone can reach the logging road, they have to pass a small pawnshop and a jewelry shop, both of which have surveillance cameras outside. No one else in the town has them. No one else monitors the comings and goings—because in a town this small, why would they? But if I can get their footage for the nights of the homicides, that might show me our victims before their deaths—maybe even the killer. We know they were on foot. We just don't know where they came from.

On the side of town where the logging road is, there aren't many businesses, or houses. It's a heavily wooded area that's been known to shelter the cars of teenagers from time to time as they go to make out. Some people walk their dogs down there as well. But for the most part, it'd be known to a killer that they could have limited privacy there. No one in town would think anything of seeing two people going for a walk at night down the logging path.

I glance up to the signs above me, passing a tailor, a laundromat, and a dry cleaner before turning into the small jewelry shop. I wait at the door for them to buzz me in—they're serious about their security. Once inside, a woman who's likely in her seventies with a poof of white hair offers me a cold smile. A thick golden chain is tight around her wrinkled neck. Her arms are loaded with golden bangles as well. The amount of gold she's wearing seems a bit ostentatious, but if it makes her happy —I'm glad. On the other side of the shop, there's a woman glancing in the cases.

"Good morning, Detective," she says to me before I even get the opportunity to introduce myself. Her tone makes it clear that she knows exactly who I am, introductions aren't necessary. Word has obviously gotten around about who I am, or at least, that's what she wants me to know.

"Good morning, Mrs. Ashton. I was hoping I could talk to

you for a few minutes," I say. From what I've heard from others in this town about Mrs. Ashton, she's got eyes on everyone. She may look frail, but she watches everyone and pays attention to everything. She's got a mind like an iron trap, apparently. And I intend to utilize that, if she'll let me. However, I've also heard that she hates outsiders with a passion. So my chances of her helping me are probably fifty-fifty.

"I suppose, but if a customer comes in, I have to give you the boot. I'm sure you understand. Mariska, are you done looking? We both know you're not buying anything," Mrs. Ashton says to the woman on the other side of the shop. Mariska snaps her head up, looks to Mrs. Ashton, and glowers before stalking out of the shop.

"Of course, I'll get out of your hair if anyone comes in," I say, a little surprised she kicked Mariska out. "As you know, we're investigating the two homicides in town, as well as the disappearance of Ellie Gordon."

She laces her fingers together and places them on the counter. Her knuckles are knobby, her thick fingers corded with blue veins. Though her eyes are milky, they're still sharp when they settle on me.

"Yes, I am aware," she says clearly.

"You're one of the few businesses downtown that has a surveillance camera facing the street, and there's a chance that you might have captured the women who were murdered on video," I say, just giving her enough details that she can piece it all together herself.

"So, you want a copy of my videos," she says with a wan smile.

I nod. "I was hoping that you wouldn't mind."

"Normally, I really think that the privacy of our citizens is paramount and that the police should require a warrant for video evidence."

My stomach tightens. She really might make us get a

warrant to get the footage. Witnesses like this are exhausting. She's not grandstanding because she really cares about the privacy of the other residents of this town. She hoards their stories like a dragon with gold. She likely has a chip on her shoulder toward the police and now wants to stand in the way of helping us solve a double homicide, rather than giving over a few hours of video. I can't say this is the first time I've encountered something like this, and it definitely won't be the last.

"Mrs. Ashton, I can assure you that we are not looking to violate anyone's privacy here. We're not interested in the everyday gossip that happens in this town. There are two women dead, their bodies have been burned at the edge of this town. That should be of serious concern to anyone that is a resident here. Not only does that have implications for the upcoming tourist season, and I hate to say it—but we don't know if this killer is done. More women could die if we don't act, and if we don't act fast. So please, I urge you to give us the footage."

She looks at me so hard, I'm sure she can see straight through me. Her expression hasn't thawed even a little though. Finally, she lets out a little sigh of defeat. My speech must have gotten to her.

"Fine, I'll give you those days only. Two days of footage, no more. But if you come back here looking for more, you better come with a warrant or a subpoena," she says before her lips purse.

I nod. "Thank you. I really do appreciate your help."

"I will need my grandson to pull the files for you. He'll email them over to the station later today if I can get him over here."

"Thank you," I say.

"Oh, and I'm not sure if you're interested, but I do have some information on Ellie, if that could be of some help to you," she says smoothly, as if she's been holding on to these words, waiting for the right moment to unleash them. Delight shimmers in her eyes, as if she loves nothing more than to spill information about the others in this town.

I take out my notebook for show, though I don't have much faith that this woman has any real information to offer. I know it'll likely just be town gossip; that's what all the tips thus far have been.

"Ellie was the type of girl who a lot of people talked about." She lets out a dry little laugh. "If I hadn't been careful in my youth, I would have ended up just like her. But things are a little different now. It's harder to hide some things, with the internet and all that nonsense. I thought the talk about her was a little unfair. She was doing exactly what a girl that pretty should do. She was just looking around for the best option."

I'm surprised that this woman has a much better attitude on Ellie's dating than Ellie's own mother did. That's not what I expected at all. I take a few notes, but I don't interrupt Mrs. Ashton.

"The last night that I saw Ellie was April 13th. She was walking downtown, first toward the bar over on Elm Street. I was here late that night. Vivica Fowler had decided that she wanted to upgrade her wedding ring and she wanted to come in late so no one could see her do it. She wants everyone to think that Baron thought about it all on his own and surprised her with it." She rolls her eyes, but I'm sure this is the kind of thing she accommodates often. "She asked if I could be here around eleven to meet her, and I agreed because I knew she'd be spending quite a pretty penny. She loves nothing more than spending Baron's money, so I'll accommodate that if she likes. Anyway, I saw Ellie walk by the first time around ten, and then she walked back as I was leaving around eleven thirty or so."

I note that down. This, at least, is helpful gossip. It can help me establish a timeline. Though I will verify everything she's saying with the footage.

"Was Ellie with anyone?" I ask.

She shakes her head. "No, she was alone. And it stood out to me because she was smoking. I'd never seen her smoke before. I didn't think she was a smoker."

That's the kind of thing that small-town people notice.

"How was she dressed?" I ask.

She furrows her brow, trying to remember. "She was wearing a dress, a short one. Not anything too flashy, just a typical cotton dress. I think it was green."

"Did she have a bag or anything with her?"

"Just her handbag," she explains as she shrugs slightly.

"So, it didn't look like she was planning to leave town?"

"Not at all. She looked like she was just going to see some of her friends or something."

I note that down as well. "Did you see Ellie's car anywhere?" I ask.

She shakes her head. "No, but she doesn't normally park over here. She walks around town from the bookstore. She was very fit and liked to stay active. She was always on some kind of new fad diet that she'd talk your ear off about."

That's good to know as well.

"Is there anything else you can think of?" I ask.

"No, I don't think so. That's all that I recall about that night. But hopefully the tapes help you," she says.

I finish up with Mrs. Ashton and give her my card so that her grandson can email me the files once he has them. Then I cross the street to the pawnshop that's almost directly across from Mrs. Ashton's shop. The front window is barred, but through the bars I can see guitars and amplifiers lining the windows. Several large tools also line the windows: saws, chain-saws, a lawn mower. I open the front door and a loud chime echoes through the shop as I enter. The store smells like diesel and oil. The source is clear when I see several aisles piled with machinery, tools, and generators.

To my left, the store is filled with household items, guitars, bicycles, designer purses, video games, and several flat-screen TVs. On the back wall, behind the counter filled with jewelry, they've got a full wall of guns. Pawnshops always look the same. I've been in thousands and I can never tell any of them apart. It's like they're copied and pasted all over the country.

A man in a camo T-shirt and camo hat sits behind the counter on a barstool. He nods to me as I come in, his thick beard bobbing up and down with the movement. He's very pale, his blue veins clear beneath his translucent skin.

"What can I help you with?" he asks in an accent that almost sounds southern.

I introduce myself, and the man stiffens. Despite hearing a lot about many of the other residents in town, I don't know anything about this guy. I've never seen him out in town. The way he looks at me tells me he knows exactly who I am, though. It looks like someone dragged him up here kicking and screaming from Georgia, but who knows if that's actually the case.

When he doesn't say anything further, I ask, "What's your name?"

"Max Moody," he says somewhat reluctantly.

"Is Eric Moody your brother?" I ask. There's an Officer Moody at the station. He's much younger than this guy, probably at least ten years his junior. He's one of the youngest beat cops they've got here in Saranac Lake. They don't even really trust him to do patrols yet.

He nods slowly. "Yeah, that's my younger brother. Why? Did he say something to you?" he asks. "Because I didn't do nothing."

I shake my head and explain the reason for my visit, that I'm looking for surveillance footage for the night of the homicides and for Ellie's disappearance.

"Can't help you," he says simply. Each of his words is punctuated, like each is a nail in a coffin.

"And why is that, exactly?" I ask.

He shrugs and holds his dimpled chin high. "Because I don't have to. It's my right as a red-blooded American to object to unlawful search and seizure by a law enforcement officer. You have no right to my surveillance footage and I don't have to give it to you without a warrant. This is some fishing expedition." It's not the response I expected from the brother of a fellow law enforcement officer.

I know he's only seconds away from going full-on conspiracy theorist. Next, I'll probably want to activate him with MKUltra. I force myself not to roll my eyes at him. He's right after all. He can refuse me. It just looks incredibly suspicious and makes me wonder what exactly he's hiding or who he's hiding.

I take out my notebook and catalog the exchange. I'll need to get started on a formal request for the footage before I can move on to a warrant. If we make an arrest at some point, I can subpoena the records, but we're not at that point yet. But I'll be prepared should we get there.

"Did Ellie ever come in here?" I ask.

"Nope," he says simply, and I can tell by his tone it's the same response he'll give to every single question I ask. The surveillance footage from Mrs. Ashton's shop should be sufficient, so at least there's that.

"Well, thank you for your time then," I say.

"You're not going to find anything," he says as I turn. There's a roughness to his words, and something else—maybe a veiled threat. This seems a strange hill to die on.

"Oh?" I turn back, facing him again.

"No one in this town did this. They couldn't have. So, I think you all should start looking outside this town. There's enough going on with the deaths in the wilderness. You aren't helping us. You're just bringing media attention that we don't need." He sneers as he speaks to me. It's treatment that I'm used to. In this line of work there are plenty of people who dislike law enforcement. I used to take it personally, but not anymore. There's no point. It's not me, it's the job.

"I'll keep that in mind. But we've got to investigate. We can't just move on at your urging. And as much as you may not want to face it, someone in this town *could* be capable of murder and you'd never know it. Would you really like us to rush this along, move on, and for more women here to die?" I ask, paying close attention to his body language. He's still stiff, his eyes narrowed, his nostrils flared. I know he just wants me out, and I'll leave... at some point.

I glance at the jewelry case in front of him, and a necklace catches my eye. The crucifix with the sapphires and silver ivy that her mother had described. I pull out my phone quickly and snap a picture.

"What the hell are you doing?"

I shrug with one shoulder before pocketing my phone. "Getting an early start on my Christmas shopping," I say before turning and leaving the shop. I know that Max was lying to me about Ellie never being in the shop. That's clearly her necklace that he's got in his case. I text a picture of the necklace to Ashley after carefully cropping it, and within seconds she confirms that the necklace is her daughter's.

I text Sergeant Dirby about the case and ask him if there are any updates on Plattsburgh. It's been a while since he told me about the surveillance footage. In a few seconds, he texts me back that there's been no movement yet. A knot I hadn't realized was in my stomach eases ever so slightly. I'm okay for now.

16

HIM

Being out in a town like this was a risk. Especially during the day. His pulse raced as he strolled through the streets of downtown. Even in small towns like this, there were ways to blend in, ways to disappear. Today, he'd chosen a clipboard, a hard hat, and a navy-blue jumpsuit as his camouflage. Not a single person in town had made eye contact with him.

It was perfect.

He walked past a small coffee shop, the smell of the fresh brew pouring out onto the sidewalk as he passed. For a fleeting moment, he was tempted to slip inside. But he restrained himself. Though the disguise would dissuade glances, questions on the street, ordering a coffee raised the chance that someone would remember him.

Ahead, he saw her slipping out of a jewelry store before eyeing the pawnshop directly across the street. What was she looking at? It took a minute for him to see it, the ridged dome budding in front of the store. A security camera.

He made a mental note to stay away from that particular shop.

As Harlow jogged across the street, she looked back toward

him. Her eyes narrowed on him automatically, as if she'd felt him staring. His heart threatened to burst from his chest.

But as quickly as she looked at him, she glanced away again. For now, she was safe.

For now.

17

My phone rings as my feet hit the pavement on Main Street again. The afternoon sun warms my neck as I walk down the street toward the coffee shop. I grab my phone, glance at the screen as it vibrates against my fingertips and see Lucas's name on the screen. I pick it up and press the phone to my ear.

"Lucas," I say simply, waiting for him to talk. My stomach clenches. I hope this isn't about another body. If we get a third body right now, that will mean that we officially have a serial killer on our hands. Though my gut tells me that's where this is going eventually, to face a serial killer again so soon after Platts-burgh, that would be difficult. And for two serial killers to be hunting this town at once... that's extreme.

"We had some interesting calls to the tip line today," he says.

"Oh?" I wouldn't say that's all that uncommon. There are always so many calls that come into the line, but most of them are garbage and don't lead anywhere. But if Lucas is calling me about one of them, I'm intrigued.

"First, someone called and said that they saw a strange man

lurking around the town at night carrying a gas can," he says. There's skepticism in his voice.

"Well, then I guess we should have a patrol circle the town tonight to keep an eye out for creepy-gas-can guy," I say, trying not to let sarcasm put an edge on my voice.

"Next, the tech team looked into the phone that we found behind the pawnshop—"

"The phone I found, you mean," I interrupt.

Though I can't see him, I know his pause means he's rolling his eyes at me. "Anyway. They confirmed the phone is Ellie's from the SIM card, but they weren't able to pull anything off it except for the contacts saved on the SIM card. Too much water got into it or something," he says.

"That's huge," I say. First the necklace in the pawnshop, and then Ellie's phone behind it. That's a lot pointing toward the pawnshop.

"And, a woman named Twila called. She thinks that one of the bodies found might be her best friend," he explains.

"Where's she at?" I ask.

He reads off an address to me.

"Does she want to come to the station or does she want us to come to her?" I ask.

"She owns one of the boutiques downtown. I can meet you over there in a couple minutes," he says.

I plug the address into my GPS and find that I'm a seven-minute walk from the shop. I finish up my call with Lucas, grab an iced coffee, then walk over to the store. The boutique sits on the ground floor of a large brick building. Large windows give me a view of racks filled with pastel outfits and brightly colored handbags. All the colors make it look like it's a candy shop, not a clothing store. When Lucas strolls up, I open the door and wave him inside.

The inside of the store smells like rich vanilla and sugar, which suits the vibe, and as we approach the counter, I see the source is a flickering candle next to a computer. A woman with long red hair and pale skin sits at a desk clicking away on her laptop. She's got on thick glasses that seem a bit big for her narrow face. The woman is thin, lanky. When she stands, I realize how long her hair is as it falls to her waist.

"Are you the police?" she asks as she glances between the two of us. Her eyes are a bit too wide as they appraise us, giving her a deer-in-headlights look.

I nod and introduce myself and then Lucas, but I'm surprised she hasn't already heard who we are through the gossip mill. Maybe she was expecting Chad.

"You're not what I expected," she says, with a bit more honesty than I think she means to. Her cheeks flush as she looks to the floor. "I didn't mean that in a bad way. I just—I guess I expected uniforms and a siren, I don't know."

"Nothing to worry about," Lucas says, trying to put her at ease.

I glance around the store to see if there are any lingering customers, but the shop seems to be empty. "Are you comfortable speaking here or did you want to go somewhere with more privacy?" I ask. I'd invite her to the station, but since our space looks like a storage locker, and sitting in the police station makes most people uncomfortable, I decide not to mention it.

"Here is fine. This is usually our slow time. Most of my orders are online anyway, but typically lunch hour is my rush. I think because people end up staining their shirt." She lets out a nervous laugh.

"So, you called us about your friend—" Lucas says, clearly trying to steer the conversation.

She nods. "Yes, Chloe. I haven't seen her in a few days. Honestly, the last time I saw her was right before the body was found. I've been calling and calling... She's never been the kind of person who wouldn't call back. I tried going by her apartment, and she's not answering the door either. So, I'm really concerned about her," she explains.

I get Chloe's address from Twila and note it down. That'll be our next stop. A wellness check to see if Chloe is at home is the easiest step that we can take here. But before we do that, I have a few more questions for her.

"Does Chloe have any family in town?" I ask.

She shakes her head. "No, her mother passed away last year. She doesn't have anyone else here in town. I think her brother lives in Manhattan maybe. They're not close."

I nod and make a note of that as well. "What's her brother's name?"

"Jack," she says.

"What was Chloe doing the last time that you spoke to her?" I ask.

"Um, I don't remember. I think she was cleaning her apartment or something. It wasn't anything out of the usual. There isn't anything that really sticks out to me about that day," she says. "I'm just so worried about her."

"And when was the last time you physically saw her?" Lucas asks.

"The day before the call."

"Did Chloe drink or do drugs?" he asks.

Her eyes bug. "Drugs? God no! She drank occasionally, but not to excess."

"Is there any chance that she had a trip planned and went out of town or maybe she's busy with work?" Lucas offers.

She shakes her head. "No, not at all. She works at home as a freelance graphic designer, so while she does get busy with work sometimes, she still has a pretty flexible schedule and keeps in touch. We never go more than a day without talking at least once. I've never not heard from her for days. This is not like her." There's an edge to Twila's voice as she wrings her hands. It's clear how worried she is about her friend.

"We'll check on her. I promise you that we will get to the bottom of this and track her down. I'm sure that it's nothing," Lucas says easily. I'm sure it's a phrase he's said a thousand times.

She nods stiffly. "Thank you."

"Was Chloe dating anyone? Could she be at a boyfriend's house?" Lucas asks.

"She wasn't dating anyone seriously enough to be at their house for days. She wasn't a long-term dating type of person." Her eyes go wide seconds after the words are out of her mouth. "Oh, God, that sounded bad. I didn't mean that in a bad way. She's not like a slut or anything. She just really wasn't that interested in dating or relationships. She was more focused on her work and being happy by herself."

I nod and note that down as well. "Did she mention being scared to you recently or feeling like anyone was watching her? Did she have any enemies? Anyone in town who gave her a hard time?"

She shakes her head. "No, nothing like that at all. She was a really nice person. She didn't have any enemies at all. Even when we were back in high school everyone loved her."

I look to Lucas to see if he has any more questions and he shakes his head. I finish up with Twila and glance over my notes. I think that we have everything we can get from her. My phone buzzes as we leave the shop. I glance at it and find another email from my mother. She's pressing yet again for me to call her, to reach out in some way. Apparently, she and my father have been speaking again and they're both very worried about me, based on a lot of the news coverage. I swipe the email away and sigh before shoving the phone back into my pocket.

18

Night thickens outside my motel room. The smell of French fries and fast food fills the air around me, so permeating it's making me question my choices. I feel like I'm marinating in it. As I click on my laptop, going over an open missing persons case, the dull hum of the news changes in pitch and catches my attention. I don't normally watch TV, but with all of the homicides in Saranac Lake, I've been trying to keep up with it a bit more. I want to know what's being leaked to the media.

But it isn't a reporter on the screen that has my attention. No, it's Ashley Gordon. She's got on a satin blouse. She's leaning forward in the shot, her elbows on her knees, the worn couch filling the background of the frame. I blink several times, as if it might make Ashley disappear. My stomach is in knots as I watch.

"So, Ms. Gordon, why did you ask us here today?" a reporter who's off screen asks.

Ashley picks at the bridge of her nose and her face finally conveys some emotion. During our first interview, her missing daughter seemed like an inconvenience.

"My daughter has been missing for over two weeks and the

police are doing nothing about it." She grinds the words out through gritted teeth.

Nothing? There are flyers up all over town, social media posts circulating. I've found her necklace, her cellphone; they've conducted several searches. Rage fills me until my chest tightens. I force myself to slow my breathing, when I realize just how rapid it's become.

"At the rate they're going, my daughter will never be found, and they're just letting that killer run amok in the McKenzie Wilderness. What do we even have cops for? What are they doing exactly?"

I swipe the remote off the bed next to me and turn the TV off with more force than I need to.

19

TWENTY YEARS AGO

Dinner smells awful. My mother decided to cook, and I think we're all going to suffer for it. Across from me, my dad sits at the table. Tension has swollen inside the room and it's thicker than the stench of the tuna casserole. I look between the two of them, the six feet separating them. It's the first meal we've eaten together in months, since my dad left the last time. It took him this long to get my mother to agree for him to come to dinner, so at least he's trying like he told me he would.

But I need him back here soon. I need him to be a barrier between me and her. She grimaces as she scoops the dinner onto each of our plates, and I do my best to not sneer at it. If I look even remotely uninterested in this dinner, she's going to make me pay for it later.

Silence thickens in the room, and my mother grabs the remote for the television that sits in the corner. She clicks the TV on, and switches to the news. On the screen, a woman with a crisp blue suit and short blonde hair named Sherrie Summers appears and smiles a little too broadly at the camera.

"Good evening and thank you for watching the five o'clock news, I'm Sherrie Summers and I'm going to catch you up on what's happening today in Olympia." The woman rattles off some stories on the highway, a farmer's market that won't be open as usual on the weekend, and a dog that was found that's looking for its missing owner. Then the woman introduces a man and the camera switches to him.

The man has a thick brow and a wide jaw. His suit is a creamy brown color, with a sky-blue tie. He looks incredibly serious, his mouth a grim line.

"Thank you, Sherrie. Tonight police are searching for the killer or killers of a young woman whose body was found in her home yesterday evening. So far, the police have not released her identity, but they have reason to believe this woman's death may be related to a string of homicides that have haunted Olympia for the past three years. Law enforcement is concerned that this is not the last, and that we may see further killings if the public doesn't come forward with tips."

I swallow hard, but my throat has gone so dry, it's like my mouth is filled with sand. I glance to my mom and then to my dad. My mom's eyes are glued to her plate as she stabs her fork into the casserole over and over again, but it keeps dissolving under the force. My father's eyes cut to me, and he motions to my plate as if he didn't hear a single thing the man on the TV said.

"Eat your dinner, Harley Jane."

20

Back in the office, the weight of Ashley Gordon's appearance on the news presses down on me. The roar of the bullpen as we climb to the third floor helps calm me, get my head back in the game. On the top floor, I find Chad and several members of his team circled around a table in the back. Unfortunately, this shared space has to fit all of us, and though I knew I'd end up seeing him here at some point during the investigation, I was hoping that it wouldn't be today.

Chad looks up from the table as we walk in, a sick smile creeping across his lips. Though he says nothing, I can see the barbed words he wants to say in his eyes, the way he looks at me. He's holding back, why I don't know. He's never been the type to hold back for any reason.

"Afternoon," Lucas says to Chad. But Chad says nothing in return.

I ignore the lot of them and walk to my desk. As I throw my bag down, my phone rings.

"Detective Durant?" Racquel says as soon as I answer the phone.

"Yes?"

"We just got a hit on the DNA database for the first victim," she says.

It's surprising that we got a hit *now*. It's been over a week since the first victim's DNA was placed into the database. If there'd been a hit from the family's DNA that we plugged in, that should have been within a day or two.

"Who is it?" I ask.

"Ashley Gordon was a match," she says.

Frustration nags at me. We got the match right after her theatrics on TV. Perfect. Just perfect. "It took this long for a familial match to come back? I thought that would only take a day or two based on what the ME told us," I say, frustration needling me. This family has been waiting for answers for over a week, and we're just now getting them? I feel thrown off. The shoe prints didn't match Ellie's size, so I didn't think it could be her. Am I losing my edge?

"There was a mix-up in the lab with the results. One of our junior techs added the file into the wrong stack meant for negatives. As I was going through the stack today to update case files, I noticed the positive result. I do apologize for the hold up. It came back about a week ago," she explains softly.

"It's not your fault. Thank you for calling to let me know," I say before finishing up the call with Racquel.

I turn to Lucas as I shove my phone in my pocket. "We've got to head to the Gordons'. The mother was a match for the first victim. That was Ellie Gordon," I explain as I gather my things again. Lucas is as surprised as I am. At least this will get me out of the office again, so I don't have to deal with Chad and his team.

"You mean after her stunt on TV we're going to prove her right?" He shakes his head.

"Yeah, I know, the optics aren't good. But there's nothing we can do about it."

Back in my Jeep, I take a deep breath and gather my

thoughts. I've got to ready myself for the inevitable conversation we have to have with Ashley, to explain to her that her daughter was butchered and burned at the edge of town. This will not be an easy conversation to have, but thankfully Lucas is a little better at that kind of delivery than I am.

We pull back in front of the Gordons' house. The shades are all down, the house dark. Ashley's SUV sits in the driveway. It doesn't look like it's moved since the last time we were here. Ashley was already on edge with her daughter's disappearance, so I can only imagine how she'll take this news. Lucas climbs out of the Jeep first and I follow. My boots click against the walkway as we approach the front door.

It takes a minute for Ashley to open the door, and when she does, she looks worn. Her eyes are dim with dark circles beneath them. She looks like she's aged ten years in the week since we last saw her. Her auburn hair flares out from her head, twisting this way and that, like Medusa's snakes. Her eyes dart between the two of us, and she waves us inside. The movements of her body are so slow, it's as if a malaise has gripped her, like maybe she's been dipped in grief and it has forever changed her.

"How are you holding up, Ms. Gordon?" I ask as we walk into the foyer.

"I've got to do an interview to get the two of you back over here? Interesting timing." She glares at me. She waves us through to the dining table before she speaks. "Are you checking in so I'll stop running my mouth on TV?"

I ignore the jabs, knowing the impact of the news I'm about to deliver. The last thing I need is her calling another reporter over here.

"I think you should take a seat," Lucas says, but Ashley refuses to sit, her hand gripping the back of one of the dining chairs. Her hand clutches it so tightly, her knuckles are flashing white at me. It's like an SOS message—she needs our help. But for now, it's not help we're extending.

Tears fill her eyes; Lucas's directive has already set a tone. The room fills with a cloud of grief. It shifts, as if all the air has gone out of the room completely. She collapses into the chair across from Lucas. Her head hangs loose on her neck, then she finally looks up to him again.

"Just tell me." She chokes the words out.

"This morning we got a positive identification on the first victim that we found. Unfortunately your daughter has passed away," Lucas says.

Ashley sobs, tears and hysterics gripping her. She's breaking apart in front of us, the weight of her grief thickening in the air like poison.

"We are so sorry for your loss, and I know this must be incredibly hard right now. But we're going to do everything that we can to find her killer," I say, hoping that my words will soften the blow somewhat. I need this woman to know that I will fight for her daughter, that I will find the monster who did this to her. And I will do everything in my power to keep this man from killing again.

"I just need a minute," she says as she shoves up from the table and disappears down the hall. Lucas and I glance at each other as we hear her sobbing from somewhere in the bowels of the house. I know how alone she must feel, like the world has been kicked out from underneath her. It's something I wish no parent ever had to feel.

A few minutes later, Ashley returns. Her eyes are raw, the tip of her nose red. She's got a bundle of tissues in her hand as she takes a seat again.

"Let's get this over with," she says as she looks at the table.

I ask her some of my usual questions verifying her where-abouts the night of her daughter's disappearance. It's not that I think she had something to do with her daughter's death, but statistically speaking she's more likely to have done it than anyone else in this town.

"Is there anyone you can think of who would have had a reason to hurt your daughter?" I asked her this before when we first spoke, but with her death hanging in the air between us, she might think of someone who hadn't come to mind before.

She shrugs weakly. "I don't know, any one of the men who she felt the need to meet up with?" She sniffles and shakes her head. "If she'd just been more guarded, this wouldn't have happened. She should have been more careful." She clenches her fists atop the table, and anger rises inside me. I can't believe she's already turned to blaming her daughter for her own death. But then again, I guess I shouldn't be surprised based on our previous conversations with Ashley.

"Could you please provide us with a list of close contacts that Ellie had?" Lucas asks. "We did find her phone, so we were able to get her contacts off of that—but anyone else you can think of would be helpful."

She nods. "I'll email you a list of everyone I can think of. You already spoke to her boss? Ellie was having trouble with some guy from work."

"Yes, we spoke to her when we were originally investigating Ellie's disappearance." I had called and told Ms. Gordon about searching the apartment and speaking to Raven. But I guess none of that stuck in her mind, or the news is making it hard for her to recall right now. Either way, I explain it all to her again.

"Go talk to Margo," she says.

"Margo?" I ask. That's not a name that I've heard before.

"Margo Fowler. She and Ellie were friends for a while, but they had a falling out not too long ago," she says.

"How long ago?" I ask as I write that name down, wondering why she didn't mention this to us before.

She shrugs, seemingly shaking off all her sadness. "I don't

know. I don't really keep up with those things. Maybe a month, maybe less. I don't know."

I nod and thank her for the information. We finish up with Ashley and I set my sights on Margo. If Margo and Ellie had a falling out, that's a good lead that I need to follow up on. We need to know what happened between the two of them, especially if they had been close. I can't believe Margo was never mentioned during our first conversation.

Across town, in upper-scale townhouses, we find Margo Fowler's home. There are four townhouses pressed together here, very much in the style of New York brownstones. I glance up and down the street; high-end cars stand outside each of the homes. Lucas and I both approach the home. The bay window in the front has the plantation shutters closed.

Lucas reaches up and knocks on the door. In a few minutes, a woman with long blonde hair that darkens toward the ends opens the door and looks between the two of us. She's got on heavy makeup and a designer dress. Is she going somewhere or is this how she dresses every day?

Lucas handles the intro, and Margo reluctantly waves us inside. Gold bangles jingle on her wrist as she moves. Based on the look of her home and her outfit, I'd wager they're real gold.

"I'm not in any trouble, am I?" she asks as she signals for us to take a seat on her large leather couch. She lets out a little laugh that tells me she's not serious.

I take a seat next to Lucas. "No, not at all," I say before explaining the reason for our visit. I watch her carefully to see her expression as we relay the news that Ellie has passed away.

She raises her hands and covers her mouth as she gasps, perched on the edge of the couch. Her eyes flood with tears. "No, that can't be right."

"We are so sorry for your loss," Lucas says. "But Ashley

Gordon recommended that we come speak to you about Ellie. She said that the two of you were close."

She nods. "Yes, we were."

"She did mention that you and Ellie had a falling out recently," I say.

Her eyebrows pinch together and she looks from me to Lucas. Then she shakes her head. "No, we definitely didn't have a falling out."

"You two didn't have a fight or anything before Ellie's disappearance?" I ask as I take out my notepad.

She shakes her head again. "No, and I don't know why Ashley would say that. Then again, she never did like me. She thought I was a bad influence on her daughter." She sits up a little straighter; as if she needed it, her posture was already perfect.

"And why would that be?" Lucas asks while I write a note.

Margo glances at my notebook, and I know she's wondering what I wrote down. Whenever I'm questioning a suspect, I make sure that I take plenty of notes—whether they're valuable or not. Sometimes, just the act of writing something down can intimidate a suspect into spilling the beans.

"Because Ms. Gordon didn't like the fact that we were both single women in our late twenties who weren't interested in getting married. She didn't see any path for her daughter that didn't include an early marriage and at least three children."

"So... were you two dating?" Lucas asks.

Margo lets out a shrill laugh. "Oh, God no," she says as she presses her palm to her chest. "We dated men. Sometimes, Ellie did a little escorting if we went to the city. She was a very pretty girl and got a lot of interest. But here we didn't do any of that. Word would have spread like wildfire and ruined our lives."

Escorting? This could be the info we've been missing that could help the rest of the details click into place. Did Ellie have a bad experience with a client? Did something go wrong?

"Did she ever have any bad experiences during her escorting? And where did she escort?"

"Manhattan, mostly. And no, she'd only done it three or four times. It was fun, she told me, but at the end of the day it made her feel cheap to take money from these men. I thought it was ridiculous because most of them were incredibly wealthy. They could easily afford a few hundred dollars for her time and thought nothing of it. They probably spent that much on their socks." She waves her hand in the air as she speaks, dismissing the idea completely. Something strikes me about Margo's posture, her demeanor. It's as if she didn't just find out her *dear* friend is dead. It's like she's speaking to the goddamn press about a store opening downtown.

"Did anyone else here in town escort with Ellie?" I ask, thinking of our new victim.

She shrugs. "I'm not sure."

"Margo, what do you do?" I ask.

She furrows her brow. "What do you mean?"

"For work, what do you do for work?" I clarify.

She shakes her head. "No, I don't work. My father is Baron Fowler." The way she says it, I know that I'm supposed to know what that means. But I have no idea who Baron Fowler is.

"Oh, right. You're not *from* Saranac Lake." She lets out a little laugh that's too airy and musical for the tone of the room, as if my outsiderness is the reason for my obvious ignorance. "My father is a lumber magnate and he owns the motel. He's quite wealthy, so I don't work. Well, not like most people work. I do some appearances for the family, things like that. But I don't have a day job or anything. I did used to work as a model, but it all just became too much, you know?"

I don't know, so I look back at my notepad and pretend to look over my notes. I'm not sure what else to say or ask. My guess is that Margo is some sort of socialite, based on her answers. And she clearly doesn't want to be much help.

"Did Ellie go out with anyone before her death?" Lucas asks, picking up the thread of the conversation while I'm distracted.

"Like for escorting or for fun?" she asks.

"Either one," he says simply.

"She did go on a date with Gavin Croswell before she disappeared," she says, as if the thought just occurred to her.

I wish she had told us about that at the beginning of this conversation. "When was the date?" I ask. Why didn't Raven know about the date?

"I think the day before she disappeared, maybe? It's hard to keep track," she says with a noncommittal shrug.

"Did she call you after the date? Or send you a text?" I ask, making a few notes.

For a moment she contemplates my question, then picks up her phone. She taps on the screen, then scrolls several times with her finger, her long nails clicking on the screen each time it moves.

"No, it doesn't look like she did."

"So, the last time you heard from her was before the date," I confirm.

"Yeah, she texted me about an hour before to say that she was excited," she says as she looks down at the texts, then shows me the screen.

"And you didn't think anything about not hearing from her after or her disappearing for over a week?" Lucas jumps in. His tone is a little more accusatory than I'd like it to be, but who am I to tell him how to question this woman. I'm not exactly happy with her either, but I can't say that I'd do better if I were in her shoes. I drop the ball with texts all the time.

She shrugs again. "Look, I'm very busy. People text me all the time. I'm easily distracted. It honestly didn't even occur to me that I hadn't heard from her until you both showed up here today," she says, a little too nonplussed. Maybe it's because of her upbringing. I've met people like this, those who are so rich that they see everyone else as disposable. Maybe she's used to friends coming and going with no discussion.

"Did Ellie ever mention Grover Stark to you?" Lucas asks as he glances at his notebook.

She nods. "Yes, she saw that creep standing outside her apartment on the street all the time, watching her windows. He'd follow her around the shop when she was working in the bookstore. He wouldn't take no for an answer. Every time that Ellie rebuffed him, Grover would joke about her playing hard to get." Margo lets out a disgusted sound that sounds a bit like a cough.

"Do you think that he'd be capable of hurting her?" Lucas presses.

"There's no way of really knowing what someone is capable of, is there?"

"How long were you and Ellie friends?" I ask.

"I don't know, since elementary school. We went to school together. So at least twenty years, or more."

"And during that time, how often did you both typically speak?" I ask her as I note the timeline.

She stiffens, and scoots back on the couch. "I don't know, sometimes every day, sometimes not for weeks. I traveled a lot, sometimes I wasn't easy to reach. I really didn't look that much into silence, Detective. It's very common in my life. You may think that wealth gives you a certain type of life, that it sets you up for amazing things, but it can be incredibly lonely. It can mean that I don't talk to anyone for weeks at time, except for those who I've hired."

She wants me to feel sorry for her, that's clear. Poor little rich girl. I'm sure this is a role she plays often. I don't think I'm going to get anything else helpful out of her though. And if I press my luck too much, she'll lawyer up. I'm lucky she didn't ask for counsel for this conversation.

"Is there a reason that Ellie wouldn't have told Raven about her date with Gavin? You're the first person who's mentioned it to us."

She lets out a low laugh that manages to be condescending. "Gavin is a playboy. He's always jumping from woman to woman. And most women don't want to admit they want to date him. So she wasn't proud of it."

I finish up with her and resolve to go back to Raven. She'll likely know more about the falling out between Margo and Ellie if it happened. Going secondhand off of information from Ashley isn't the best option, but right now we've got nothing else to go on.

We drive across town to the bookstore, and stroll inside to find Raven behind the espresso machine making a customer a latte. She nods at the two of us as the door chimes, and we wait patiently near the hallway that leads back to Raven's office. When Raven approaches, there's sweat beaded on her brow, along her hairline. It's cool in here, so I make a mental note of that.

"Do you have a few minutes?" I ask as I wave my hand toward the hall.

She nods. "Of course, let's go in my office," she says as she motions for us to follow her.

We take a seat in front of her desk and Raven takes her seat as well. Her chair squeaks in protest as she slides it toward us. She looks between Lucas and me, waiting for us to speak.

"I'm sorry to be the one to tell you, but we positively identified the victim who was found on April 13th, and unfortunately it was Ellie Gordon," Lucas says. "We are very sorry for your loss, and we know this must come as a shock."

Her mouth hangs open as she looks between the two of us like she's waiting for us to say that we're joking. Tears well in her eyes, then spill down her cheeks.

"No, no, no, no," she says over and over again as she chokes out a sob. "She can't be. She was just here, she was alive—and why would—who could—I don't understand." She chokes the words out through her sobs.

"I know this is a shock and incredibly hard, but we have a few questions so we can track down the person who did this to Ellie and to keep them from hurting anyone else," I say. "Moving quickly here is incredibly important."

She nods weakly, then grabs a tissue from the desk and blots her eyes. Glittery mascara streams down her face with the tears.

"What do you need to know?" she stammers.

"First, I need to know why you lied to me about firing Grover Stark." I need to level-set with Raven. If I'm not confident that she's going to tell me the truth, then there's no point in continuing with the questioning.

"I didn't lie to you about firing him. I fired him after his last incident with Ellie," she says, her head cocked a little to the side, her brows furrowed.

"Grover showed us a text where he quit," I explain.

She shakes her head. "He texted me like four or five times while he was working here saying that he quit, then would come back in the next day begging for his job back. It was always the same thing. He'd tell me that he was drinking, that it was a stupid drunken text. At that point, he wasn't causing major problems and we needed the help, so I hate to say that I let him come back far more times than I should have."

I glance to Lucas to see if he buys that. It seems like a reasonable explanation to me. When Lucas nods, I continue.

"Did Ellie ever talk to you about her relationship with Margo Fowler?" I ask.

Raven nods. "Yes, she talked about her quite a bit. They were very close. But I think their relationship was very different from the one that Ellie and I had," she explains. "Margo has always seemed..." Raven has a hard time grasping the right word. "Cruel?"

"What do you mean by cruel?" Lucas asks.

"Margo has the uncanny ability to pick your biggest weaknesses or things that you're self-conscious about, then she belittles you about it until you feel so small."

I note that.

"Do you think she'd be capable of violence?"

"I'm not sure, possibly." She's silent for a moment. "Margo is very rich. I'm just a normal person. Ellie had some money. She wasn't rich or anything, well not on Margo's level. But she was comfortable. She worked here for fun sometimes, but it was pretty clear to me that she didn't *have* to work. Margo let her get out some of the desire she had for that luxurious lifestyle, because I definitely wouldn't ever be an outlet for that. They went shopping, went to the city together, went on double dates. I'm more of an introvert, so none of that was my scene."

"Were you ever jealous of their relationship?" I don't mean for my words to sound judgmental; being jealous of friends is normal, it can happen. It doesn't mean that Raven ever acted on the jealousy, but I need to know if her opinion of Margo is colored by anything.

She shakes her head. "No, not at all. Their relationship seemed a bit superficial and the things they did weren't really the types of things I was interested in. I own my own business, I'm very involved in literature programs for the youth in upstate New York, I curate events, I own my own home. In my own way, I'm quite comfortable too, not rich. But I do have money to throw around if I wanted to. I just choose not to." She stumbles over her words a bit. "I'm not judging them, so please don't take it that way. It's just a different lifestyle choice is all."

I nod and I do think she's being genuine. Nothing about her words or her tone seems off to me, and I don't get the feeling that Raven would be a very good liar. Margo on the other hand, I get the feeling she lies easily and often. "Did Margo and Ellie have a fight before her disappearance?" I ask.

She looks between the two of us before letting out a low sigh. "Yeah, they did."

Strike one for Margo. "Do you know what the fight was about?"

Raven rolls her eyes. "A guy. Their fights were always about guys. Oh, and then they had a fight because Margo thought that Ellie had stolen some of her jewelry. Which is ridiculous. Ellie was not the kind of person who would steal."

I make a note about the alleged jewelry theft. I don't know why Margo wouldn't have brought that up if it was a problem.

"Any *guy* in particular?" Lucas asks as he arches an eyebrow.

"Gavin Croswell. There's a lot of history there, and it's kind of a mess," she warns me. Surprise, surprise, I give Margo the opportunity to tell me more about Gavin and she dropped the critical information.

"Please go on. I've got time," I say as I make a few notes about Gavin.

"So, the Croswells and the Fowlers are the richest families in this town. The families actually helped found this town together like two hundred years ago or something. They both owned lumber companies here, then expanded. The Fowlers own a motel and a ski resort here. The Croswells ended up branching out too. They own some restaurants, a motel, and several other small businesses downtown. Because of the competition between their businesses, the families eventually had a falling out and there was a lot of bad blood between them... That is until Margo and Gavin started dating while they were in their early twenties. They were heavy into one another. It seemed like maybe they'd get married. But Gavin is a play-boy. He cheated on Margo, the families separated again. It all went up in flames basically." She stops for a moment to catch her breath. "So, a few months ago, Gavin started trying to get

Ellie to go out with him. Ellie always refused—the girl code and everything—but Gavin didn't want to take no for an answer."

"Margo told us that they went on a date," I say.

She nods. "Yeah, Margo was pissed. She'd asked Ellie not to date Gavin. She still had her eye on him, hoping that one day they'd reconnect or something, I guess. But anyway, Ellie tried going on a date with Gavin in secret—but nothing stays a secret in this town."

"So, they had a falling out over this secret date?" Lucas asks.

She bites her lip, and I know she's holding something back. Her eyes fall to her desk, like she's debating something.

"Raven, it's okay, you can tell us," I say.

"Please don't be mad, but I didn't tell you the whole truth when you were here the first time, because I was trying to protect Ellie. I thought that maybe she'd run off, that maybe she was hiding out somewhere."

"Why would she be hiding out somewhere?" I ask, trying to get to the bottom of this. I'm not angry that she kept information from us, but if it can help us track down the killer now, I need her to start talking.

"It wasn't the first time that Ellie had been out with Gavin. They'd actually been going out for a while. But the night that she went missing, that's when Ellie told me she was going to tell Gavin that she was pregnant. I thought when she disappeared that he took it badly and she left for a bit to clear her head or to figure out what she was going to do. I didn't think she was dead. I didn't think that—"

"So, let me get this straight, she told Gavin that she was pregnant right before she went missing?" This is not good news. The number one cause for a pregnant woman's death is homicide. Could Gavin have blown up because he didn't want to be a father and killed Ellie? Why didn't Raven tell us about this in the beginning? This is the most frustrating part of being a detective. You never get all the answers the first time you ask a question.

She nods. "Yes, well at least she told me she was going to tell him. I never got confirmation from her that she told him, obviously. I was waiting for her to call me at some point to tell me what happened, but when she didn't, I assumed things went bad and that she might need some space to figure things out."

"Did Margo know about the pregnancy?" I ask.

Raven holds her hands up. "I have no idea. Unless it's possible that she overheard when Ellie was telling Gavin," she explains.

"Did Ellie's mother know about the pregnancy?" Lucas asks.

"I don't think so," she says.

I know that Ashley would not have been happy for Ellie to get pregnant outside of wedlock, but it was clear that she wanted her daughter to settle down. That would put her on the path to settling down, so I'm not so sure this would have been bad news for her mother. We finish up with Raven and head out.

I grab my cellphone and scroll through my contacts to find Dr. Pagan. She picks up on the second ring, and I can hear the beat of techno music in the background.

"Hello, Detective," she says as the music gets quieter. "What can I help you with today?"

"Did you test Ellie to see if she was pregnant when she died?"

"Let me check my notes," she says, and I hear the rustling of paperwork in the background. "No, it doesn't look like my tech ran a pregnancy test. That's odd, most of the time we do run one."

"Could you please expedite that test?" I ask.

"Of course."

"And if she is pregnant, I'll need the DNA collected from the fetus, along with an estimated gestation," I say.

"I'll get that over to you as soon as I can," she explains.

We chat a bit more and end the call. My biggest concern is Gavin and Margo. We need to speak to Gavin, and get more information about Margo before we talk to her again, because she's clearly lying to us already. If we're going to speak to her again, I've got to lay a trap.

21

The office is quiet on the third floor as I sit among the dusty tables and stacked furniture. Lucas took off already, but I'm not quite ready to pack it in and head back to the motel. My phone pings in my back pocket, and I grab it to glance at the screen. In my inbox, an email waits with several attachments. It takes me a moment of scanning them to realize it's the surveillance footage from the jewelry store. I open my email on my laptop and download the videos.

My heart races as I wait for the progress bar to finish. When it finally does, I take a look at the time stamps. There are five days' worth of videos here, more than I expected to get. But I'm not going to complain about that. I skim the first few days, and notice something odd on April 11th. At around 3 p.m. I see her walk across the street from the jewelry store and disappear into the pawnshop. I continue to go through the next days, but she doesn't go back to the shop. I cue up the video from the day of Ellie's death. For hours, I watch people in the town filter past the camera as they walk the streets of downtown. The sky is overcast, making the video darker than some of the others.

At 5 p.m., I see Ellie for the first time. She walks down the street in a nice dress and heels, the shoes I suspect she was wearing when she disappeared. But I still can't piece together why the footprints at the scene didn't match her size. Maybe they weren't Ellie's footprints at the scene at all. Though I can't tell exactly what shoes she's wearing in the video, the footprints at the scene were flats, not heels. And while it's not uncommon to change out of heels and into flats, especially while going for a walk, there's no way there'd be such a large size discrepancy.

I fast-forward through several hours of low traffic, until I see Ellie again. This time, she's got a man at her side, a man I suspect is Gavin. The man grabs her, kisses Ellie slowly, then backs away. They chat for a moment, then go their separate ways. The man disappears off screen, while Ellie remains in view. A few moments later, she continues walking in the opposite direction of her date. I keep watching, waiting to see if the man follows her, but he doesn't. It isn't until a few minutes after Ellie's walked away that I see something else: a pickup truck driving past, following her. I need to find out if Gavin, Grover, or Max owns a pickup truck, and if one of them followed her that night.

My first stop is to the pawnshop after I confirm that it's still open. I send a few screenshots from the surveillance footage to my cellphone before I pack up my stuff and head out of the station. Part of me wonders if I should grab Lucas for this, but I don't think that Max is going to react any better if two cops show up on his doorstep, so I decide to go it alone. The sun is burning low on the horizon as I walk from the station down the main drag of downtown. I pass the bookstore, and glance in to see Grover hovering just behind a woman in the shop.

I jog across the street toward the pawnshop, the door jingling as I slip inside. The scent of grease and gasoline hits me as soon as I cross the threshold. Before the door even shuts behind me, Max is leaning on the counter, glowering at me. He's got a baseball cap pulled down over his shaggy hair.

"What the fuck do you want?" he growls as I approach.

"I had a couple questions for you," I say.

"I'm not answering any of your questions," he snaps, barely waiting for me to finish talking.

"Okay, let's call them rhetorical then. You told me that Ellie Gordon had never been in here," I say as I pull up the screenshot of her going into the pawnshop on my phone. "But I got surveillance footage of her coming into the shop right here."

"That could be anyone."

I look down at the jewelry case in front of him. The crucifix necklace is still prominently displayed. I tap on the glass right above it. "And it's interesting, because Ashley Gordon confirmed that the necklace right there belonged to Ellie. So I have to ask, how exactly did that end up here?"

"I promise all of my clients anonymity," he says. There's a pink tinge to his cheeks, as his frustration rises to the surface.

"So, she was a client then," I say.

"I never said that," he snaps right back at me, then presses his lips together.

I don't want to mention the phone to him yet. I'm going to save that for later. "What kind of vehicle do you drive, Max?" I ask. Though I could just pull this information from the Saranac team, I'd prefer to ask Max myself.

"A Ford F-150," he says with a little shrug. "Why?"

"No reason," I say. "Does Grover ever buy pieces from clients?"

He shakes his head. "No, he helps me catalog, clean the store. He wouldn't be able to tell a diamond from a broken piece of glass."

I nod slowly and take a mental note of that.

"Why are you asking questions about Grover?" he asks, his eyebrow quirked. I guess word of him being fired from the bookstore never made it over here. Though, I get the feeling from Max that he keeps to himself.

"He has some connections to Ellie Gordon, so we're doing our best to flesh out the leads that we've gotten. We owe it to her family to do our best to follow up on some tips." I keep it as vague as possible. Max takes a step back from the counter and leans against a barstool that he's got near the wall. He crosses his arms loosely over his waist as he appraises me.

"Between the two of us, he's an odd duck. I've had some trouble with him talking to customers unprofessionally. He's made some people uncomfortable..."

"Has he mentioned Ellie?"

He shakes his head. "Not that I remember. He doesn't talk much, not to me anyway. He seems to save it for the customers."

"If he says anything to you about her, would you mind giving me a call?" I ask as I slide my card across the counter to him.

"As long as you don't show up back here asking for my footage," he says.

I'm not about to make him any promises, but I nod. I know if I want his footage, I'm going to have to come back here with a warrant.

22

A call to Saranac Lake PD tells us exactly where to find Gavin. Lucas and I stand outside one of the few modern buildings in the entire town. This monstrosity, a marketing firm that Gavin has spun up with family money, stands just a few blocks from the police department. A gawdy statue, a metal form that I think is supposed to mimic the curves of a woman's body, stands outside of the building.

We walk into a lobby that's stark, minus a glass reception desk that stands in the middle. A small woman with thick black glasses sits behind it, her eyes focused on a monitor to her right. When we approach, she looks up.

"Yes?" she says simply, and I explain the reason for our visit.

"Well, you see, Mr. Croswell is very busy. I'm not sure that he has time today to speak with *detectives*," she says, her words clipped. Clearly, she was trained to deflect any requests to speak to him.

"Okay, well if it's better for Mr. Croswell, then he can come down to the station to speak with us there. But as a courtesy we were coming here to speak with him so that he didn't have to deal with the media possibly getting wind of him speaking to law enforcement," I say smoothly. I know how to deal with people like this, how to give them the space to dig their own grave.

She clears her throat and glances toward the phone.

"So, if he'd like to meet us at the station today, let's say at six this evening..."

"Actually, if it will just take a few minutes, I can see if I can give you a little bit of time in his schedule, just give me a moment," she says as she picks up the phone.

I hear her low explanation into the phone. Her words are punctuated in a way that tells me that she gets yelled at often. She hangs up and then looks back to us.

"He can give you twenty minutes," she says as she motions toward a door behind her.

We walk toward the entry, our shoes echoing in the giant lobby. I push the door in to find a long hallway beyond. The scene before me reminds me of a labyrinth before a Bond villain's lair. Shiny walnut wood lines the halls, illuminated by lines of LEDs along the floor and the ceiling. At the far end of the hall there are two small doors inset into the wood on either side and a glass door where the hall ends. Gavin's name is etched into the glass, the letters frosted. I glance at Lucas as we walk. This all seems a little much, and his expression seems to match my feeling on the view in front of us.

When we approach the glass, I can see into the office. A man sits at an ornate desk, the fixture carved of wood that's almost obsidian, while all the details are gold. A laptop stands open in the center, a coffee cup to its left. The man has his back to us, his legs propped up on the far end of the desk. From here, I can see that his black hair dusts the collar of his sports coat. It's slicked back, parts of it feathered with silver. I rap my knuckle on the door and he waves us in without turning.

The door hisses open in front of us, as if he's pulled some lever, but I didn't see him move. Two cerulean velvet chairs rest in front of the desk, where I imagine he'll want us to sit. Inside, I can see the full expanse of the office. It's massive, at least a thousand square feet. Along the back wall sits a TV along with a few leather chairs and a glass table. Several cabinets filled with awards line the walls; framed ads from the fifties decorate the office instead of art. This is Don Draper's wet dream.

Gavin turns, looks to Lucas, then his eyes carve their way up my body. I'm aware of every inch of my flesh where his gaze falls, and it makes my skin crawl. I hate to admit that Gavin is a good-looking man. He's got broad shoulders, chiseled cheekbones, and a straight nose that fits his face just right. A whisper of a beard frames his square jaw and his full lips.

"Well, I wasn't expecting this," he says as he arches his eyebrow. "Well, *you*, I should say." His voice is as smooth as velvet, and I can absolutely see why this guy has a playboy reputation. It's been three seconds and he's already flirting with me.

I try my best to force a smile. Maybe if this guy thinks he has a chance with me, he'll give me the answers that I'm looking for.

"You know, if you'd like, we could have this interview over dinner," he says to me, ignoring Lucas.

"While I appreciate that, I think we can handle this here," I say.

He nods slowly and a smirk quirks his lips. "Oh, I bet we can. Please, take a seat," he says as he signals to the chairs.

I let Lucas sit first, hoping that'll get Gavin's focus off of me. It doesn't work. He watches me too closely as I walk across the room and take my seat. Gavin leans back in his chair and swivels slowly back and forth as he looks me over, like he's sizing me up.

"So, Mrs...?"

"It's Detective Durant," I say, clarifying my name for him. He's obviously digging for information, but I'm not going to give him the satisfaction of knowing that I'm single.

He nods slowly. "What questions did you have for me, Detective?" He says *detective* in a voice that's trying desperately to be sensual. I'd laugh at him if I didn't need answers.

"We're here about Ellie Gordon," I say, watching his body language closely. To his credit, his expression doesn't falter for even a moment when I say her name.

"What about her?" he asks.

"We heard from several people in town that you and Ellie were dating." Lucas jumps in as I take my notepad from my pocket. I don't plan on spilling who passed the information, but I want to make it clear to him that I have several sources.

He nods. "Yes, we were. But I guess I wasn't her type, because I stopped hearing from her after our last date about two weeks ago."

"You didn't find it alarming that you didn't hear back from her?" I ask.

He shakes his head. "Women ghost sometimes. It happens. I wasn't going to force myself on her if she didn't want to talk to me. I have plenty of options," he says, his grin widening before he winks at me.

Ugh, do women really find this charming or alluring? I feel like I'm being hit on by a used-car salesman. I'm not sure if he wants to fuck me or see me slip into a late-model Toyota with low mileage.

"What did the two of you do on your last date?" This is a bit of information that no one else has had, so I intend to double-check any of the information that he gives me.

"We went for a walk around the lake, then we went to Charley's. It's a steakhouse that my family owns. She loves the place, so that's typically where we go," he explains. "After the date we walked around downtown a bit, got ice cream, and then we went our separate ways."

I note that down so that I can check with the staff to see if he was there. I do at least know they officially parted ways downtown, thanks to the security footage, but whether or not he followed her after is still unclear. However, if his family owns it, they may cover for him if he wasn't actually there.

"Do you own a pickup truck?" I ask.

He shakes his head. "No, that's not really my style."

"Did Ellie say anything to you during that dinner that surprised you?" I ask. I don't want to flat out ask him about the pregnancy yet. I want to see if he offers it up first.

His brows furrow as he considers but his forehead doesn't wrinkle. Botox? "Like that she didn't want to see me anymore or something?"

"Anything at all out of the ordinary," I clarify, trying not to lead him. I want him to give me the info here. What he remembers could tell us a lot.

He shakes his head. "No, not that I remember."

All right then, time to drop the bomb. "So, she didn't tell you that she was pregnant then?"

His eyes nearly bug out of his head as he glances between the two of us. "That's not possible. Or if she was, it wasn't mine. She definitely didn't tell me about that at dinner, if that's true."

"That couldn't be possible? Why?" Lucas jumps in. He leans toward Gavin.

He lets out a low laugh and shakes his head. "You're going to make me blush, Detective. I don't typically kiss and tell. But believe it or not, Ellie and I had never had sex."

Now that, I don't believe for a second. A guy like this isn't going to wait for true love. He's obviously finding plenty of women to sleep with. You don't get a playboy reputation for being chaste.

"You really expect me to believe that?" I nearly laugh. "Would you be willing to give a sample of your DNA?"

"Well, yes, Detective, I do. There's no reason for me to lie. If Ellie was pregnant with my baby, I'm sure you'd be able to verify that information with her when you find her, so I'm not sure what you think I stand to gain here." He shrugs. "And if you really need my DNA to determine a baby isn't mine when you find her, fine. But I'm sure she can tell you yourself."

He doesn't know that Ellie's dead. I forgot that detail. If he's lying, he's one of the best that I've encountered.

"I'm sorry to inform you, but Ellie's body has been identified. She passed away," I say, my words a little harsher than I mean for them to be. "Her death was ruled a homicide. That's why we're here."

His brows fall, and his mouth hangs open for a moment. "What happened to her?" he asks, his voice low.

"That body found on the edge of town two weeks ago, that was Ellie. She died the night of your last date," I say.

He shakes his head. "No, that's not possible."

"Unfortunately, it is," I say. "So, I'm very curious what was said during your dinner, and what might have happened to Ellie after your date."

"I didn't have anything to do with this. I would never hurt her. You can talk to every girl in this town who I've dated. I've never hurt or threatened any of them. I might have some problems with commitment, and I might not be the best guy in the world, but I am not capable of *that*."

"Oh, I do intend to ask them all. I will talk to everyone in this town and find every skeleton in your closet if I have to, to track down who did this. If you did this, you cannot hide it from me," I say. There's no veiled threat in my words. The threat is completely clear.

He nods and steeples his fingers atop the desk. "I don't doubt that for a minute, Detective. If Ellie was pregnant or if she died the night of our date, I didn't have anything to do with either of those things."

"What happened between you and Margo?" Lucas asks. I'd almost forgotten to ask about her.

He shakes his head. "We just didn't want the same things."

That seems like a cop-out to me, and I'm not sure I believe him. Lucas glances at me, his expression saying the same thing.

"I know that Margo and Ellie had a falling out. Margo accused Ellie of stealing a bunch of her jewelry and pawning it all," he says.

I write that down.

"Where did you go after your date?" I ask.

"Ellie and I left the ice cream place separately. I went home. I can show you the footage on my video doorbell if you'd like. I was home about thirty minutes after we got ice cream," he offers.

I nod, and he pulls out his phone, tapping a few times before showing me a video. Sure enough, he strolls up to the door at about ten fifteen in the evening. I scan the video, looking for blood on his clothes, but there's nothing. He doesn't seem upset, angry, anything. Nothing seems out of sorts about him at all. It would take an extreme sociopath to go from torturing and butchering a woman and setting her body on fire to walking home casually as if he'd gone on a stroll, and it would have likely taken him over an hour.

"Can you please send me a copy of that video?" I ask as I pass him my business card.

He nods. "Absolutely."

I shove up from the chair, and we collect the DNA sample from Gavin. We need to get back out there. Gavin couldn't have done this based on our timeline, but someone in this town did. And I have to find them.

"Oh, and Gavin," I say as I turn back to him.

"Yes, Detective?" he says with a smirk.

"That contact information is meant for that video or tips only. If you reach out to me to flirt, you will regret it."

He leans into the desk, closer to me. "Will you use those cuffs on me?"

I roll my eyes and storm out of his office. As we reach the

parking lot, there are several news vans parked, cameras out, their reporters hanging around like seagulls waiting for someone to drop a French fry. I stalk toward my Jeep, and the questions begin to rise around me as the media shouts toward me. When I finally make it back to the station, I put in a request for a warrant for the records for the pawnshop. I need to know how Ellie's necklace made it into that case. Did she sell it? Did someone else? I've been going over the conversation with Max in my mind over and over again, and unfortunately a warrant seems the only way forward.

There's a knock on my motel door, and I open it, expecting my dinner delivery. Instead, I find Grover standing on the other side of the door. I glance back into my room, toward the door where I've got my service pistol stashed. I curse myself for already taking it out of my holster and making myself comfortable.

"What do you want, Grover?" I ask without skipping a beat.

"You got me fired," he says, his eyes narrowing on me.

"No, I didn't," I say as I lean against the doorframe. I've got about four inches on Grover, so I can't say I find him particularly threatening. Every few minutes someone walks down the hall, so we're not secluded enough for Grover to do any real damage.

"Yes, you did. You were at the pawnshop asking all types of questions about me. And then Max said that I shouldn't bother coming back tomorrow! I just got that job," he says. Each word rises by an octave until I swear the pitch could shatter glass.

I sigh. "I asked some questions because of your connections to Ellie Gordon. If that got you fired, then I'd say you were already on pretty thin ice. I've heard that you continue to make it a habit of harassing women who come into your workplaces. If you're looking to hold a job for more than a few weeks, maybe you should switch up your behavior a bit."

He takes a step toward me, and I straighten, rising to his nonverbal challenge.

"Take one more step, I dare you," I say, and he takes a step backward.

"Stay out of my business, Durant. Or you'll regret it," he warns.

"We could clear this all up right now. Where were you the night of April 13th?"

"Suck my dick," he says as he storms off down the hall.

I let out a low laugh before I slam the door.

23

We've got nothing. I've sent Gavin's DNA to the lab, but based on his reaction, his body language, I'm not sure he's good for this. Every single minute that this case goes on, I realize how little we have. There's so little evidence, so few leads. But I won't let this case go cold. I won't fail these two women who are relying on me to find their killers. I look up from my desk. Lucas sits across from me, his laptop open as he looks over a case file. The office is empty except for the two of us.

"We need to talk to Margo again. She lied to us the last time we spoke; I want to see if she's lying to us about the night of Ellie's disappearance," I say. She didn't give us an alibi for the night of Ellie's death, and right now, she's the only one with any real motive to go after Ellie. Unless the father of her baby is out there somewhere.

He nods. "I'll see if I can get her to come down to the station at some point today."

"Just phrase it gently. I don't want her to lawyer up. Make it clear that we're not sure about Gavin's story or something," I say.

"Do *you* want to call her?" he asks pointedly.

"No, you're a safer bet. You've got a softer approach than I do. I might put her on edge."

"Never thought I'd hear you admit that out loud," he says with a chuckle.

"Shut up and get her in here," I say as I shove up from the desk and stalk over to the coffee pot to refill my cup. I look out over the lake next to the station. A man is walking around the park, making lazy circles. From here, I can't tell who he is.

I turn back to watch Lucas as he dials a number on his cellphone, then presses it to his ear. Within a few minutes, he's scheduled an appointment for us to talk to Margo later this afternoon. That's one thing I'll be able to cross off of my list.

My phone vibrates in my pocket and I grab it. Racquel's name flashes on the screen before I accept the call and press it to my ear.

"Hey, Racquel."

"Hi, Detective. We got the DNA back on the second victim. We were able to match it to the DNA sample that you had sent in from Manhattan," she says.

"Did anything come back on checking to see if Ellie was pregnant?" I ask.

Racquel clears her throat. "We were able to recover some tissue; she may have been in the very early stages of pregnancy. We have not been able to run the DNA of the tissue against the database yet or to the sample that you sent over. But it does appear she was pregnant."

"How early on?"

"Likely right at four or five weeks," she explains.

"Did you find anything else?" I ask.

"No, that's all I've got for you," she says.

Racquel and I finish up the call. I thank her and shove my phone back into my pocket. I turn back to Lucas and update him.

"So, we need to talk to Margo, run Gavin's DNA, question Twila again, and call Chloe's brother, Jack," he says.

I grab my laptop and walk to the conference room; my first call has to be to the only family that Chloe has, even if it's just her brother. Luckily, we were able to get his number from Twila.

I dial the number and wait for the call to connect.

Static on the other end of the line and an uneasy male voice saying "Hello?" tells me that someone has answered.

"Hello, is this Jack Williams?" I ask.

"Yes, this is Jack. Who is this?" he asks, his words unsteady.

"This is Detective Durant; I work with the New York State Crime Bureau. I spoke to you recently about your missing sister..." I say. "I was hoping to talk to you for a few minutes about your sister."

"Oh, right. What do you need?"

"I'm sorry to inform you over the phone, we typically prefer to do this in person, but your sister has passed away," I explain.

A sharp intake of breath tells me that he heard me clearly.

"Mr. Williams, I am so sorry for your loss."

"What happened? Was it a car accident? What happened to my sister?" he asks quickly, his questions running into one another.

"Unfortunately, your sister was the victim of a homicide," I say carefully, suddenly wishing that I had Lucas on this call. I'm not sure my delivery is soft enough for this.

"Someone murdered her?" he asks, an edge to his words.

"Yes, I'm very sorry," I say.

"Who killed my sister?" he asks, his words sharpening.

"We haven't made an arrest and I was hoping that I could talk to you a little more about your sister to see if you can give us any insight that might help in our search." I want to pace the room. I hate doing this over the phone. This isn't an easy conversation to have under normal circumstances, but over the phone with someone who's long distance, that makes this even harder.

"What do you need from me?" he asks. "My sister and I weren't very close. I'm about ten years her senior, and after our parents died, we continued to grow apart. It's not for lack of love or anything, we just didn't really have much in common."

"When was the last time that you spoke to your sister?" I ask.

"For Christmas, I think. Or she might have called for my birthday. I don't really recall."

"During any of your last communications, did Chloe mention that she was having problems with anyone? Did she have any concerns?" I ask.

"She'd had trouble on and off at work with some guy who was basically stalking her. She mentioned it offhandedly a few times, like it was some kind of joke, but I told her that she should take something like that more seriously. She ended up not working at the bookstore anymore. She started doing graphic design from home instead."

Chloe worked at the bookstore as well? "Do you remember his name?"

"No, unfortunately I don't. I don't think she ever told me his name."

I clear my throat and look over my notes. "Do you know of any enemies or bad blood that your sister had with anyone?"

"No, I don't think so. Chloe usually got along with everyone. Except for our mother, but obviously she's not around to cause problems anymore."

I don't think that Jack is going to be able to give me anything else of use, so I thank him for his time and promise to keep him updated on anything that we find on the case. I end the call with him, close my laptop, and grab my things. A figure emerges at the top of the stairs. Sergeant Dirby's cheeks are pink as he scans the room. I hadn't expected him. Another figure comes into view behind him. Dirby's eyes are apologetic when they land on me.

"Got a minute, Durant?" He asks almost like he hopes I'll say no.

"I was about to head out," I say motioning toward my closed laptop.

"I'll just take a few minutes," Sheriff Crowley says. "Let's go to the conference room."

"Do I need my union rep?" I ask, anxiety needling me. This can't be good.

He shakes his head. "No, this will be quick."

I follow the two men into the conference room as my palms slick with sweat. My heart pounds so hard, I'm slightly light-headed. This can't be good. Both men take a seat and I follow suit.

"Detective, do you remember seeing anyone else at the station when you left the night of Officer Green's death?"

I shrug. "I don't remember. There may have been others in the building still. I didn't check the building before I headed back to the motel." Though I doubt there was anyone there but me and Green, I don't mention that.

Sheriff Crowley takes an image out of a folder and slides it across the table to me. The grainy black-and-white picture comes into focus as I pick it up. My Jeep stands in the dark parking lot, a figure next to it. But it's clearly not me. I look up to Dirby and Sheriff Crowley, confused.

"Who is that?" I ask.

"That's what we were hoping that you could tell us," Sheriff Crowley says as he lays out a few more pictures, sharing a slideshow of a man entering and exiting my Jeep before I leave the station. The final images show the man approach the building after I've left.

"It looks like this person entered your vehicle, then went

into the station after you. Did you see anyone in the parking lot?"

I shake my head. But I realize the implication here. They can't pin Green's death on me. Someone else was there, but who was this man, and why was he in my car?

Dirby and Crowley leave the office, and a few minutes after I head down the stairs. As I walk down, I bump into Chad —literally.

"Oh, hey there, Durant," he says as he glares at me.

I want to groan and to kick him down the stairs, but I don't. "Chad," I say simply.

"Where are you off to in such a hurry?" he asks.

"Why aren't you off anywhere in a hurry? How many bodies do you have piling up? Twenty now?" I throw the words at him like daggers.

"Jealous?" he asks with a sick grin.

"Jealous... of all the victims that you're going to be held accountable for if you don't find their killer? No, not exactly," I say, sarcasm dripping from my words.

"Don't worry about my case load. I can handle it," Chad says as he steps closer to me. I take a purposeful step back. "Unless you want to offer your services?"

"If you're still scrambling after I'm done solving my case, I'd be happy to help you if you don't know how to solve a homicide." The jab lands. He glares at me for a moment, but as soon as I register the look, it's gone, and he's replaced it as if it were never there at all.

"Good luck with your case, Durant," he says as he squeezes by me, his shoulder slamming into mine. I grit my teeth and keep walking, though I know he did it on purpose.

I walk downtown, make a short call to Raven to confirm that Chloe did in fact work at the bookstore for a short time and that she also had problems with Grover. Then, I focus on heading to Twila's clothing shop. She's the only other connection that I have to Chloe in this town so far, so hopefully she'll be able to offer some answers that will help. I've put in a warrant request to search Chloe's apartment, but it could be another twenty-four hours before we have it in hand. The judge is notoriously slow. Chloe's landlord hasn't gotten back to me about entering the apartment, so even if we had her brother's permission, there's not much we can do without the warrant.

Eyes follow me as I walk the streets downtown. These days I'm unsure if it's because everyone knows I'm investigating the homicides in town or because I'm still an outsider to them. That's the thing about these small towns: word travels fast, bad words travel faster. I was surprised that Gavin hadn't heard about Ellie's fate for that reason. Typically secrets move through towns like this at the speed of the wind.

I push open the door to Twila's shop. She stands at the back, rearranging clothes on a long rack. She turns when the door dings, and her hands drop the garment she was holding. Twila scrambles to pick up the shirt, put it back on the hanger, and shove it onto the rack before turning to me. My presence clearly frazzled her.

"Do you have news about Chloe?" she asks, her eyebrows inching up her forehead as she walks toward me. Her high heels click against the wood floor as she walks.

I wave toward the chair she's got at her desk toward the back of the shop. "You should take a seat," I say, knowing that the words are a grim preview of what's coming.

Her face falls as she looks from me to the chair, but she follows my directions anyway. I trail behind her as she walks and cross my arms.

"I'm really sorry to inform you that we confirmed this morning that Chloe has passed away," I say.

"The news said that they identified one of the victims, but they didn't say who it was. I was really hoping that it wasn't her," she says as her gaze falls to the floor. She shakes her head and sniffles. "I can't believe that she's dead."

"I know it must come as a shock, and I want to let you know that I understand and I am so sorry for your loss," I say. "But I do need your help so that we can find whoever did this to Chloe."

She nods stiffly and finally looks back to me. "Did you talk to Jack?"

"We did. I spoke to him a short time ago. He has been informed about Chloe's fate," I explain. "Jack told us that Chloe had dealt with a stalking situation at work. Did she tell you anything about that?"

She sighs. "Yes, she didn't take it seriously though. It was more of an inconvenience. She was annoyed that the guy seemed to be so interested in her, but she didn't really take any steps."

"How exactly was he stalking her?" I ask. "Her brother wasn't able to provide many details."

"At first, it started small. She'd catch him watching her at the store. He was always keeping tabs on her calendar—where she was going for lunch, trying to make sure they worked the same shifts. He'd park next to her at work to have opportunities to *run into her*. Those sorts of things. She thought back then it was a little crush and didn't think much about it. But then he started texting her, like all the time. They'd gone out for lunch together once, Chloe thought as colleagues, but clearly this guy thought it was more. After that, she caught him waiting outside her house in the middle of the night several times. Once, she thought she saw him looking in through her windows with a drone or something."

I note all of that down. It sounds incredibly creepy and very suspicious, but not at all unlike what we heard about Ellie's experience. If I were her, I would have gone to the cops. But many times law enforcement doesn't take women seriously. For all I know, she did try to get help. "Did she inform anyone about the stalking?" I ask.

"No. She thought that she would get in trouble at work for it since she'd originally gone out to lunch with him of her own free will. Back then, she thought that Raven and Grover were very friendly, so she was afraid that it'd paint her in a negative light."

I'm sure she was also concerned about the rumors that might spread through the town. It'd be so easy to gain a reputation as a *problem employee* in a town like this if you brought up concerns with your boss. I'm sure all the business owners speak to one another.

"So, what happened with it?" I ask.

"She ended up quitting the bookstore and started freelance graphic design instead so that she didn't have to deal with it anymore. It worked out. She was actually much happier in the end, but it was a huge risk on her part. She had done graphic design years ago, but didn't really care for the industry. She liked working with people more, and books."

"Was there any more stalking after she left?" I ask.

"A little bit. He did continue to try to reach out to her via text and on social media despite her frequent blocking," she explains.

"Did she take any steps then?"

She sighs and crosses her arms. "You have to understand that Chloe was very stubborn and fiercely independent. She was the type of woman who didn't believe in asking for help or letting anyone know that she was in a position of vulnerability. She didn't take the threats seriously, not that she ever told me, and when I told her to reach out to law enforcement, she brushed me off over and over again."

"Unfortunately, that's what typically happens in these cases," I say. What I don't say is that it then escalates into homicide. I've seen women before who tried so hard to not bring attention to themselves, to their struggles, because they didn't want to be that woman who *cried wolf*. Women are taught that we need to be independent, that we need to stand on our own, so reaching out for help, asking someone—even the police—for help, that seems like a failure.

She nods weakly. "I wish that she'd listened to me."

"I know, it's so hard," I say, feeling like the words aren't enough. "Do you know if Ellie Gordon and Chloe were friendly?"

"Honestly, I'm not sure. Chloe mentioned her a few times because they worked together at the bookstore, but I don't know if they spent much time together outside of work," she explains.

I wrap up my questioning with Twila once I'm sure that I've gotten everything that I need. Next, I stop back by Margo's to try and confirm the story about her missing jewelry, but she's not home and she missed our appointment. I make a note to reach out to her again later—unfortunately it's all too common for people to flake out on our appointments. As I weave through downtown with a fresh cup of coffee in hand, I overhear several women chatting about the McKenzie Mauler. Apparently a man has been seen lingering at the edge of the woods, watching residents near the lake. As the number of victims has grown, I can feel the crackle of electricity in the air, the fear, the slight edge to everyone's voice. There are two hunters stalking this town, and it's only a matter of time before they strike again.

24

TWENTY YEARS AGO

It's been three weeks since my mom let my dad move back in. And I feel like we're all walking around holding our collective breaths. I keep waiting for *something* to happen, because they haven't yelled yet. It's like watching a bomb tick down. An explosion is coming, but the clock is stuck on three seconds. I glance between them, the tension filling the room. I wait for the tick, for the last moment before the screaming begins.

But it hasn't happened. Nothing has happened.

And so now, I wait. I wait for my mother to take out her anger on me, I wait for my father to disappear for hours, for her to lash out because he's gone. But—there's nothing.

"We should all get ice cream," my dad says as he pops his head in the living room.

His voice startles me. I've been watching TV on mute to not upset my mother, and she's in the back of the room, looking over books about knitting. She glances to me, then her eyes narrow before moving to my father.

"Why?" she snaps.

Here it comes. I know it.

"Because I think getting ice cream would be nice," he says.

She raises a brow to that. "You never want to get ice cream. You're lactose intolerant," she says, grimacing at him.

"Come on, it would be nice. We should try to reconnect as a family," he urges.

I can see the argument brewing behind her eyes. The curses I know she wants to lob at him. I can almost argue it for her. She'll start by saying that it's his fault that we need to reconnect as a family in the first place. And why is he so concerned about it now? He didn't care for thirteen years.

But she doesn't say that. Instead, she sighs, nods defeatedly, and walks toward him.

"Let's go, Harley," she says to me without even turning around.

I click the TV off, and trail after them. In the car, my heart races. Because I still feel like something is coming, something is off. Maybe it's just me being paranoid. The news has been talking nonstop about the dead women, trying to find their killer. And I know who the killer is. He's driving the car.

Some days I wonder how many women he's killed. Others, I try to forget because it makes me sick. I can't get the image of that dead woman out of my mind. I've drawn her a few times to see if seeing her in person again will erase the lines of her face from my memory. But it doesn't help.

The car rolls out of the driveway as my father turns left. In a few minutes, as we're closing in on the ice cream shop, my father slows down.

"So, I'm thinking about moving my practice to Tacoma," he says. My dad has moved his practice three times that I remember. He started small, in our town, and then as it grew he moved closer and closer to Seattle. I think one day he plans to live there, but he hasn't made it that far yet.

"Tacoma?" My mother sputters the name of the city like it's something foreign to her, a dirty word.

"Yes, if I move the practice to Tacoma, then I can get

some patients from Seattle. That would really help me grow. I've had some inquiries from patients asking if I'd be willing to open a satellite office there. So I've really been considering it."

Tension blooms inside the car, and I can practically feel my mother's anger crackling like static. I shrink into the seat, hoping that it'll swallow me. This is what I was waiting for. This will be the spark for the powder keg. Now she has a reason to go off, to rip into him. And he had to do it now, so I'm stuck here to witness it. I wish he'd left me at home.

She lets out a raw laugh. It's humorless, almost pained. "Is this what you were waiting for? Why did you even bother to come back if you were just going to move to Tacoma?" Each of her words is sharp, punctuated with rage.

"Waiting for? What do you mean?"

"You came back just to tell me that you were leaving again? You strung me along for months giving me hope, weaseling your way back into our lives for what? To leave again?"

"No, no—" he says, trying to calm her. This is when he'd usually yell back, when tensions would flare. But something is different this time. His tone has changed completely. "I want you both to come with me. I want to sell the house and to buy a new house there." Silence blooms in the car. "That is, if you're willing to," he finally says after a long silence.

My heart squeezes. This could be it. This could be the moment when it all implodes or when we finally have a good path forward. If she doesn't want to go, I'll fight to stay with my father. I can't stay with her. I've already told him that.

"Do you really mean that?" she asks.

He nods. "Yes, I do." He turns into the parking lot of the ice cream shop, but I'm frozen, waiting for my mother to decide our fate.

"Houses there are very expensive..."

"We have a lot of equity in our house. With how the practice is doing now, with the new office, I don't think we'd have any problem affording a house there," he says.

My mother is silent for a long time again. When she's silent is when she's the most dangerous, the most terrifying. I'd rather her scream, at least then I'd know what she's thinking. Sweat prickles on the back of my neck as I look between the two of them. I feel like my head is on the chopping block as I wait for an executioner to decide my fate.

"Okay," she says, finally. And I swallow hard, feeling very much like my heart is lodged in my throat.

"Okay...?" My dad drags the question out, wanting more from her.

"We can try it out. I like living near the water. I've never lived in the city like that, but I would be willing to give it a try," she says.

Tears prickle my eyes as I feel something that I haven't gotten to feel often, especially not for the past few years. Hope. My dad pops his car door open, and I follow suit. I want to thank my mother, to tell her I'm so happy about moving to Tacoma. But I don't. If I tell her that I'm happy, if I act like I like this decision, she may change her mind to punish me. So instead, I press my lips together and stare at the ground as I walk.

My dad wraps his hand around mine, and squeezes it gently. "What do you think, kiddo?" he prods.

I offer a noncommittal shrug. I'll celebrate with him later, when my mother isn't hovering, listening. For now, I'll smother my happiness and drag it back out later when I can enjoy it.

As we walk into the ice cream shop, the woman who owns the place stands behind the counter, a newspaper open in front of her. She's chatting with another woman. Even though the door dinged, they haven't looked at us. They're too deep into their conversation.

"Goldie, have you heard about this killer?" she asks, straightening the newspaper, making it wrinkle loudly.

"That Seattle Sleeper guy? The one who's killing all the women out there in Olympia?" she asks.

"Yeah, that guy."

"What about him?" Goldie asks.

"They've got a sketch of him!" she says, as she pulls the paper over to the woman, pointing her finger at it, rustling the paper as she does.

I walk closer, and glance at the page. My heart sinks the moment that I see it, when the cold eyes stare back at me from the page. There's no denying that the man on that paper, the rudimentary sketch, is my father staring back at me.

I look back to my dad, but the place where he stood next to me is empty. He's already back in the car, the reverse lights flashing white on the wet concrete.

25

At four in the afternoon, the slowest judge on the planet finally approves our search warrant and our request for the records from the pawnshop. I've never had one take this long, especially when the goal is to check on the well-being of someone who's missing. But I guess now that we know she's dead, that's kicked him into gear. I wait outside Chloe's apartment with Lucas and some of the other guys from the station. We've got to wait on the forensics team to arrive in case this is a crime scene. We're still not sure where Chloe died and what evidence may or may not be present here.

The winds have kicked up and blow in thick clouds, shading the afternoon sky. Though my sunglasses are pinching the bridge of my nose, I keep them on. Lucas is silent beside me, but he looks at me every few minutes like he wants to say something. I take a slow sip of my coffee, the lukewarm liquid coating my throat as I look over the parking lot again.

"How long do you think this is going to take?" Lucas asks, as he crosses his arms.

"Are you in a rush?" I ask as I raise my eyebrow before appraising him.

"Maybe," he says as he presses his lips together.

"Oh?" I wonder if he's looking for conversation because he's bored with the wait for the team. I knew it would take us a while; another body was found in McKenzie this morning. Racquel already has enough on her plate, and it makes me wish yet again that we had more resources, so our team wasn't spread so thin.

"There's this guy I've been talking to... I was supposed to talk to him tonight."

"Well, I'll make sure you get out of here on time," I say as I flash him a smile. Lucas and I chat about the guy until Racquel and her team pull up. I let out a bottled breath as the team starts to spill out of their white vans. My pulse picks up as I move toward the building, Lucas flanking me.

Now, it gets real. Now, we might be able to actually get some answers. It takes a few minutes for everyone to get ready, and for the landlord to open the door for us. The air inside smells stale, and slightly sour, like there's food inside that's gone bad. Given how long her apartment has been empty, that doesn't surprise me. I slip on my foot covers, yank on my latex gloves, and ensure that my hair is pulled back. Typically, I hang back and let the forensics team do a first sweep of a crime scene to lower the risk of contamination. But I'm too anxious to stand outside waiting for news. I need to go over the scene myself, to try and piece together what happened to Chloe.

The soft light spills in through her windows, illuminating a small dining area with a worn wooden table, a kitchen that's tidy other than a pile of dishes in the sink. To the right of the kitchen, after we walk into the apartment, we find a living room with an L-shaped couch, a flat-screen TV, and a coffee table atop a fluffy rug. The lamps are in their places on the night-stands, books stacked on the coffee table, and a vase in the corner. There are no signs of struggle here at all.

The flash of flashlights from the forensics team searching

for details in the space flickers around me, strobing the walls, the floor, the ceiling. Though I can hear the rest of the team moving behind me, there's an abandoned feel to this place, as if it knew that Chloe wasn't coming back. The life I'm sure Chloe built here is gone, snuffed out of the world like she was. I continue past the living room, down a hall. I pass a small office with nothing but a desk and a laptop in it, then at the end of the hall I find the bedroom. The covers are thrown half off the bed, part hanging onto the floor.

I creep farther into the room, careful of my footing. In my pocket, I've got a flashlight, which I retrieve and click on. There are dark droplets on the floor in the bedroom, creating a trail that leads to the bathroom. It looks like dried blood to me, but I'll need the team to double-check. If that's blood, that means that Chloe was likely attacked in her apartment, then led or taken to the logging road. I look at the windows, trying to find any evidence of entry. But there is none. That means Chloe likely let her attacker in. This was someone she knew, someone she was comfortable enough with to be left alone, someone she wasn't surprised knew where she lived...

In the living room, I find Lucas chatting with Racquel about the scene. I let them both know what I've found, my suspicions. They both walk back toward the bedroom, and I follow. Racquel and one of her assistants confirm that the droplets are in fact blood. And that changes everything. Because now we know for sure that Chloe was taken from her apartment. She let someone in.

It takes us several hours to finish processing the scene, but I send Lucas home early so he doesn't miss his chat. There's nothing he can accomplish here anyway. Technically I could leave as well, but it makes me feel better to be at the scene, to wait to see if any new information is uncovered. The light fades, giving way to night, and the scene quiets. Slowly the team begins to filter away, and I finally leave the apartment. Several news vans are parked around the parking lot as I head out. My footsteps echo too loudly on the pavement, and I swear I can feel the tension expand in the air as the teams take note of my presence.

A woman in a red dress and with a microphone in hand runs toward me with a camera operator trying to keep up behind her. A sinister smile splits her lips, her red lipstick startlingly bright.

"I'm Libby Langston with WMHT. Did you find a body in that apartment? Evidence of a crime? Is this connected to the recent bodies that have been found around Saranac Lake?" She fires off the questions at me without even taking a breath in between them.

"I'm sorry, but I cannot comment on an ongoing investigation," I say, the words bubbling up inside of me automatically.

"Is this related to the death of Ellie Gordon or Chloe Williams?" she asks, her words all blurring together.

"Again, I can't comment," I say again.

"The public is concerned. The members of this community are concerned for their safety," she says, trying to guilt me into saying *something*.

"If the public is concerned, then I recommend that they come forward with any information that might be helpful for law enforcement." I keep walking toward my Jeep, Libby and her camera operator hot on my trail. As she starts to speak again, I climb inside, shut my door, and lock it. She glowers at me from the other side. But I pull away, leaving them and the scene of the crime behind me.

26

We haven't had any news back on the samples that were taken at Chloe's apartment this morning. And so far, every lead I've tried to chase down about Ellie's escorting has led me nowhere. Because we were on scene at Chloe's apartment all day, I haven't been able to look at the pawnshop records that Max sent over from our warrant. The evening sun burns on the horizon, casting the desks in an orange glow. Though I should probably finish up my day and grab dinner, I can't leave yet. I've got digging to do and I need to start combing through the records. Though I'd asked Matthew to help us with the investigation to dig through the social media accounts of Ellie and Chloe, thus far, no one has had the time.

Lucas throws open the door to the third floor, bags rustling in his hands. I sent him home from Chloe's apartment hours ago, so I didn't expect to see him back tonight.

"What's all that?" I say, motioning toward the bags.

"Burgers," he says, as he drops the bags on my desk.

The smell of French fries hits my nostrils the moment he sets it down. I sigh, as I realize how hungry I am. Sometimes I'm able to get serious tunnel vision and block out how much I need food. Hours later, I'll emerge shaky and regretting my decisions.

"You are an angel," I say.

"Yeah, yeah, remember that the next time you're pissed at me."

I mock shock. "Name one time I've been pissed at you," I say a little too dramatically.

"Um, at least twelve times a day." He rolls his eyes at me.

I scoff at him. "I am not nearly that moody."

"You are far more moody than that. I'm just being generous today." He laughs.

"I'll let that slide because you brought me food," I say as I snatch one of the bags and unearth a burger inside of a greasy wrapper. I shovel the food into my face as I swivel my laptop so I can eat and scroll at the same time.

"How was your chat?" I ask as I wiggle my brows at him.

He shakes his head. "I don't kiss and tell," he says before he turns his attention to my screen, as if it'll make me drop the questions about his date. "What are you looking at?" he asks, glancing at my screen.

"Just opened the files from Max. He's got an Excel sheet with records. He was able to argue to limit what he gave us. So the records are limited to the specific necklace and what Ellie specifically pawned," I explain.

"What have you found so far?"

"Nothing, I just opened it up," I say as I turn the screen so he can see what I'm looking at.

We start to go over it together; there are many more records than I'd expect. There are over fifty records of Ellie pawning jewelry.

"Where did she get all this jewelry?" Lucas asks as he scans the entries.

"Do you think she got it from escorting?" I ask.

"Margo said she only did it a few times. I don't see how that could have added up to all this..."

"Margo did accuse her of stealing jewelry though." I hate to bring it up, since we haven't been able to confirm this story with Margo yet. Gossip isn't the same as real police work, but when there are pieces like this that align, it's hard for me to argue with it.

"Have you been able to meet with her? I know you mentioned you were going to try to swing by after she didn't show up for her appointment," Lucas says.

"She wasn't home. But I think that's our best lead for tracking down this jewelry."

I grab my cell and give Margo a call, but it goes straight to voicemail. I leave her a short message to give us a call back when she gets a moment.

"So, it looks like Ellie isn't the one who pawned her necklace..." I say, as I finally reach the entry for the necklace on the spreadsheet.

"Grover?" Lucas says as he finally catches up.

"Well, tomorrow morning we're going to have to track him down again," I say.

Lucas shakes his head. "I think it's time that we have him come to the station... There's a lot pointing in his direction."

I agree. The necklace, the stalking, the cellphone, none of it looks good for Grover. But we have to connect these dots with real, solid evidence. Right now, as much as I hate it, this is all too circumstantial. And nothing crumbles faster than a case based on circumstantial evidence.

"Has the team been able to go through the social media posts yet?" Lucas asks.

I shake my head.

"We should look through and see if we can find any connections between Ellie, Chloe, and Grover," he suggests.

"Good idea," I say.

Digging through social media feeds for evidence is some of the most mindless work. But in about thirty minutes, we're able to confirm that Grover was liking and commenting on posts frequently by Chloe and Ellie. I add that to my notes.

As I scroll through posts made nearly a year ago, I notice a major status change for Chloe—a relationship update. She went from being in a relationship with a man named Jordan Holebrook to being single. I jot the name down. It's not one that I've heard so far from Twila or anyone else in town. Why wouldn't anyone have mentioned the breakup? Maybe it was too long ago? This is the frustration about working in law enforcement. These little details matter, but most people think they don't.

"Looks like Chloe changed her relationship status a lot," he says, his eyes bugging a little bit as he scrolls. "Like a lot a lot." He clicks his tongue in a judgmental way.

"What do you think that means? Lots of potential enemies?" I ask, popping a French fry in my mouth.

"I don't think so. If she moved from guy to guy this often, it doesn't seem like she had enough time to make enemies. Enemies take time. This seems like she had a short attention span."

"I sense a little bit of judgment lingering there," I say, pointing a French fry at him as I talk. But her history sounds similar to Gavin's.

He rolls his eyes.

"Or—is that jealousy? How long have you been single now?"

"Oh shut up, will you."

"Ah, so jealousy it is." I relish this. I really do. So often he takes potshots at me, and I always forget that his relationship status is the bane of his existence. He is a hopeless romantic with nowhere to focus that energy, and it eats at him. "You know, there are a lot of self-help books that talk about how important it is to learn to love yourself single bef—"

"Oh, stop it. But I will say I'm not surprised that you have read those *single-lady* self-help books."

"I haven't read them, but I've seen them all in the bookstore. If you want me to pick you up a copy because you're too embarrassed, I'd be happy to," I say.

"Ugh, will you stop it?" he says as he shoves his burger in his mouth.

"Okay, so back to the case then, since you can dish it but you can't take it." I have to add one more little jab before I move on.

He rolls his eyes at me again.

"We know that Ellie went out with Gavin. I don't see that Chloe went out with Gavin, no connections there. They didn't work at the same place. They did go to the same schools, but so did everyone else here in this town. What else did they have in common?" I ask.

"They didn't go to the same gym. They didn't date the same guy. No overlapping friends that we've found so far. I'm not seeing any connections at all; they don't even look alike. All we've got is that they live in the same town. No indication that Chloe was escorting too."

"So, could the killings have been completely random?" I offer. That is something that happens, though it's on the rarer side. Though this isn't technically a serial killing, because of the ritualistic nature of the deaths my mind is already screaming *serial*. When it comes to serial killers, there's always something that connects the victims. Whether that's where the killer found them, or what they look like, they fit some type of profile. But so far, the bookstore and Grover are the only things connecting these women.

"Oh, here I see that Ellie dated one guy for more than three months," he says, still scrolling through her timeline.

"How long were the other relationships?" I ask.

"Usually less than six weeks," he says, with obvious disapproval. "Why even change your status at that point? You probably don't even know his last name."

"If you added them on Facebook, you know their last name," I snap back, though I know he's not being serious. I feel like he's judging this victim harshly. He didn't even know Ellie. "Anyway, how long did she date this guy?"

"Five months," he says. "Jordan must have been a keeper."

"Jordan Holebrook?" I ask.

He nods. "Yeah, how'd you know?"

"Because Chloe dated him too. About a year ago," I explain as I pull up the status change and show him.

"That was the same time that Jordan was dating Ellie..."

"Okay, let me get this straight, he was Facebook official with both girls at once? That's bold."

"But also worth looking into..." he adds. And he's right. We need to talk to Jordan, that's our only connection between these victims. But before we do that, I need to get some background on who this guy is. So far, I feel like I've heard about every person in this town, and Jordan is a name that's never been mentioned once. Why is that?

I pick up my phone and call Matthew Chen. As always, he picks up on the first ring, though he sounds out of breath this time.

"Hello, Detective Durant, what can I help you with?" he asks.

"Do you happen to know Jordan Holebrook?" I ask.

Matthew clears his throat. "Why are you asking about Jordan?" he asks me, his tone wary.

I give him a short rundown, trying to sum up the connection with the victims in a few sentences. I know that Matthew is quite busy, so I don't want to eat up his day with minutiae, but I want him to also understand that this could be an important piece to our case.

"You're going to run into some problems with Jordan if you

question him," he says, the warning hanging on each of his words.

"What do you mean?"

"Jordan gets into trouble with us a lot, to put it nicely. It seems like every week he's getting picked up for something. It's usually minor. But he's good enough friends with the Croswell family, even if it was something major, they'd hire a lawyer for him. He grew up with Gavin as his best friend, and Gavin got him into—and right out of—trouble all the time," he explains. "Gavin grew out of the troublemaking, but Jordan didn't."

"Can you give me some examples of what he's doing?" I ask. There are a lot of paths that *troublemaking* can lead to, especially in a small town.

"Let's see, most recently, trespassing, breaking and entering, selling stolen property. We caught him trying to steal a boat a few months ago. The list goes on," he explains.

"Any drug issues?" I ask.

"Mostly marijuana, but we've stopped prosecuting for that. He's never carried anything harder that I know of."

"Where can I find him?"

Matthew relays the address to me, and I jot it down, then thank him for his help. While this guy's background doesn't exactly make him sound like the hardened criminal who would butcher two women and then burn their bodies, I can't exactly rule him out without talking to him. Especially if he's spent his whole life being bailed out of trouble over and over again. There might be a reason he keeps going back to crime.

We carve our way through the city toward Jordan's home. He's got a loft apartment in an older building toward the edge of town. The place used to be a factory, but got converted into condos and apartments years ago. We pull into the parking lot, the four-story brick building looming over us. They haven't done much to the façade; the outside still looks very much like a factory. Huge cracks mar the asphalt, and it looks like it's withstood nearly two hundred years. Two benches sit out front, with large ashtrays on either side. We pass by them as we walk toward the front door. The foyer is open, so modern that it looks empty, sparse. Light floods in the large windows, reflecting off the white tile. It looks sterile in here, almost like a hospital. We walk to the elevator and it hisses open in front of us. While many of the old touches of character remain in this building, I'm glad the elevator is sleek and modern. The last thing I need this morning is to be trapped inside an elevator for hours.

We climb to the fourth floor, stepping out when the elevator dings. Though Lucas thought we should haul Jordan to the station to question him, I like going out of my way to corner suspects. I want to catch them off guard, not give them time to prepare. If we ask him to come to the station, he'll set up a time, schedule when he'll tell us all about Chloe and Ellie. I'm not giving him time to get his story straight, to find someone to back up an alibi if he tries to craft one.

As we turn out of the elevator, we find Jordan's door and Lucas knocks. The large door is carved from solid wood, the grains obvious under the bright hallway lights. Age has darkened the edges of the wood, making it look like it was hauled off of a pirate ship or like it has a much richer history than sitting here in this old factory.

Jordan answers the door shirtless, his long dirty-blond hair mussed, pajama pants hanging loosely on his sharp hip bones. A tattoo of a dragon snakes up his chest, just under his collarbone, while a large cobra circles his left arm. He looks between Lucas and me, and grimaces.

"What did I do now?" he groans, and waves us inside.

The space is open, a contemporary space that still holds a lot of industrial flair. Above us, exposed air ducts crisscross the ceiling. Light spills in from the original windows that run the full height of the room. Aged wood covers the floors, pockmarked from years of abuse.

To our left, there's an open kitchen with butcher block countertops and shiny red cabinets. In front of us, a sectional sofa is placed haphazardly in front of an enormous TV. Jordan waves us toward the sitting area.

Based on his demeanor, even if Matthew hadn't told us about Jordan's background, I'd know that he'd run into law enforcement many times. He's too cool, too calm as we stroll inside. From his bed, he grabs a balled up thermal shirt and throws it on, then looks to me.

"We're here to talk to you about Chloe Williams and Ellie Gordon," I explain.

He raises a brow to that as he scoops up a pack of cigarettes, shakes one out, and lights it. "Why?"

"Because they're dead," I say, my words a little more punctuated than I mean for them to be. I probably should have softened the blow, but I want to throw this guy off. I want to make sure we get the truth. I'm not here to make him feel warm and fuzzy about the deaths of his exes.

"What do you mean *they're dead*?" he asks as he glowers at me.

"I'm not sure how to make that statement more clear than I already was." I cross my arms and look to Lucas. He gives me a warning look, which I intend to ignore.

"You dated the both of them, correct?" Lucas asks.

He nods and takes a drag from his cigarette as he starts to pace the room. Hollow thuds echo with his progress through the living room. His eyes are shadowed by his lowered brow.

"Yeah, like years ago. It's been a while," he says.

"It's actually been one year," I explain, looking at the timeline on my notepad.

"Well it feels like more, but whatever."

"Did you date both of them at the same time?" I ask.

He raises a brow, and looks to Lucas like he expects Lucas to defend him.

"We're not here to judge, man," Lucas says as he holds his hands up. "We're just trying to get to the bottom of what happened to them."

"I did date them both at the same time, but last I checked that's not a crime." Smoke pours from his lips as he speaks. He grips his cigarette so tight, I'm surprised that it hasn't snapped in half.

"No, it's not a crime. But it is suspicious that you dated them both and then they both ended up dead," I say. I'm not sure if this guy is as sharp as a sack of wet mice, or if he really can't see the implications here.

He lets out a dry laugh that sounds more like a cough. "Are you questioning everyone who dated *both* of them, because there are at least ten guys in this town who match that criteria," he explains.

"Not that criteria and such a recent timeline," I snap back.

"Okay, fine. So I dated both of them at the same time. But they both knew about it. We weren't exclusive or anything. It was over a year ago. They were both seeing guys from Tinder too. It's not like I was fucking up or anything or hiding something from them. They knew what was up," he explains. He sighs. "Maybe it's a generational thing. I'm sure at your age people see things differently." He adds a sharpness to the phrase *your age*, but I ignore the jab.

"So why did you split up?" Lucas asks.

"Chloe wanted to take a break from dating. She said it was getting too exhausting. Ellie didn't like to stay tied down, so she said she wanted to keep exploring her options." He shrugs. "They moved on and so did I. I didn't take it personally; neither of them were the *one* or anything."

"You're saying there was no bad blood between the three of you?" I ask.

"I know for a little while Ellie got jealous of Chloe, but I told her that was being a little ridiculous. I wasn't jealous of the other guys she was seeing. After that, she never mentioned it again. So I don't know if they had a secret feud going on or anything," he explains.

"Where were you the nights of April 13th and April 27th?" I glance at my notepad, then back to him.

"Playing with my band in Albany," he says as he walks over to his bookshelf and grabs me a couple flyers that are stacked there.

The papers show several different dates with this band Grease Monkey; the pictures in the middle of the flyers are of Jordan. While I doubt that this guy would print up flyers to have credible alibis for the nights of the homicide, I will need to double-check them to be sure.

"There are pictures of me at the venues all night all over social media," he says as he waves his hands at the flyers. "You can keep those."

I fold the flyers and tuck them into my pocket. "Thanks, we'll check on these. So, if you weren't involved in their deaths, did Ellie or Chloe ever tell you anything that made it clear they feared for their safety or had enemies in town?"

He shakes his head. "Not that I remember. But as I said, it's been a while." He looks toward his door. "I think we're done here," he says, making it clear in his tone that our time is up.

As we leave, I pull up the pictures on Instagram that Jordan referenced, and sure enough throughout the nights there are images posted showing him at each of the venues. Mentally, I cross Jordan off the list.

Dark clouds clot the sky as Lucas and I leave the apartment. In the shadow of the building, I pause and scan the parking lot. A van sits in the corner, a camera set up, but no one is standing behind it. Of course the media followed us here. They're hungry for answers. Luckily, they've given me a bit of a break as Chad's case has been far more interesting. I should send him a thank you card for not finding the killer already.

My phone rings, and I accept the call, hoping that it's Margo or Grover returning my call. I need to get both of them into the station to talk to them. But instead, it's my mother's voice that cuts through the silence.

"What do you want, Mother?" I ask. I've been avoiding her emails for weeks. This is how it always starts when she tracks me down. Despite my name changes, unfortunately it's only a matter of time before she tracks me down again. Everything leaves a trail. I know eventually she'll find out where I'm working and she'll show up. She's already mentioned seeing the media coverage about Plattsburgh in her emails.

Lucas glances at me, clearly trying to determine whether or not leaving is actually the best course of action, before he gives me a little distance. With a few feet of space between us, I can unload on my mother in peace if I need to. The last thing I need is for him to hear everything I've been holding back, wanting to say to her for all these years. He doesn't know what she put me through—not the full extent of it anyway. So if I say all the things I've been bottling up in front of him, he will judge me and think that I'm cruel. He'll think that I'm the one in the wrong in this situation.

"It's so nice to hear from you too, Harlow." Sarcasm drips from her words. "Why aren't you answering my emails? Your father and I are worried about you."

"You're worried about me? That's rich," I snap back as I turn my back on Lucas, as if it'll give me some type of privacy. To think that the two people in this world who let me down completely as a child are now worried about me as an adult is a hilarious turn of events I never would have expected.

"Of course we're worried about you," she says, and there's an undercurrent to her words that really makes me question why she's tracking me down *now*. It's been about five years since she really targeted her energy on finding me. But I always wonder what sparks it. "I was hoping that you'd cooled off a bit since the last time we spoke."

"Cooled off?" I choke out a laugh with the words. This woman has no soul. She can't. "Why would I have cooled off? Do you think that my feelings on your abandonment were fleeting? That if I'd only sleep on that, I'd change my mind in the morning?" My father's words are pouring out of my mouth and I want to stop them, but the years of training are hard to shake off.

"You're being ridiculous, Harley. Those things happened twenty years ago. It's time for you to move on," she says. She's got an air of untouchability around her now, a confidence to her voice that I've never heard before.

"It's not ridiculous, Mother." I spit out the word *mother*, like it's a curse. "Dad built a life off of helping people heal wounds that were over twenty years old. I figure you of all people would understand the damage you did with your choices. It may have been easy for you to move on, but you don't get to decide how I feel about what *you* did. That's not how this works." I pace as my words sharpen. "And let me make this clearer for you, because I don't think you took me seriously last time. But if you can't accept that you don't get to dictate how I feel or how I live my life, you don't need to be here. No one invited you, no one here needs you. This isn't closure I asked for, and I'm more than happy to go on living my life without you in it," I say. I still can't wrap my mind around how exactly she expected this reconciliation to go. She really thought I'd step back and welcome her into my life again with open arms?

"Your father and I are concerned about you," she says again.

My jaw locks and I grind my teeth together as the words finally register. I was too distracted by my anger the first time, but now it's hit me. She's talking to my father again? Did they ever stop talking? I assumed they did. I heard about their divorce in the news when I was in foster care. A kernel of hate blooms inside me with her words. The idea that these two monsters, the two people who tore my life apart, are conspiring together to talk about how they're worried about me now is the most ridiculous thing I've ever heard. Why would they get any say in my life *now*? Why would they care?

"You're *concerned* about me?"

"Yes, when we spoke last week, I told him how it seems like you're running yourself ragged, and for what, Harley? For what?" There's concern in her words like I've never heard before. The words seem genuine, but I don't buy them. Not from her.

"To atone." The words tumble out of me unbidden. It's a truth I don't think I've ever shared with anyone, never meant to share with anyone. And yet here they are, being laid bare between us.

"To atone for what?" she asks, her voice creeping higher. There's noise in the background, like she's close to a busy road. "For how you broke apart our family?"

"I did not break apart our family. My father did that—well, he started it and you landed the killing blow. The two of you worked together. He killed women and you killed the family when you abandoned me. So don't even start with me." My voice inches higher, and I step farther from Lucas. I think back to the months after she cast me aside, the first few months in foster care, when I'd sneak to the phone and sob for her to take me back. I should have never done that. I should have accepted that she abandoned me and moved on with my life.

"Someday, you'll understand. Maybe once you have children." Her words are so patronizing.

"I will never have children," I say with finality, though it's none of her business. I will not give this woman the satisfaction of continuing her bloodline. She doesn't deserve grandchildren. Neither does my father.

"You can't possibly mean that. One day—"

"No, not one day, Mother. Never. You seem to think I'm still the child you abandoned. That I'm still that meek teenage girl who was so scared of you, of what the world would do to me. Because I saw true evil up close. I saw it with my own eyes. That girl died the moment you left, the moment Dad went to prison. And this is who's left. You don't know me. You haven't seen me grow. You don't know who I had to become to survive what you did to me. And to be frank, you don't deserve to know me. You don't deserve to be in my life. So go back to Dad and you can bond over the daughter you lost and leave me the fuck out of it," I say as I turn. From across the lot, I can see Lucas in my Jeep, watching. I give him a nod to let him know it's okay as I walk toward him.

"I don't know how you live with yourself," she says right before I end the call.

27

Lucas is silent beside me as I drive back to the station. My phone vibrates in my pocket over and over again. And though I don't pull it out of my pocket to check it, I know what the notifications mean. They're piles of requests for interviews, my mother trying to get me back on the phone. Some part of me hopes that if I ignore them long enough, maybe they'll go away. But I know they won't. I pull up out front of the station and unlock the doors. He turns to me, raising his brow as he does. I'm not kicking him out of my car, per se, but I'm doing so in the nicest way possible. For at least a little while, I need to think.

"You coming in—" he asks, motioning toward the building.

"I need the night to think," I say.

He looks confused. "You're taking the night off?" Disbelief hangs on his words. And I know why. Time off isn't something I do. With my last case, even when I was stabbed, I refused to take time off to heal. I can't sit. I can't take a break from a case. But right now, we don't have a whole lot of leads, and I need time to think.

"I am," I say with finality. I don't want him to challenge me on this or to try to talk me out of it. I need him to accept what I'm saying and go.

"Okay... well, if you need me."

"Yeah, I know. Good night," I say, trying to hurry him out of the car. Right now, I'm barely holding it together, and if I'm going to break down, I can't do it in front of him again. I can't look weak in front of him or in front of any other officers. I'll do that back in my motel where I don't have to pile guilt on top of everything else I'm already feeling.

He slides out of the car hesitantly and looks back at me one more time as he shuts the door. Frustration is clear on his face. I know he wants to fight me on this, to try to reel me back in. But thankfully, he doesn't. For now at least, he's respecting my wishes. When I was nearly kicked off the case in Plattsburgh, he helped me recover from a night of wallowing. And I know if I need that tomorrow, he'll happily show up to kick my ass.

I drive the two minutes to the motel, pull my car into a space in the back, then weave my way toward my room. Once inside, I grab a bottle of whiskey I squirreled away for this type of occasion and pour myself a healthy amount into a paper cup. Drinking cheap whiskey out of a paper cup pretty much sums up my entire life right now. Why do I even do this?

My phone dings and I scoop it up and look at the screen. An interview request from the *New York Times* sits on my phone, the preview text making it very clear that they know who my father is and that they want my take on it. Everyone knows. That's just the thing I need right now, for the media to figure out who I really am. They're going to blow this all wide open and destroy my life—again. They don't see the damage that they're doing to me, to my career, to my life. They think they're peddling a story that their readers will buy, that'll drum up some ad revenue. A sharp pain pierces my heart and tears prickle my eyes.

I didn't ask for this. For this life. For these parents. To be the child of a notorious serial killer. I should have become an accountant, disappeared into a room full of cubicles, and no one would have ever asked about my past or where I came from. I wouldn't have mattered.

I choke out a sob as tears run down my face; several drop into my whiskey before I finish it off. The heat of the burning liquid spreads like fire through my chest. But it doesn't burn away the pain, the abandonment, the years and years I suffered. I think that's what's the worst in all of this. No one sees that I'm a victim too, that like the women who died, I lost my life too. I lost a piece of me that I'll never get back. Who knows who I could have been, what my life would have been like.

But no one cares about that. No one sees that side of my life.

So where do I go from here? Do I give up? Try to fade into a normal job where no one would ever think to look up my past? If I did that, a part of me would die. That I know for sure. I *need* detective work; it helps fill a hole that's always existed inside me. But then again, one day I think this job may consume me. It may take absolutely everything that I have to give—and I'd let it, if that meant that somehow I'd atoned for what I did. For all the women I let my father go on to kill.

I've done the math. Over fifteen women died because I said nothing. It could be more. But because I was selfish, because I didn't want to be left alone with my mother, I let my father go on killing. I let him ruin lives, rip apart families. Maybe I don't deserve to feel better about what I did. Maybe that's something I can never balance out.

Knuckles rap gently against my door, and I walk to it, glancing at the peephole. Lucas stands on the other side of the door, two large paper cups in his hands—I'd put my money on it being coffee. I debate whether or not to answer it, but the siren call of the caffeine is too much. When I open the door, he shoves the coffee toward me and steps inside, before I can even think to shut the door and lock him outside.

"Sure, come on in," I say sarcastically as I slam the door behind him and lock it.

"Are you done wallowing or am I just in time for the finale?" he asks, his words clipped. He takes a sip of his coffee and looks me up and down. "Whiskey does not suit you. Neither does moping."

"Stop with your judgmental shit," I grumble as I drink my coffee.

"Stop making it so easy to be judgmental. You feel sorry for yourself and give up every time things are hard," he snaps at me. "Get your shit together and learn how to keep fighting."

If my coffee wasn't so good, I'd throw it at his head. I scan the room for something to throw, but nothing is in reach.

"I don't give up every time something is hard," I say, an edge to my voice.

"Really? Because you almost gave up on our last case. And you give up every single time someone discovers your identity in another town. Do you ever even give it an hour to see how it might go? To see if anyone actually cares?" There's genuine anger in his voice, and I'm taken aback. "You're lucky that you can pick up and move on anytime you feel like it, not everyone can do that."

Anger rises inside me so high that spots explode in my vision. Who the fuck does Lucas think he is? He acts like he's an expert on my life. He's never seen any of this shit firsthand. I've lived it. "How dare you. I've been kicked off the force several times because of my history. I don't just move on because it's fun for me. I move on because I have to. After my history surfaces, no one wants to work with me. I'm damaged goods. I get it, and I go." I hold my hands up as if I'm surrendering. Because I don't know what else to do. That's the barrel I'm staring down again. My days here are numbered, my career in

New York. I actually liked it here too. I liked working with Lucas. And now, I just want to lash out at him so it's not so hard when I have to leave. If he hates me now, then I've got nothing to hold me here.

"You might have been kicked off a few times, but I know that wasn't the case every time," he says as he glowers at me.

"Oh, and how exactly do you know that?" I ask.

"I called. When I heard about your past, about what you were going through, I called some of your old departments and I asked what happened. Why you moved on, when."

"Are you fucking kidding me? You invaded my privacy." Though I don't mean for it to, my voice rises until I realize I'm almost yelling at him. My chest tightens with the rage bottled there. Did he not believe me? Does he think he has some right to dig around in my past as he sees fit? I'm not a suspect to be investigated.

"I didn't invade your privacy. Working in law enforcement doesn't grant you immunity from anyone ever finding out about your past, quite the opposite actually. Those records are available for everyone. You bailed in Texas and didn't even tell anyone you were leaving, same with Michigan. There were people on your teams looking for you. They were worried that something might have happened to you, that one of the cases you solved led to you getting hurt."

Tears prickle my eyes. But I don't believe him. That couldn't have happened. It's not like I bonded with anyone. Why would they give a shit when I left?

"That's not—"

"They nearly opened missing persons reports on you. The only way they knew you were okay was because you'd terminated the leases on your apartments, and they were able to find out from the leasing departments that you'd left. They cared. They wanted to know what happened to you," he says.

My heart twists. But disbelief tamps down my emotions.

Because that can't be true, it can't. No one in Texas or Michigan gave two shits about me. I don't know where Lucas is getting this information or if he's making it up.

"Why would I lie to you?" Lucas asks. "I gain nothing here. Hell, I could lose something if it convinces you to go back there. I want you to stay here. I want to keep working with you. But I want you to stop doubting yourself, for you to stop thinking the entire world is against you. Because it's not. I'm here. I'm on your side. And I know you don't believe me, but every time things get hard, you're going to find me standing beside you. Supporting you." He pauses for a moment. "If you'll let me, that is."

I cough out a humorless laugh; he has no idea what I've been through. I want to argue with him, but I can't find the right words. Instead, I shake my head.

"Why do you have to come in here and do this to me every time?" I ask as I look up at him. Tears burn my eyes and I hate him even more for making me cry. "Do you ever think that, to me, maybe it's easier if no one cares?" I know what my father would say about it. That I build walls around myself, that I push everyone else away so that I never give anyone else the opportunity to abandon me, because of my deep abandonment issues. Times like this, I wish I could scour my father's words from my brain, but I can't. There's no getting rid of this.

"I have to do this because I'm not going to let you give up, Harlow. You don't get to quit here. There are victims that need you. And after we solve these two homicides and find out who did this to these women, we're going to break open Chad's case and figure out what's going on there," he says.

I look at him with disbelief. "We are *not* taking Chad's case," I say. That would be career suicide, and I'm not about to sign up for that.

He laughs a little. "No, we're not. But wouldn't it be hilarious if we made him think that we were?" A sick smile twists his lips, and I can't help but smile too. It would be great, and I would love nothing more than to see the horrified look on Chad's face if we started sniffing around his crime scenes.

I hang my head and stare at the dirty motel carpet. The fibers are shaggy, fraying. I count them, trying to get my mind off of this situation.

"So, what are you going to do?" he asks.

Outside that door, the unknown looms. My mother, Chad, what the media may say about me—my connections to the most notorious serial killer in the past fifty years. I don't want to face what's out there. Today, I want to give up, to climb under the covers and stop being *strong*. I've spent my whole life fighting everything and everyone, and today, it would be nice to have someone to fight for me. Rather than fighting on my own.

But then I realize, that's exactly what Lucas is doing. He's trying to help me fight this. He's trying to help me face what might be waiting for me outside.

Tears well in my eyes as I look back at him. I walk toward him, my hand still gripping my coffee, and I plop down on the chair next to him, a small table between us.

"I'll stay," I say. The words *for now* rise in my mind. A promise. A warning. I'm not sure which one.

"You've got to learn to let me help you. We're partners. That means we help each other. You wouldn't let me quit. You wouldn't let me walk away. So I'm not letting you do it either," he says as he shoves up from the chair. "Finish your coffee, have a good cry, and tomorrow morning get in the office ready to catch a killer."

Before I can say anything else, Lucas leaves. The door slams behind him, and for once, I feel what the impact could be if I leave. I know I'd miss him. I know I'd feel like I really let him down if I left. I slip out into the night air, my head still heavy with the weight of my thoughts, my past. I'm hoping that the cool, night air will help clear my head, and some food will help me shake off my buzz. The darkness envelops me as I walk across the parking lot, the click of my boots on the pavement the only sound.

I turn left out of the motel and cross the street to the sandwich place that I pass at least three times a day. After I've gotten my sandwich, I walk down the street, the bag crinkling in my hand. The trees sway over me as I walk, wind rustling the branches. At the end of the street, I follow the path into a small, circular park with several benches and a fountain in the middle. The cold hisses against my thighs as I sit on one of the benches and retrieve my sandwich. Water trickles from the fountain as I shovel the sandwich into my mouth. Halfway through, a sharp sound cuts through the night.

My heart jumps.

Was that a scream?

I listen intently, the silence building around me. I heard something; I know I did. My heart pounds as I stand up, abandoning my sandwich. The throb of my pulse echoes in my ears as I strain to hear something, anything. Another scream cuts the night. It couldn't be anything else. The noise came from my right, probably a few blocks away. I jog toward the source, my feet pounding against the pavement.

The houses and trees blur around me as I force myself to run toward the sound. I could call someone—Lucas maybe, and have him meet me out here. But I don't think there's time. The sound was so close, the scream.

Down the street, I hear a car door slam, and an engine rev as I turn the corner. Taillights flash at the end of the street as a pickup truck peels off. I fish my cellphone from my pocket, and call Saranac Lake PD. I need someone on patrol to chase down this truck.

"Detective Durant, good evening," Matthew says as he answers the phone.

I ramble off the information about the truck, and instruct him to have patrol keep a lookout for it. He takes my instructions, and I run down the street to where the truck had been parked. There's a pool of blood in the middle of the street beside where the truck stood.

28

Dawn's light claws at the horizon, slashing the purple sky, streaking it with orange. Stars still barely freckle the sky, their dying embers fading. I squint against the light as I peer out the motel window. There's a chill in the air this morning, reminding me of the freak snowstorm that hit in March. Are we in for snow again? I punch my arms into a jacket, hike up my jeans, and lace on some ancient boots. Last night, I spent a long time combing the neighborhood where I saw the truck for more blood, but I found nothing. Saranac Lake sent out a patrol, but no one but me saw the pickup truck.

I want to get out before Lucas wakes up, to sweep the neighborhood again and the surrounding streets to see if I can find anything. I throw my bag over my arm and head out of my motel room, the door slamming behind me. It takes me three minutes to weave through the motel and get to my Jeep. Condensation beads on my windows, and I'm thankful that it's not frost yet. Last year was a hard winter and I'm not looking forward to the next one.

The city is empty as I weave through the streets, stopping to grab a coffee. After the rich aroma of dark roast fills my car, I drive north up Bloomingdale Ave toward the edge of the city. If I keep going north, I'll hit the mountains and skirt the edge of McKenzie Wilderness, where the bodies keep surfacing. But I don't plan to head that way. The last thing I need is to run into Chad over there or to find a vic for this case. I drive slowly through the neighborhood, but I find nothing new, even in the early light of day.

As I approach the edge of the city, I turn left onto the logging road where we found the bodies. I park at the end, wanting to walk the same path that the victims did. From where I've parked, the curve of the road and the thick trees hide the spot where both victims were dumped. The dirt is soft beneath my boots, molding to my feet. Footprints mark my progress as I trudge toward the end. The faint smell of fire on the wind curls my nostrils.

But it can't be—it must be in my imagination. I pick up my pace, walking quicker toward the end of the road. As my stride lengthens, the smell grows stronger. It can't all be in my mind, and there's no way that the smell of the previous victims is lingering. The glow, the thickening stink, it all hits me at once. My hand trembles as I reach for my phone, adrenaline already hitting my blood. There's another body, a third victim.

A serial killer. There are two serial killers hunting in Saranac Lake.

I call the forensics team, the sergeant, then Lucas. I stand back, keeping as much distance from the scene as possible. It's important that we do whatever we can to preserve this evidence, whatever may be left anyway. It's already so hard to try to find anything with the bodies burned up. But if there are footprints, something the killer dropped, those little details may help us track down a killer. They may help us solve this.

I scan the ground, searching for any boot prints like the first or second scene. Near the body, there are marks on the ground that could be footprints. There's also blood, flesh.

This victim was tortured here, disfigured where anyone can see. This is their stage and they're killing for all the world to see.

Lucas pulls up first, the wheels of his rental car spinning in the mud at the end of the logging road. I told him not to get a sedan, but he argued that there was no way he needed a pickup truck while we were here investigating, since I have my Jeep.

"You okay?" Lucas asks as he jogs up to me. His pace is slower than it usually would be, his large boots clopping against the dirt road.

I nod. "Yeah, I'm fine. I was out for a walk, and—" I wave my hand toward the body.

"So... we're up to three," he says.

"Yup, so we've got two serial killers in this little town," I say. It's not something I would have expected. Having two active serial killers in the same area like this, it's incredibly rare.

"When is everyone going to get here?" he asks.

"They're on their way now."

It takes about twenty minutes for everyone to arrive. The cars pull up, and after the forensics team starts to climb out of the vans, more white vans pull up behind them. I grind my teeth. The media.

Camera crews swarm out of the vehicles, setting up at the edge of the crime scene. There are at least five different stations here. At this rate it seems like this one is all going to be on the news cycle for a few days.

Racquel nods to us as she approaches, a clipboard in her hands. A few months ago, Racquel was promoted, and now she manages all the crime scenes. She did the work before without the title, but I'm glad they finally gave her the recognition she deserves. On her clipboard, I know she's got lists upon lists of how they need to process the scene so that everything is cataloged appropriately, so that none of our evidence is compromised.

"So you came upon the scene?" she asks me as she glances down at the papers in front of her.

I nod. "Yes, about thirty minutes ago."

"We're going to have our team extinguish the flames and start to collect evidence, but I need to know how close you got to the body," she explains.

The team starts to approach the body, with a large foil blanket to smother the flames without the potential of destroying evidence.

"I walked to about there," I say as I point toward some of my footprints about thirty feet from the body. "Once I saw the flames, I stopped and called it in," I explain.

"What were you doing out here?" Lucas asks.

"I wanted to clear my head before I went into the station today, so I decided to come out here and walk." There's no blood remaining in the street, no evidence the pickup truck was there at all. Did I imagine it? Did I drink more than I thought?

His eyes narrow as he inspects me, but he says nothing.

"Sorry, I've got to ask for procedural reasons, so we can answer in court if necessary. Did you or anyone else touch, move, or otherwise molest the body?" Racquel asks.

I shake my head. "I didn't. And, no, not that I saw." I don't take the questions personally. I know well enough that they're all part of procedure, not that she thinks I actually tried to move the body or compromise the evidence.

"Did you see any weapons or any evidence on the ground as you approached?" she asks.

"To be honest, I wasn't looking for anything like that. So no," I admit. Maybe I should have been paying closer attention. "The fire had my attention."

"This scene looks a bit more gruesome," she admits.

"How so?" I ask. I didn't get close enough to discern anything like that. I didn't want to disturb the scene. And I'm not sure how it can get more gruesome than the other scenes.

"It looks like there was more of a struggle this time, and that there was more anger involved. The other scenes, it looked like the killer lured the victims here. This time, there are lots of streaks and slashes in the dirt, there's a lot of blood outside of the area directly next to the body. And it's clear that the breasts were removed, sheared off actually, because they were thrown next to the body this time, they weren't burned. But the victim didn't sustain as much damage from the flames," she explains.

"Why do you think that would be?" Lucas asks no one in particular as he crosses his arms and glances toward the body.

The team has put out the fire, but the smell still clings to the air. The air is thick and smells rather fatty. The acridity of burned hair still lingering.

"Do you think they got interrupted? Or startled?" I ask.

Racquel looks toward the scene. "That's always possible, especially in an area like this," she explains. "It's very public. But if you didn't see them..."

"Last night, while I was out getting dinner, I thought I heard a scream. I ran to a neighborhood nearby, and I swore I saw blood on the ground. But it wasn't there this morning." I shake my head, trying to clear my jumbled thoughts. Was the scream related to this? Was it not? "I can't understand how anyone can butcher someone like this on a logging road and make it home covered in blood without anyone noticing. Whoever did this had to look like they'd just smeared blood all over themselves. There's no way to get out of this clean," I say. That's been my biggest hurdle here. In a town this small, I'd think that someone would have seen something, heard something. We're close enough to some cabins, houses, that if there was a victim screaming out here that someone would have heard them. We're not so far out into the woods that two people can disappear completely.

Lucas shoots me a look, and I know he's annoyed that I

didn't call him. "How long will it take to process the scene?" Lucas asks.

"At least three hours, but probably more like five," she explains. "We need to collect soil samples, log all the boot prints that are here, try to reconstruct the struggle based on where the blood splatter is. The other scenes took us a little less, but with the scattered evidence this time it'll likely take us longer."

"So, we're looking at talking to Dr. Pagan about this tomorrow sometime," Lucas says.

My cellphone vibrates, and I glance at it. Saranac Lake PD is calling me. I accept the call and press the phone to my ear.

"Durant, we just had a call into the tip line that might be helpful to you," Matthew says.

"Oh?" I ask.

"A woman named Veronica said that she was friends with Chloe Williams and has information about what Chloe was doing the night that she died," he explains.

I take down the woman's information from Matthew. "Is she willing to come in to talk to us?" I ask.

He clears his throat. "She's currently out of town, so you're going to have to call her. She said that's why she hadn't reached out sooner. She just saw on social media that Chloe died. So, she wanted to fill us in on what she knows."

"Okay, I'll give her a call, thanks," I say before ending the call.

I excuse myself while Lucas and Racquel talk more about the scene, and I call Veronica. She doesn't answer, so I make myself a note to try again later. But as soon as I've written it down, my phone rings.

"Detective Durant," I say as I answer.

"Oh, hi, Detective. Sorry, I don't answer numbers I don't recognize," Veronica says. "I didn't expect to get a call back so quickly."

"Well, we try to move as quickly as possible in homicide

investigations. Time is of the essence," I explain. "So, you have information about Chloe? How did you and Chloe know each other?" I ask as I pace the edge of the scene.

"Chloe and I were good friends. We'd worked together," she explains. The woman has a deep voice that makes me think she must be quite a bit older than Chloe. But that makes more sense that they knew each other through work.

"So what information do you have?" I ask, when she doesn't elaborate beyond the work relationship.

"Oh sorry, I've never spoken to the cops before. I'm rather nervous. Chloe and I talked quite a bit even after she left the job. But she'd told me that night that she was going on a date."

I take out my notepad and jot that down. "Who did she go on a date with?" I ask. Most calls to the tip line are garbage. That's one thing I learned early on working as homicide detective. If there's a stabbing, someone will call saying they heard gunshots. If a woman is missing, someone will crawl out of the woodwork saying they knew her in elementary school. That's why many times stations are reluctant to even point out the tip lines to the general public. I'm not sure if it's attention seeking or if they want to feel like they're a part of something.

"I don't know. She was reluctant to tell me his name."

I grind my teeth. Then why bother calling me at all? This information isn't helpful. "Did she say where she was going on the date at least?" I ask, hoping that there's something here.

"Yes, she went to Charley's," she says simply.

That name strikes a chord with me, and not just because it's one of the few restaurants in town. Where have I heard of that restaurant before? I know it's not because I've passed it a thousand times. Though I know I've heard someone talk about it, I just can't place the source. I'll have to check the restaurant to see if they remember seeing Chloe and who she was with. Given this small town, I'm sure that someone has some gossip about who Chloe dined with.

I finish up my call with Veronica and hang up the phone. Lucas still has his eyes on the body, and Racquel is ushering the forensics teams around, snapping pictures, and logging the scene. I fill Lucas in on the restaurant tip. We'll have to follow up on it later today when it opens. For now, it's far too early.

29

TWENTY YEARS AGO

We moved three weeks ago. Our new house is nestled in the middle of Tacoma, only ten minutes from my father's new practice. I can walk there, if I want to—but I don't. We packed up everything and brought it here with us, including the animosity between my mother and father. Before the move, for a while, things were better. They didn't argue so much, my dad was spending more time at home, and for a short time my mom actually seemed happy. Though I didn't think that was even possible.

But now that we've unloaded the boxes and we're settling in, something has shifted. It's like a poison fog has trickled in from the musty basement, filling the house again with anger. Last night, when my father returned home from work, my mom threw a glass at his head. It shattered into a thousand pieces, littering the foyer in sparkling shards. This morning, I noticed a dent in the drywall, a scar.

I still don't really understand what the fight was about. My dad moved us, he's been home more, and yet—somehow my mother thinks that he's cheating. That his late nights must be caused by women gobbling up his attention. Little does she know, he is with other women, but they don't live through it. Sometimes I think about telling her, telling someone to unburden my soul.

At the top of the stairs, I clutch my legs to my chest, my eyes homed in on the dent above the door. Downstairs, my mother is stomping in the kitchen, her anger resonating through the house. The floorboards groan, the windows rattle. It's just a matter of time before it all boils over again. Before one of them leaves, and I'm left behind, like a forgotten plant that's withered in a windowsill.

"Where the fuck is he?" my mother rages to herself. Well, not so much to herself. She projects her feelings on everyone else.

I stand up slowly, and slink off to my room, careful of the floorboards that I know will warn my mother of my movements. Once I'm safely inside, I hold my breath as I close my door, praying the hinges don't squeak. I take a deep breath once it's closed and tiptoe to my bed.

She's mad because my father's office hours ended twenty minutes ago. In her mind, he should have been here ten minutes ago, so every second that ticks on by, she grows more and more enraged. I live with a grenade that had the pin pulled long ago. I know we're ticking closer and closer to an explosion, but no one can guess when or where it'll happen.

An hour after the time my mother decided my father should be home, he comes through the door. He calls to us, letting us know that he's arrived, a lightness in his tone. I want to warn him, to shine a light down the stairs like a lighthouse to let him know of the danger that's looming. But I can't. If I leave this room, then I'll be a target. And I won't stand between the two of them when they fight. I've thought about it, but I'm too much of a wuss to face my mother because I know what my mother is capable of once he's no longer here to shield me.

"Harley Jane!" my dad calls from downstairs.

"Where the hell were you?" my mother growls seconds after my father calls for me.

I grind my teeth and head to the window, where I shoulder it open. My window looks out onto the roof covering the back porch, giving me a little landing to get away if I want to. And I do, often. It's my refuge when they fight; though it doesn't keep me from hearing everything, somehow I feel safer.

"I was working. You do understand that I still have to see my patients and sometimes there are sessions that have to run a bit long. You need to be reasonable and understand that I can't always be here within a few minutes of my office hours ending," he says, in a voice so calm, it puts me on edge. How can he stay so even when she screams at him? "There's traffic, sometimes sessions run late. My assistants have questions..."

"Working?" She barks out a laugh. "Is that what you like to call it? Who is *she*?" my mother screams at him. Her voice rises so high it cracks.

I can hear her through the shut window, which tells me how loud it must be inside the house. I press my back to the slope of the roof, the rough shingles digging into my back. The cold of the roof is soothing as I look up into the inky sky. Sometimes I wonder what life would be like without my mother. If I could finally breathe, if I could walk through life without worrying if I'd get hit or screamed at. I've heard the term *it's like walking on eggshells*, but that doesn't quite describe it. It's more like walking on broken glass because the stakes are so much higher than a broken egg. One wrong move could break something else; it could break me.

"You really need to get it out of your head that there's someone else. I just uprooted my career, moved to a new city with you to put you at ease. Do you really think I'd be able to start a new relationship in this town in days? You're being unreasonable and irrational," my father shouts back.

Some days, he's able to keep his composure, to not yell. But I guess today isn't going to be one of them.

"You really expect me to believe that you're out there working with your *patients* all this time? That you need to spend hours with them even after your office closes? This is absolutely ridiculous. You don't care about this family at all," she shouts, and I can hear the pain in her words.

The back door opens, and someone—probably my father—stomps out onto the deck. My mother follows him, her voice lowering as she follows. I guess she doesn't want the whole neighborhood to hear their fight, so at least there are some small blessings.

"Yes, I expect you to believe it. Because that's what I'm doing. Not everything in the world can really be as bad as it is in your head. You make up these grand, elaborate things that I must be out doing, but there's no evidence for any of it. Please, show me some proof for all this alleged cheating that I'm doing. I would love to see it."

"You can't explain where you are half of the time. You're always answering emails on your laptop or taking calls. There's no way that all of it is work. It just can't be," she says, her voice growing more and more shrill by the second.

"I have a large practice. I have nurses and two other psychiatrists who work with me. I have to answer to my employees and to my patients. I'll give you the logins for my email if you're so sure that they're suspicious. Want to check my cellphone too?" he asks, and I think he hands it to her. I can barely see them beyond the sharp edge of the roof.

For a long moment, my mother is silent. Then finally, she says, "Just because there's nothing in there doesn't mean anything. You probably deleted all the evidence already."

All of this fighting, for what? So he can keep going out to kill his patients? So he can sneak off and another woman will die. The news has talked recently about how there hasn't been another murder, how they think that the killer may have moved on. My guess is all of my mother's nagging is keeping him from going out, from putting more of his clients out of their misery. It's a perilous road to walk, because on one hand I want my mother to keep him here, to keep him from killing again. Because then maybe that will keep him out of prison. But I don't know that this is something my father can quit. It's a compulsion, something he feels like he has to do.

"This is becoming tiresome. I don't know what I have to do to prove my loyalty to this family, to you. But I need you to figure it out. Because I don't know how much longer I can do this," he says, and he sounds so defeated.

"You brought me here, you took away my friends, the family I had left. You've taken me away from everything and then you leave me here all alone. And you want me to be happy with that? You want me to grovel at your feet and thank you for this life that you've built for me? For this gilded cage?" she asks, her words so sharp they may as well be punctuated with daggers. She has so much hate for my father and me. I don't know why she clings to this. I don't know why she wants to keep us both here. She should just let us go.

"You volunteered to come. You thought it would be better too. I didn't take you from anything. You barely left the house before. So don't act like I did something terrible to your life. Nothing has changed. And you're not alone. Harley is here, but you don't want anything to do with your own daughter. You'd rather sit downstairs and sulk because nothing is the way that you want it to be."

My heart twists and my stomach sickens as I listen to them. I'm a pawn for them to throw back and forth at one another. I don't even know why they had a child in the first place.

"You know as well as I do that Harley is barely my daughter. You wanted her. You got me pregnant and talked me into keeping her. So don't act like this is something that I chose," she hisses at him.

My heart sinks. And I don't know why. I've always known that she hates me. I've always felt like she didn't want me. But hearing those words out loud, it's a different kind of pain. I didn't want to be right.

30

The conference room in Saranac Lake PD is a bit too cold for my liking. I've already put on my jacket, but wrapping my hands around my warm coffee cup is doing more for my warmth than anything else. We finally heard back from Grover regarding our request for an interview, so we've rushed back to the station to question him. The late morning sun sneaks in through the small window in the conference room, casting daggers of light over the shiny wood table.

Lucas pops open the conference room door and ushers Grover in. Today, he's got his greasy hair slicked back. His eyebrows are low as he looks at me. His lips are pursed, like he's annoyed with being here, but someone urged him to come in. Some part of me thinks that it may have been Max who had a hand in that, if only to keep us from getting a warrant for more of his records.

"Take a seat," I say when he hovers a little too long at the door.

He looks at me like he has half a mind to argue, then plops down in a chair across from me. "What do you want?"

Lucas sits to my left, a legal pad in front of him. I've got my small notebook open, a pen already clutched in my fingers.

"We wanted to talk to you about Ellie Gordon and Chloe Williams," I say, though I know that much should be obvious to him.

He shrugs halfheartedly. "This feels like a conspiracy to pin this on me because you're desperate to find a suspect," he says as he crosses his arms and leans back in his chair.

"Well, then if you could just answer a few questions we can clear this all up and you can be on your way," Lucas says, reining in his usual edge of sarcasm. I can tell that he's holding back.

"Fine, that's what Max said too. He said if you guys clear me, I might be able to get my job back. So"—he waves his hand through the air—"let's get this over with."

"So, can you confirm for me that you worked with both Ellie and Chloe." My words are nearly a question, but we all know that he did. I just need it on the record.

He nods. "Yeah, I worked with both of them. I also went to school with them too. But so did everyone else in this town. You do realize how many people there are here that worked with Ellie and Chloe too, right? Raven worked with both of them, but I don't see you hauling her in here."

I press my lips together and take a deep breath before continuing. "Did you try to date both Ellie and Chloe?" I ask.

"Chloe and I went on a couple dates. Ellie and I had lunch. There was mutual interest." He holds his chin higher, like he's proud of himself for these details.

"So, Chloe and Ellie never told you that they weren't interested? They never indicated that they were no longer comfortable with your advances?" Lucas pushes, because we've heard now from several people that they rebuffed Grover. Maybe this guy is just delusional and thinks that all women are interested in him.

He shakes his head. "No, I actually ended up moving on because I was no longer interested." For a moment, he swivels back and forth in his chair, but then ceases the movement suddenly, as if he just realized he was doing it.

I write down a few notes about his version of the events, even though I don't believe them in the slightest.

"When did you see Ellie Gordon last?" Lucas asks.

"I don't know, probably on the 10th or the 11th," he says.

"And how did you come to possess her crucifix necklace?" I ask.

He presses his lips together in a thin line. "I didn't—"

I lean forward and place my hands on the table, then lace them together in front of me. I level my eyes on Grover. "We have the records from the pawnshop that you pawned Ellie's necklace on April 14th. That's the day after Ellie died."

"That doesn't look good, man," Lucas adds as he shakes his head.

"I didn't—"

"Then where did you get the necklace? Why did you pawn it? And most importantly, why did you pawn it the day after Ellie died?"

He throws his hands up. "I found it. It was outside of Charley's restaurant on the ground. I knew it was hers, and I was so mad. She was on a date with that douchebag Gavin because she'd chosen *him* over me. Fucking bitch." His cheeks are painted with red as his anger rises. "I wanted to get her back, so when I found that necklace, I decided to pawn it. I knew she was in the pawnshop all the fucking time pawning jewelry, so I knew she'd see it and it'd piss her off."

I glance to Lucas, trying to discern if he believes this little outburst.

"I'd have been mad too," Lucas says, playing the sympathetic friend. I know the tactic, and sometimes it works. "So, you were outside the restaurant watching Ellie and Gavin?"

He nods. "Yeah, I was hoping that she'd get mad at him and leave, then I could swoop in and make her feel better. But that didn't happen."

I hate to say that I believe him, but I don't see why he'd admit to watching Ellie from the parking lot.

"Did Ellie ever mention where she was getting all this jewelry to pawn?" I ask.

"Some of it she stole. She told me that she'd learned from Jordan about how much she could make by pawning stolen jewelry when they dated. She'd also said something about getting cheap jewelry online and flipping it. Some of it was counterfeit but was able to be passed off as real. Max was really mad a couple of times because after paying out Ellie for a large lot she brought in, he figured out that she would slip a few fakes into the mix."

So she was stealing jewelry, selling it to Max, and ripping him off. That's the kind of game that seems like it could make Ellie a lot of enemies. But how does Chloe connect to all this? Grover is still the only real link I have.

"The night of April 12th, you were outside of the restaurant before Ellie went missing... Where did you go after?"

"I went home with the necklace, hid it in my dresser. Then I watched TV for the rest of the night," he says.

"Can anyone confirm that's where you were?"

He shakes his head.

"And the night of April 23rd?" Lucas presses.

He picks at his fingernails. "I was at the shop. I worked until about ten," he explains. Chloe likely died after that, so it isn't much help that he was at work.

"What did you do after work?"

"I went home, made myself dinner, and went to sleep, like I always do," he explains.

We finish up the interview with Grover, and we've got no choice but to let him go. There just isn't enough evidence to hold him yet. Right now, everything is pointing solidly in his direction, but we need evidence that he took the necklace from Ellie after she died and we need a murder weapon.

31

For a month solid, I've eaten nothing but fast food, and I feel it all the way to my soul. If I don't eat some real food, or a salad, my heart may actually give out before I solve this case. It probably also doesn't help that I'm on my fourth latte of the day, but that's neither here nor there. Since this morning I've hinted to Lucas that I want to grab some real food tonight, but thus far he's ignored me. And in this town, I will not go sit in a restaurant by myself. The media will swoop in or, worse, Chad.

"Want to go to Charley's tonight?" I ask, for what's probably the fifth time. I want to scope out the restaurant, and see if anyone there might know anything about Chloe, who she was with the night she died. Not to mention, they actually have real food on their menu.

He looks at me over his laptop, his brows drawn; the rest of the room is empty, cast in grays from the thick clouds outside. "Do you only think about food, Harlow?" he asks, in his usual judgmental tone.

"If I eat another burger tonight, I will die," I say, more dramatically than I need to. But how else will he see my point? "And then you'll have to worry about this case all by yourself. I swear that I don't have any blood left in my body. My heart is just pumping around burger grease."

"We can go out for one hour. I've got too much to do to spend an entire night in a restaurant," he says.

"You're awfully grumpy today," I say, closing out some of the tabs I opened earlier for research.

"No, I'm trying to make some headway in this case. I feel like we're just going in circles."

"You're just anxious because we have to go talk to Dr. Pagan in the morning to find out the initial report on the new victim," I say. I'm anxious about it too, but at the very least, killing an hour or two in a restaurant will help. There's nothing I can do on the case right now anyway. We don't have enough to move on Grover, Gavin, or Max. Right now, Grover is my lead suspect, but we still need something solid.

"Don't you think it sends the wrong message?" he asks.

"You think that needing to eat because we're human sends the wrong message?" I ask, raising an eyebrow.

"You know what I mean."

"Look, if we spent every evening in a bar drinking and never actually doing any police work, then sure. But we do deserve a couple hours away every now and again." Usually these conversations go the other way around. It's Lucas trying to talk me into taking a few hours away. The irony isn't lost on me.

"Fine. Stop whining. I'll go with you. You're such a baby, you should be able to eat in a restaurant by yourself," he says as he shuts his laptop and shoves it into his bag.

"No, I should be able to get my partner to go to dinner with me without begging," I say as I pack up my own computer.

Lucas and I bicker the entire way to the restaurant. As we pull into the parking lot, it's abundantly clear that this is the hot place for dinner in town. The lot is packed, music thudding from inside. Lucas glances at me, then at the building. It's tall, with a Tuscan vibe, ivy climbing the terracotta walls.

"You sure this is where you want to eat?"

"It has really good reviews. Come on, you're the social one here. Is this really going to scare you off?" I ask, motioning toward the crowd. "Don't you miss being around other humans?"

He shrugs, like he still doesn't think this is a good idea. But he climbs out of the Jeep all the same. The low hum of voices cuts through the night as we approach the door. There's a lull in the music, and the voices rise in the space where it used to be.

"Table for two?" a woman in a tight black dress asks as we approach the front door.

"Yes, please," I say.

She nods, and waves us inside. As we follow her through the restaurant, we pass tables filled with patrons, many of whom I recognize from the streets of the city. One person in particular sticks out, Gavin. He's seated with a woman I've met before while canvassing, Mariska Sanchez. I nod to Gavin, then his eyes crawl my body and I regret it. I look away, and keep my eyes on the hostess.

Finally when we reach our table, I sigh, thankful that Gavin's back is to us so he can't eye me the entire time we eat. Lucas sits in front of me, and frowns at the packed room.

"Would you rather go somewhere else?" I ask him.

He shakes his head. "No, it's just stuffy in here."

"We could get a table outside," I offer, suddenly feeling like the more space between me and Gavin, the better.

He shakes his head. "No, this is fine."

I nod and start to survey the menu the hostess dropped off for us. We grab drinks and order our food. Lucas makes sure to mention several times that we're in a hurry. I excuse myself and head toward the bathroom, feeling the eyes of patrons on me as I pass. A few people whisper that I should get the hell out of their town, that I'm causing problems, but I ignore them. If they want to volunteer to solve these homicides, they can feel free, but until then, it's my case and I won't be intimidated to leave.

Before I make it to the bathroom, I spot a woman in a pantsuit who's obviously the manager of the restaurant. I flag her down, and chat with her for a couple minutes about Chloe. Though she did see Chloe in the restaurant the night before her death, she doesn't recall who Chloe had dinner with. I thank her for her time and continue on my way.

I duck into the bathroom, relishing the reprieve from the noise and body heat. But when I emerge again, I nearly run right into someone's broad chest. I look up and clench my jaw when I realize it's Gavin.

"Oh, there you are," he says.

Was he waiting outside the bathroom for me? What the hell is with this guy?

"It's not like I did some vanishing act. I was sitting in the corner if you needed something. Got any tips for my case?" I ask, trying to steer the conversation before it heads in the wrong direction.

A smug smirk twists his full lips. He moves closer, his body nearly touching mine. He props his hand on the wall right above my shoulder, and the forced proximity makes me want to knee him in the balls. But I don't.

"I was hoping you'd come back to my office to talk to me. It's been so lonely without you," he says, the sour smell of alcohol on his breath.

"You're literally here with a date, right now," I say, motioning toward the dining room.

"I'll tell her to leave if you want to come sit with me—or sit on me."

"As intriguing as that offer is, I'm going to pass, thank you." I duck under his arm and head back toward the table. But Gavin grabs my arm, attempting to tug me back. I grab him by the wrist, and twist it behind his back, utilizing every bit of my training. I slam him, harder than I need to, into the wall. His chest hits the drywall and the force knocks the breath out of him. I press my chest into his back, grinding his jaw against the wall.

"You ever touch me again, I'll break this arm off and shove it up your ass." I force the threat out through gritted teeth.

I walk back to the table, my heart racing, and my legs unsteady. I plop down next to Lucas, regret and sickness swelling inside me.

"What's wrong?" Lucas asks.

I shake my head. "Nothing, let's just get our food to go," I say.

Thankfully Lucas is so jazzed to get out of this place that he doesn't argue. I grab our orders, shove them into a to-go bag, and head out the door. Whispers follow us as we walk, curses and ill wishes curling around us like a toxic fog. They want us out of their town. They're not worried about the homicides, the fact that there are two killers hunting in this town at this very moment. No, they're concerned that as outsiders we're harming their town.

When we get outside, several reporters rush us. Cameras and microphones shove into our faces as the reporters ask over and over again if we have any leads, where we are with our case, why there are two serial killers hunting the same town, and most importantly—if I have any comment on the latest statement from my father. Apparently, my dad spoke to the media and told them how proud he is that I grew up to be a homicide detective. It's enough to make me roll my eyes, but they're absolutely eating it up.

Lucas tugs me back toward the restaurant. There's no path to the car without walking through a sea of reporters, so I follow him back inside.

"I'm going to go find us a different table; maybe if we eat here they'll clear out a bit," Lucas offers.

I feel bad that I got us caught in the middle of this mess. If I'd listened to Lucas and eaten more fast food, none of this would have happened. I cross my arms, lean against the wall, and watch Lucas weave through the sea of patrons for a new table for us.

A woman with sleek blonde hair and a skintight dress walks toward me. Her hips sway a little too exaggeratedly as she approaches. A feral smile curls her lips, and I raise a brow to her. I have no idea who this woman is and why exactly she's looking at me like *this*.

"I saw you talking to Gavin," the woman says. Though her words are straightforward, somehow they hold a veiled threat.

"I'm not sure I'd call it talking. Who are you exactly?" I ask. She's acting like Gavin's protective girlfriend, but as far as I know, he's as unattached as it gets.

"Christine Parsons," she says in a way that it's clear that I'm supposed to know who she is.

"Okay, nice to meet you," I say awkwardly.

"Are you after Gavin?" she asks, and I see Lucas waving his hand across the room. I guess he found a table.

I let out a little laugh. "Not even remotely. If you want that, he's all yours. Good luck," I say, as I shove off the wall I was leaning against and start to walk toward Lucas.

Christine's hand brushes my shoulder, and I turn back.

"I've seen you speak to him a few times, and you went to his office—"

I raise a brow at that. Is this woman watching me? Following me? "Look, Christine." I say her name the way a kindergarten teacher might. "I'm here investigating a homicide. I'm not trying out for a season of *The Bachelor*, in which Gavin is somehow a prize. Please, stay out of my business." I turn back around, not giving Christine another second of my time.

32

We try to sneak out of the restaurant several times, but it isn't until nearly closing time that we're able slip past the media and make it to my car without questions. Guilt is tethered to me when we make it back to the motel. I ate up Lucas's entire night, which I shouldn't have done. But then again, a few hours off won't kill him. He's constantly telling me that I need to relax.

As I climb up the stairs to my motel room, my phone rings. Racquel's number flashes on the screen and I accept the call.

"Hey, Racquel," I say as soon as it connects. I put it on speaker so that Lucas can hear the update as well.

"This morning after we finished processing the scene, we put DNA for the victim into CODIS immediately, and we already got a match," she explains, excitement clear in her words.

"Already?" I've never had DNA come back this quickly.

"Yep, there was already a familial match in the database for this victim. Her name is Tazia Miller. She was twenty-six years old, lived in Saranac Lake her entire life," Racquel explains. "It looks like her father's DNA was in the database because he worked in law enforcement for a few years. They also noted that, like the other victims, Tazia had no smoke in her lungs, so she was set on fire after she was deceased."

"Thanks, Racquel, we'll inform the family and start investigating," I say.

I glance at my watch; it's nearly 11 p.m. We really shouldn't inform the family this late of the death of a family member.

"It should wait until the morning," Lucas says, as if he hears my thoughts.

I nod. "Seven?" I ask him as I continue up the stairs.

"You're a masochist." He practically growls the words at me as he heads to his own room.

I sit back on my bed, trying to decompress—well, that's what I should be doing. Instead, I'm combing the missing persons database, looking for any new hits in Plattsburgh. It's not my business, technically. I should probably stay out of it, but something keeps calling me back to it. Something hits my door, like something was thrown at it, and as I slide off the bed my heartrate kicks up a notch. As I look out the peephole, something slams into the door again. The view comes into focus, and I see Chad kicking the door. I sigh and unlock it.

"What do you want, Chad?" I ask as I open the door a few inches.

He pushes the door and invites himself inside.

"Yeah, sure, come on in," I say as I move out of the way.

He sways slightly on his feet as he walks to the chair on the other side of the room, and slumps in it. There's a cloud of booze that's thick around him. Great, babysitting a drunk Chad was exactly what I wanted to do with my night.

"How the fuck do you do it, Durant?" he asks, looking up at me through squinted eyes. He's hunched over, his elbows on his knees.

"Do what, exactly?" I ask.

He waves his hand in the air, as if he's scooping up the words from the ether. "You know, like all this. How do you hunt a serial killer?"

I raise a brow. Did he seriously come over here for advice? "You do realize I've only found one serial killer, right? If you need help, you should call in the FBI," I say. The last thing that I want to do is be pulled in on Chad's case. So if that's what he's here to do, I don't have the bandwidth to work both. I'll have to tell him no.

"That's what Dirby's about to do. He's going to take this away from me and bring in the FBI. Then I'll remain a second-rate detective who can only solve a one-off small-town homicide," he rants. "This killer, they're depraved. We've got them on video stalking around the town at night. A man in a trench coat hunting for his next victim."

"What have you got so far? Any leads?"

"This guy is like a fucking phantom. There's no evidence. Nothing. We can't figure out what the murder weapon even could be. He's got to have some type of setup with multiple weapons." His words slur slightly as he speaks.

"There's nothing wrong with needing help," I say, as if I'm capable of asking for help myself. Though I've been able to let Lucas in, to ask him to take some of the load off me, it's not something that's ever come naturally. "Is there anything linking the victims?"

"So far, no. The victims are mostly women, a couple men though. Some seem to have been in the woods hiking before they were attacked, others were kidnapped from properties near the lake." The more he talks, the more clearheaded he seems.

"I think you'll figure it out. Don't worry about them taking the case from you," I say, trying to pretend it's a normal colleague I'm speaking to, and not Chad.

He shakes his head and lets out a humorless laugh. "As if you'd let them take a case from you."

"They'd have to pry a case out of my cold, dead hands."

"I don't know if we're going to be able to catch this guy, honestly," he says as he hangs his head.

I can't believe that Chad is making me want to help him. I tell myself I'm helping the victims, my team, not Chad. "Your killer is in berserker mode. It's only a matter of time until they do something too sloppy and you're able to find their identity. It happened with Dahmer, Bundy, all the bigs. It'll happen with this guy too."

"How do you know?" he asks, finally looking up at me again.

"Because that's the way it goes with serial killers," I say, though with every additional word of advice I give him, I know I'm risking him asking me more questions. I can always play it off that I did research during my last case, but this type of info, it's usually dangerous for me to provide. But then again, my mother is already out there spilling my secrets to the press, so what does it matter?

"Thanks, Durant," he says as he shoves up from the chair. I guess my pep talk worked.

In a few minutes, Chad is gone, along with his boozy perfume, and I'm left alone with my thoughts. Chad is lost and he came to me; that's not something I ever expected to happen.

My motel room glows orange as the sun burns on the horizon. I've already been awake for hours—for so long I'm not entirely sure that I slept at all last night after Chad showed up. My to-do list has whispered in my ear every time I've tried to close my eyes. Today, I've got to look into Tazia Miller, who she is, where she last was, if there's any connection between these three women. We've reached the magic number. We officially have a second serial killer in Saranac Lake.

I throw open my motel door and bound down the stairs. It'll still be about twenty minutes before Lucas is awake and ready to go, so I plan to grab us coffee before then. I climb in my Jeep, the windows fogged against the chill in the morning air. The first hints of spring are whispering a little louder each morning.

As I pull up to the coffee shop, it's unusually empty. I've only been in this particular coffee shop once, shortly after Lucas and I came to town. I've been partial to two of the other shops, but this is the only shop open at the moment.

Today, when I walk in, it's just me and the barista. She's got her phone sandwiched between her ear and her shoulder as she buzzes behind the espresso machine.

"Hey, Tazia, it's me again. I was just calling to see if you're coming in for your shift? It's not like you to run late, so I wanted to make sure," the woman says before she scoops her phone up and ends the call. My guess is, she was leaving a voicemail.

I place my coffee order, then try to think of the best way to open the conversation about Tazia.

"So, I overheard you on the phone. Did Tazia Miller work here?" I ask.

The woman looks a little surprised, but nods. "Yes, I don't normally work until the afternoon. It's my shop, but it's hard to get here in the morning because of my son. But this morning I got a call that the shop wasn't open at six when it was supposed to be, and Tazia was nowhere to be seen. She probably overslept or something," she says as she buzzes around the espresso machine making the lattes for me.

"How long has Tazia worked here?" I ask.

"Um, about two years, or so." Her words almost sound like a question, like she's not entirely sure.

"Has she ever been late like this before?" I try to ask conversationally, rather than like a cop digging into this woman's business, though I'm sure she knows who I am. The long looks she keeps giving me say it all.

"No, she hasn't." The barista looks up at me, finally really looking at me. Her eyes go a little wide. "Oh, you're the cop," she finally says.

I nod. "Detective Durant," I say, as I hold my hand out to shake hers.

Reluctantly she takes it. "Nice to meet you. Why are you asking so many questions about Tazia?" Just as the words leave her mouth, she pales. I can't afford for this woman to blab to Tazia's family about her possible death or disappearance, so I need to smooth this over for a bit.

"Right now, we just have a few questions about her whereabouts," I say. I can't give her all the details, but with the way news spreads around here, she'll find out by the end of the day.

"Because I told you that she didn't show up... or for some other reason?" she asks as she raises a brow at me.

"Unfortunately, I'm unable to elaborate because it is a part of an ongoing investigation," I say.

The woman's mouth reforms into a grim line, and she looks down at the coffee machine. "Is Tazia okay?" she asks, clearly avoiding my gaze on purpose.

"As soon as I know the answer to that question, I'll be the first to let you know." I hate lying, giving false hope to people who knew victims. But sometimes I have little choice. "Do you have any information about Tazia that you'd like to share?" I can't be too specific, or I may tip her off to how serious the situation actually is. And that's the last thing that I want to do.

"Tazia was a very hard worker. She took her job seriously and talked about how eventually she wanted to own her own business. I was teaching her a lot about what it takes to own a coffee shop, so she could eventually try to start something on her own if she wanted. I saw it kind of like a mentorship," the woman explains.

"Was Tazia in school or anything?"

She shakes her head. "No, Tazia didn't care for school too much. She was more self-taught. She liked looking into things on her own and learning at her own pace."

"Was she dating anyone?"

She shrugs. "I don't know. We didn't talk about her personal life. And I try stay out of town gossip. There is absolutely nothing productive about all the talk that goes on around here. But believe me, no one ever shuts up about it."

"Was there anything that happened recently with her that stuck out to you, anything concerning?" I try to keep my questions as open-ended as possible, hoping that'll spark something in her mind.

She shakes her head, but then her eyes go wide. "Oh, actually, last week I walked in on something weird." She leans toward me and lowers her voice as she talks. I nod and motion for her to keep talking. "I'd taken a break and when I got back, Max Moody was in here yelling at her and threatening her," she says before glancing around the empty shop to make sure that no one overheard her.

"Yelling at her about what, exactly?"

"Something about her coming into his shop and unloading fake jewelry. I've never seen him so mad in my life. And that's saying something, because Max is the kind of guy to chew out someone in a drive-thru window," she explains as she rolls her eyes.

"How did Tazia take all this? Did she mention anything to you about it?" I ask.

"She told him he was being ridiculous and asked him to leave. He did eventually, and she never mentioned anything to me about it. I tried to make sure she was okay, but she kept waving me off."

I nod and thank her for her help just as she slides the coffees across the counter.

I scoop them up, pay, and make sure to leave her a good tip. "I'd appreciate if this conversation could stay between the two of us," I say. I need to put in a request to expand the warrant we received for Max's records. If Ellie and Tazia were both selling fake jewelry, then ended up dead—that definitely means I need to take a closer look at Max. I also need to determine if Chloe was involved.

"Of course, I won't tell anyone about it. Or that you were even here. But, if anything happened to Tazia, please let me know," she says, and there are the first hints of tears in her eyes.

"The second I'm able to give you more information, I will."

I head out of the coffee shop, the paper cup scalding my palm. So, we know where Tazia worked, we know her identity, we have a direction to go in. Those are good starts—especially with the slow beginning we had with each of these other victims. I call Matthew Chen to find out some general details about Tazia's family, and where in town I can find them. Then, I call to put in my formal request to expand the warrant we received on the pawnshop. By the time I make it back to the motel, Lucas is wide awake and ready to go.

We drive a few blocks to the Miller residence, during which I catch Lucas up on the warrant request and my conversation at the pawnshop. The three-story colonial looks almost identical to several of the other houses lined up on the street. The only thing that differentiates them are the colors. Two of the houses are butter yellow. The Millers' burgundy home stands out among the muted colors. The white trim makes the deep red look almost bloody. I climb out of my Jeep, bracing myself for the conversation that's to come. Lucas and I have tossed ideas back and forth, what to say, how to handle it. But that doesn't lessen the uneasy feeling swarming in my guts. This always happens before breaking the grim news.

"I still can't believe you didn't wake me up before you went to the coffee shop this morning. I missed out on so much," he says, frustration edging on his voice.

"It's not like I chased down this information on purpose. I guess you could say the stars aligned," I say.

"You should wake me up next time."

"You should get an alarm clock and stop whining." I shoot him a look and he looks like he's about to argue with me, but thinks better of it.

Lucas knocks on the front door when we approach. Though it's a bit early, an Easter wreath adorns the front door, packed with gold and orange leaves. A woman, my guess is it's Jena Miller, answers the door and looks between Lucas and me. The recognition is clear in her eyes before her brow furrows.

"Detectives?" she says, caught off guard.

"Do you mind if we come in for a moment?" Lucas asks, waving toward the house.

The woman looks back into her foyer, as if contemplating the offer. Finally, she shrugs and invites us inside.

"What is this all about?" she asks as she motions for us to take a seat in the room to the left, where the living room is sparsely furnished with a simple modern sofa and loveseat. The only other furniture in the room is a teal rug and a small light. Otherwise, it looks like maybe they just moved into the house. There are no pictures, no decorations, nothing at all.

"Unfortunately, we're sorry to inform you, but your daughter Tazia passed away. Our team recovered her body yesterday, and we just got back DNA reports that confirm Tazia is a match for your family," Lucas explains. "We are so sorry for your loss. Is there anyone that we can call for you?"

"My husband is at work. Oh my God. She can't be dead, she can't be," Jena says as she shoves up from the couch and paces the room like a caged tiger. "How could something like this happen? How could my daughter really be dead?" She's talking to herself more than us. But I glance to Lucas, unsure of what to say. He's the expert in situations like this.

"Jena, would you mind taking a seat so we can ask you a few questions? I know how hard this is, but we need to find who did this to your daughter before they can hurt anyone else," Lucas says, with all the patience of an elementary school teacher.

She plops back down on the sofa, but her eyes are so far off, misted, that I'm not sure she even sees us in the room with her. She wrings her bony hands atop her knees, her linen pants shifting and wrinkling under the pressure.

"Jena, I am so sorry for your loss. But our best chance of catching the person that did this to your daughter is to move quickly. The faster we can get our questions answered, the faster we can find this killer," I explain.

"Was she set on fire?" Jena asks, her eyes sharpening as she looks from Lucas to me.

I nod. "Yes, I am sorry to say that she was."

"Was she still alive?" She's barely able to choke the question out; she trips over her emotion several times.

"Based on what the medical examiner has seen so far, we do not believe that she was alive when the fire was set," I say.

She nods. "Well, I can be thankful for that, at least. I guess." Tears roll down her cheeks, and she tries to wipe them away almost as quickly as they fall. "Maybe she didn't suffer." She chokes the words out through a sob. I wonder if my mother would grieve for me like this. Probably not.

I pull out my notebook, ready to ask her all the questions I ask the families of every victim. But Lucas reaches out, and places his hand on mine, pushing my arms to my lap.

"Jena, would you like me to call your husband?" Lucas offers. "Would it be easier to continue if he were here?"

For a long moment, she considers it. Then she shakes her head. "Tazia was a daddy's girl. Mark loved that girl more than life itself. He won't be able to answer any questions,

probably not for a long time. This is going to tear him apart."
Jena is trying to keep her composure, that much is clear. But
I can nearly see her heart breaking through her gauzy
blouse. I cannot imagine the pain she must be feeling. "Let's
just get this over with. What do you need to know,
Detective?"

"I'll make this as quick as possible," I promise. "We know
that Tazia worked at the coffee shop in town. How long had she
worked there?"

"A year, I think. Or nearly a year," she says simply. "I
always thought she could do better than working at a coffee
shop, but at the end of the day, it made her happy. So I stopped
pushing her to do other things."

"Did Tazia have any enemies or anyone that she was having
any problems with?" I ask.

She shakes her head. "No, not that I'm aware of. I'll check
with her father to see if he knows anything different, but she
didn't share anything like that with me."

"Was she dating anyone or in a relationship?" I ask as I jot
down some notes.

"She was casually dating, but she wasn't seeing anyone seriously. But honestly, her communication for the past week was a
bit—odd. To say the least." She chews her lip. "I thought I was
just being paranoid."

I raise a brow at that. "Odd how?"

"She wouldn't call us like she usually would. She kept
making excuses for why she wasn't available. That wasn't like
her at all. My daughter has always been overly communicative
if anything. She would call to talk to either me or her father
nearly every day. But the past week, she stopped doing that.
Instead we got odd texts from her that didn't sound like her,"
Jena explains.

"Can I see some of these text messages?" I ask.

Jena nods and pulls out her phone, taps on the screen

several times, then hands the phone to me. I scroll through the recent texts:

Doing great. Having a great day.

Today is going awesome.

Can't believe the weather. LOL.

None of the texts have any follow-up from Tazia, even though Jena asked several follow-up questions to her daughter. I scroll up, looking at the communications from a few weeks ago. Tazia spoke about her job, funny things that happened in the coffee shop, a book she was reading, a dog she encountered in the park along with a picture. She and her mother chatted back and forth frequently. No strange messages about having a great day or the weather.

"Do you think that someone may have had your daughter's phone?" I ask.

She nods as she takes the phone back from me. "Yes, honestly. I tried calling her several times after the strange texts, but she wouldn't pick up. There were Facebook posts identical to the text messages as well."

"Did you contact the authorities about your concerns?" I ask. Last year, while working in Plattsburgh, missing persons cases were not taken seriously. Women being in danger, people breaking protective orders, all of it seemed to slide by and law enforcement did nothing about it. Seeing how little oversight there is for these small-town police departments, I'm concerned that's happening again here.

She shakes her head. "No, I didn't think it was that serious, otherwise I would have. I should have called someone. Maybe..."

"You wouldn't have been able to prevent this," Lucas says.

So, what we know so far is that Tazia was acting strangely for a week and didn't contact her family herself *that we know of* during that time. Did the killer have her somewhere?

"Did Tazia mention any concerns for her safety? Stalking? Unwanted interest by anyone in town? Are there any old grudges anyone has toward her that you can think of?" I ask. Most of the time the family can't think of anything or they're unaware of situations like this that could escalate. But either way, it's worth asking.

"No, she never mentioned anything like that to me," she says.

"Is there anything else you can think of that might help?" I ask.

"The day before I started getting the strange text messages from Tazia, she went on a date with Gavin Croswell. She was very excited about it, but I tried to talk her out of going on the date with him," she explains, looking from Lucas then back to me. "You two aren't from around here, so you may not know much about Gavin's history, but to say the least, I don't think that any mother in this town wants her daughter dating him."

"Even though he's loaded?" Lucas asks.

"Sometimes money just isn't worth it. I know that Tazia wasn't after money, but Gavin has charm. He lures women in, and then—well. I don't know specifics, but I have heard whispers about how he treats women, about what he does when they're alone."

"Is he abusive?" I ask as I take some notes about that. Gavin has always given me a bad vibe. He seems like a skeezy playboy at the very best; at the worst, maybe he's a sociopath.

"I've heard mostly verbally and emotionally, but one of his old girlfriends showed up with bruises a few times. When they broke up, she left town and never came back."

"What was her name?"

"Lucy Hale," she says. "Everyone was shocked when she

left town. People honestly thought that she and Gavin would get married. He was with her longer than anyone else in this town. Since she left, he's barely been with anyone more than a month. I'm surprised at this rate there are still women left in this town that will date him, but it seems he hasn't been through them all yet." She rolls her eyes.

"Do you know where Lucy went or her contact information?" I ask.

"She moved to Manhattan. I'll see if I can find her contact info for you."

"So, back to your daughter's date. You're sure that she went out with Gavin the night before the strange text messages began?"

She nods. "Yes, I tried to talk her out if it. She told me about the date a week before it happened, and I spent the whole time trying to talk her down, to get her to see reason."

"What did she see in Gavin exactly?" I ask.

Jena shrugs. "She didn't give me any specifics about that. She just seemed excited that he was interested in her at all. She could have done so much better than him if that's really what she wanted. But before Gavin asked her out, she never even seemed remotely interested in dating anyone. She was perfectly happy to be single—as far as I knew."

I finish up my conversation with Jena and thank her for her time. Lucas and I head back to the station, and I pull up the name and phone number for Lucy. We need to get her take on what happened while the two of them dated. It takes two tries to get Lucy on the phone. The phone rings several times, then finally a woman with a deep voice answers and I throw the call on speaker.

"This is Lucy."

"Hi, Lucy, I'm a detective with the NYCB, and I was hoping to talk to you for a few minutes about Gavin Croswell."

She's silent for so long, I check to make sure the call didn't drop.

"Sorry, I just— What is all this about?"

"Gavin is a person of interest in a case," I say, not wanting to add more info than necessary.

"Look, Detective, I've worked really hard to get out of that town and to leave all that happened to me there behind."

While I appreciate that she's trying to put up some boundaries and separate herself from her past, I do still need to know what happened with Gavin. If he did something to her, if he abused her, then it's not a huge leap to think that he might graduate to killing at some point.

"I understand, and anything that you say to me will be kept between the two of us. But I really need to understand your history with Gavin given some of the things that are happening in the town right now," I say. I wish I could give her more specifics that might coax more of a response out of her. I can't do that though; I have to hope that she's heard from family still in this town about what's going on.

"Is it related to those murders?" she asks, her words hitching. "I saw them on the news."

"I can't go into detail about why specifically we're contacting you, because it is part of an ongoing investigation." Lucas nods at me as I speak, letting me know in his own way that I'm on the right track without going too far over the line.

She sighs. "So, it is then. I get it. I've seen enough cop shows to know what you're getting at."

She's silent for a long time, so I add, "Look, anything you could tell me would be appreciated. My hope is that we can keep other women safe by knowing the details of what exactly happened to you."

"Who told you about my history with Gavin?" she asks. "Actually, never mind. The whole town knows. It's not like it matters who told you. Gavin and I dated for two years. I was so young, looking back. But I thought I was all grown up. I was barely twenty-two. Gavin was three years older than me. He already had a bit of a playboy reputation at that point—nothing compared to what he is now—and I felt so lucky that he picked me of all people."

"Do you know why exactly he *picked* you?" I ask.

"Because I was very suggestable? Because I went along with anything that he wanted? There are probably a million reasons, all of which add up to the fact that I was just a pretty mound of play dough. He could do whatever he wanted, treat me however he wanted, and I was an enamored little girl that would fawn over him at any chance I got," she says, her voice dripping with disgust.

"And how exactly did he treat you?" I can tell based on her comments that it's not good, but she's so vague that it's not giving me enough details to go on.

"One time, I disagreed with him in front of his mother, and that night he kicked me in the stomach so hard I had to go to the emergency room. I thought that he'd caused internal bleeding or something. I lied to the doctors there and told them that I thought I had appendicitis to cover for him. In the end, there was nothing wrong with me, and he made me feel like an idiot for going to the hospital."

"That's horrible," I say. Lucas shakes his head, clearly disgusted by the story.

"Another time, he nearly broke my pinkie finger because he thought that I flirted with the waiter who was serving us at his restaurant. He always treated waitstaff like they were nothing. He didn't even say thank you when they brought out the dishes. That should have been the first red flag when we started dating, that he saw servers as *lesser* than himself." There's such disdain in her voice. I can tell that this is still a very tricky subject for her. I hope that she's gone to talk to someone about everything that happened. Unfortunately, most of the time women who are in one abusive relationship go on to be in others.

"I am so sorry, Lucy. That's awful."

"I wish I had good stories to tell about him, but honestly after the first six months of being in a relationship with him, that was every day. There was significant emotional abuse. He took money from me so I couldn't leave him. The last straw was when he started trying to get me pregnant so that I'd be trapped with him forever. That's when I really started to look at what I was doing. I couldn't let him do that to a child. I couldn't let a child grow up thinking that having a father that beat their mother was normal. I borrowed a couple hundred dollars from my mom, and I left town at that point."

"Did he try to follow you or anything? Did he threaten your life?"

She lets out a humorless laugh. "He threatened my life more times than I can count. For a long time, I kept the voice-mails because I was afraid he would find me and kill me. But eventually he lost interest and moved on. I was able to move on with my life too—after a while. The PTSD still makes it hard. Sometimes I wake up in the middle of the night with cold sweats because I have nightmares that I'm back there, that I didn't get out."

"I'm really sorry that you went through all that, but I'm glad that you were able to get out. You're brave for standing up for yourself, for knowing that you deserve better," I say. "Thank you for your time today. I don't want to keep you any longer."

"Detective, wait," she says, before I'm able to hang up.

"Yes?"

"If I were you, and women were dying in a town where Gavin is still residing, I'd look at him pretty hard for those murders. As someone who spent a lot of time with him, I can tell you with absolute certainty that I think he is capable of killing," she says.

"Thank you for that, Lucy. I appreciate the information."

I end the call and turn back to Lucas. His mouth is a grim line as he looks from me to the phone.

"Do you like him for this?" he asks me.

I laugh at that. "Of course I like him for this, but right now, all we have is her story. We knew he had connections to these women. We don't have solid evidence. This is all circumstantial. Everyone in this town has these connections to one another. If we want to go after him, we need to have something that connects these dots more. Right now, we can tie him to two of the victims, but the ties aren't incredibly concrete. One night he has an alibi for, but we don't know for Tazia or Chloe. There are also connections between Max and Grover for each of our victims, some more solid than others. I'm not sure Gavin looks any more guilty than Grover does right now."

"Gavin's alibi is a video doorbell. He could have gone out a door that didn't have a video doorbell connected to it and killed her," he says.

I nod. That could be the case. "We need to ask him about Tazia and see what his story is for that night."

"It's not a position I'd want to be in if I were him. I've got to say, it doesn't look good."

As I leave the station, the evening sun burning red on the horizon, I walk across the parking lot. I've got my laptop bag slung over my shoulder, where it digs in, biting into the bone. A woman stands behind a car, catching my eye. She's got her arms crossed as she leans against her trunk. It's Christine Parsons. What's she doing here? Her gaze meets mine, and her lips press into a thin line before she climbs back into her car and drives away.

33

There's a knock at my door so early in the morning it actually jolts me from sleep. My heart pounds as I trudge to the door. Who the hell is pounding on my door at six in the morning? I open the door and find Lucas standing outside, his arms crossed, a weird look on his face. I squint at him, waiting for my eyes to adjust to the shift in light.

"Do you ever actually sleep?" I grumble at him.

"Yes, I do. That's why I'm prettier than you are," he says as he shoves his way into my motel room.

I curse at him under my breath and walk stiff-legged over to the shitty motel coffee pot.

"Why are you here before even God has woken up?" I grumble as I pour coffee grounds into the machine.

"So, I've got some bad news," he says, then plops down on my bed. I should have known. He's already dressed and knocking on my door at 6 a.m.? That's never good news.

"Just rip off the Band-Aid then." I turn to face him fully as the pot gurgles behind me.

"They found a body in McKenzie this morning... They're

fairly certain it was Grover." He says the words like he's bracing for impact.

It takes a few moments for my brain to shake off the fog of sleep and process the words fully. "Dead? Seriously?" If I had to pick a suspect right now who I really thought was our guy for these murders, it'd be Grover. His stalking, the way he spoke to these women, the necklace, Ellie's cellphone outside of his apartment, lack of alibis, it all lines up. "Fuck."

"If he's the guy, we can still find out. It will be easier to search his place now," Lucas offers, and I know he's just trying to make me feel better. But this doesn't help the families feel any type of closure. If our suspect is already dead when we announce that he's the killer, no one is going to feel any better about the situation. "And there's one other thing... a news story dropped this morning. Gavin's father has been accused of domestic violence by his wife. She's leaving him, and it's mentioned in the article that Gavin has his own history with domestic violence."

I turn to him, trying to tell if he's serious or not. A story dropping like that—now, well. That's not going to look very good for Gavin when we start asking more questions about Tazia. Or when the media gets wind that Tazia was last seen with Gavin before she died. I fill a paper cup with coffee and choke it down.

"So, today we've got to question Gavin. We need to get to him before the media can. Or before anyone can tip him off about Tazia," I say. At least I know they won't tell him about our conversation.

He nods. "Or before he really gets the idea that we like him for this and leaves town. With the unlimited resources he has... We need to be waiting at his office when he shows up. We've got to catch him off guard."

I hate that Gavin has the means to flee the country, to disappear. That's why it's so important that he doesn't know the scru-

"I don't drink on the job, but thanks," I say.

"You two are no fun," he says as he pours a little whiskey into his coffee cup.

"Do you mind taking a seat?" I ask, wanting to test the waters of how agreeable Gavin is today. While I know he flirts with me, that doesn't necessarily mean he's going to be incredibly cooperative when we start asking more questions about his whereabouts. The rich always have hyper-protective instincts.

"Anything for you, doll," he says with all the swagger of a sleazy car salesman.

Beside me, Lucas clenches his fist, and I flash him a warning look. I don't want him to intervene if it's not necessary in this interaction.

"Have you recently gone on a date with Tazia Miller?" I ask.

His brows furrow and he looks from me to Lucas. "Yeah, why?"

"When exactly did you go out?" I ignore his question. I'm not clarifying anything for him before I get a few answers set in stone.

"April 28th. We went to my restaurant and had a bite, then we went for a drive," he explains. "What's all this about?"

"What time exactly did you return home?"

"We went back to her place. I was there until probably 1 a.m., then I went home," he explains.

"Do you have any proof that you returned home at that time?"

He glances at his phone, tapping on the screen. I'm sure he's trying to find another video from his security system claiming when he arrived. He shakes his head though.

"Looks like my internet was down, and there wasn't a video logged of when I got home." He offers a shrug with his explanation, but he doesn't seem at all bothered. This is typically the point I'd expect a suspect to start squirming.

"Did anyone see you arrive home?" I ask.

"No, I live alone. And I don't think any of my neighbors were awake. But I don't make it a habit to check in with them when I come and go."

I note that down. He's got no alibi and his alibi for the other homicides are shaky at best. That might give me enough to get a search warrant for his house.

"Again, what is all this about?" he asks, looking genuinely confused.

"Tazia Miller's body was found. We're looking into her whereabouts before her death," I explain.

"My date with her was almost a week ago," he says, trying to draw a line in the sand.

I nod slowly. But I don't intend on giving him information about our belief that Tazia was held somewhere by her killer before her death. If this guy is kidnapping women and torturing them after dates, I don't want to give this bastard any heads up about what we might know. I want to nail him to a fucking wall. I have a feeling Gavin might have also gone out with Chloe, but thus far, I have no solid connections. But I decide to try my luck.

"And when did you last go out with Chloe Williams?"

"April 23rd," he says simply.

So he did go out with Chloe too. Alarm bells go off in my mind. I hadn't found any solid connections there, though I had my suspicions.

"What can you tell me about Lucy Hale?" I ask, raising a brow at him. I've still got my pen and my notebook out, ready to take notes if he spills anything good.

He lets out a dry laugh as his eyes sharpen. "Oh, I see what's going on here. You need to find a villain, and you've decided that villain is me. So you're digging into my past to craft some sort of narrative here, aren't you?" The more words spill out of his mouth, the higher he raises his voice at me. With each subsequent word, he shows more and more teeth. Cords of veins bulge in his neck as his cheeks redden.

"I'm just asking a simple question, Gavin. I don't see why you're getting so heated if nothing happened with Lucy." I keep my voice even, low. I'm not scared of this guy, and the weapon at my side is easily within reach if I need it. I'm not afraid to press some cold steel to this guy's skull to remind him who exactly is in charge here. Not that I'd shoot him, I wouldn't. But I'd love nothing more than to assert some dominance.

"This is some kind of fishing expedition, and you're not going to get anything out of me. Get the fuck out of my office, and don't come back without a warrant. The next time you talk to me, it'll be with a lawyer." He practically grinds the words out as he stalks over to his door and throws it open. He points down the hall, urging us to leave.

I take my time closing my notebook and tucking it away in my pocket. As I leave, I pause in front of Gavin.

"I'd be careful insisting that we get a warrant. Because you never know what we might find..."

"Is that a hint that you're planning to plant some evidence?" he asks as he raises a brow at me.

I laugh. "As if we would need to. I know what you're up to."

Though I posture, now that he's aware he's a person of interest, his reaction, the next steps he takes, will really show us how guilty he is.

34

The sun is just peeking over the horizon as Lucas and I cut a path through McKenzie Wilderness toward the area where Grover's body was found. Trees crowd around the car, blotting out the light, and it feels so claustrophobic. My throat tightens, and though I try to focus, to keep my mind present, memories of being next to my father in his van as the trees flickered past outside flood my mind.

"Are you okay?" Lucas asks as I gun it a little too hard and my Jeep jumps over a hole in the dirt road in front of us. We rock back and forth as we make contact with the ground fully again, but I know it's nothing compared to what my Jeep could really handle if it needed to.

"Yeah, fine," I say, a little too quickly. "Why?"

"Oh, I don't know. You're just driving through the forest like you're trying to take over for Vin Diesel in the next Fast and Furious movie. Did you rob a bank or something?"

"Oh shut up. You always criticize my driving," I snap at him, giving a little more barb to my words than I need to.

"Well, yeah. You suck at it, so." He laughs and turns his head toward the window.

"As if you're any better. There's a reason I always drive."

We fall silent as the scene comes into view. The flash of red and blue lights strobes against the towering pine trees. Light illuminates the forest for seconds at a time before plunging it back into darkness. A small team stands on the outside of the yellow tape. Forensics vans with the doors yawning open circle the scene. The fact that they're still out here collecting evidence surprises me; usually I'd expect them to be finished up by now. I wave to Racquel as we climb out of my Jeep. She's stationed next to Chad, who's got his arms crossed as he surveys the scene.

Anxiety tightens around my stomach like a fist as my boots sink into the wet earth. As I walk forward, I can feel Lucas staring at me as he follows behind me. But I don't turn; instead I hold my head high and continue forward. I don't look forward to having to talk to Chad about his case. With how territorial he is, he's likely going to see this as an affront.

He turns, narrowing his eyes on Lucas and me, then walks over to block us from reaching the outer circle of the scene. Lucas keeps walking, catching up with Racquel while I cross my arms, anticipating the face-off with Chad. We haven't really spoken since he came to my room drunk.

"What are you doing here, Durant?" he asks.

"We got word that your victim is our lead suspect, so unfortunately our wires are going to get crossed here," I say. "I'm not interested in this case, but I'm interested in the victim."

His brow furrows, and I can tell that he doesn't believe me. But after a long moment of silence, his tight shoulders fall slightly. "We think that Grover was attacked around midnight," he explains.

"How were you able to identify him so quickly? I've heard about the killer making it difficult to identify some of these victims."

"His car was parked not too far from the scene, and he had

his wallet in his pocket. We haven't confirmed with DNA, but I don't see any reason the Mauler would have planted fake ID on the victim," he explains.

"I thought that most of the victims of the Mauler were women." That's one of the things that's throwing me off here. Why would the Mauler have even gone after Grover?

He nods. "About ninety percent women so far, but there have been a few men. We're not sure yet why men are in the mix sometimes. Maybe the Mauler was after a female victim and a man got in the way. We really don't know."

I glance around at the towering trees; how remote this space feels. "Why would Grover have been out here in the first place?" I ask. He didn't seem like the type to come out into the woods. He definitely didn't seem athletic or outdoorsy.

"We don't have any leads on that yet. We weren't able to find his phone, so we're unsure if someone told him to meet them out here."

"I wonder if he followed someone out here. He was fired from his job for stalking," I explain. Part of me doesn't want to share case details with Chad, but right now, I think a little cooperative information sharing will help us both. Maybe it'll make Chad realize that I'm not a threat to his case and that I'm just trying to solve my own.

"There were other tire tracks out here, and footprints. We know at the very least there was a woman out here, size seven or eight shoes, we think. The shoe prints are a little smudged because the earth is so wet over here."

"That's the same size that we saw at the first scene where Chloe was found," I say.

"Do you think that there may be some crossover here?" Chad asks.

"I'm honestly not sure yet. What else do you know about your Mauler? Any connection between the victims?"

He shakes his head. "No. Some of them aren't even from the

town. Some are hikers, tourists. Very few have been actual residents of Saranac Lake, which makes me wonder if those weren't the intended victims. I was really thinking that our killer was trying to ruin the tourist reputation of the town. There's been some interest in building new motels. Ground was supposed to break on a new ski resort. The town is really looking to attract new blood. Maybe the Mauler doesn't like that."

"That's a theory," I say. It's better than anything I've been able to come up with for the Mauler yet. "So, how'd he die?"

"The ME is going to have to give her call on that. It's too soon for us to tell. But like the other scenes, it's incredibly gruesome. His skull was cracked, lacerations to the face, mouth, upper body," Chad explains as he runs his hands through his hair several times. Though I want to hate Chad because he can be such a territorial douche—I can see how anxious he is, how nervous. He's not doing any better with all this than I am.

"Any thoughts on a weapon?"

"I've been leaning toward golf club, a tire iron, something that's a bit slimmer, easy to swing. All the victims have a wound to the back of the head, where we think they were initially attacked. The blow that takes them off their feet. We think the killer stays between the trees out of view, then attacks from the back," he explains as his eyes scan the trees, as if our killer might be out there right now—watching. For all I know, he could be.

I make a few mental notes about that. "Thanks, Chad. If you think of anything else, mind giving me a call?" Though I could dig a little deeper, Chad is already antsy and I don't want to ruin what little rapport that we have right now.

He shakes his head. "I'll call you once we hear back from the ME."

35

TWENTY YEARS AGO

The house is silent. A rarity these days. It's been six months since we moved, and I thought that things would get better eventually. I've held my breath, walked on eggshells, and stuck to the shadows trying to avoid the anger brewing in this house. But nothing I do helps. My mom is so angry all of the time. It feels like she's about to explode, to lash out at me every chance that she gets. Today, my mom agreed to go to therapy with my dad, something I feel is him gaming the system. But that's not my decision.

I sneak down to his office, knowing that I've got an hour or so before they're back. More and more the news is talking about women who have died, some strangled, some stabbed, some suffocated in their beds. A few weeks ago, I read a book about serial killers in the library, and it explained that most get caught because they escalate, they get sloppy. And right now, I think that's what's happening to my dad. I don't know for sure, because I don't know who all his patients are. But I have suspicions that he's killed at least twenty women. But to be sure, I've got to go through his files.

I look out the window, my heart pounding in my throat. The driveway is still empty. If I get caught, my father will be so upset with me, it may drive a wedge between us. And I don't think I could live in this house anymore if my dad and my mom both hated me.

There are boxes of files in my dad's office, but what I'm looking for isn't in them. I'm hoping that on his computer I can find a client list, something that I can check against the stories swirling all over the news about the Seattle Sleeper. I open my dad's laptop, and type in the password he gave me so that I can do research for my homework. I know better than to actually look up these women on his computer; I'll have to do that in the library.

It takes me a few minutes of poking around to find a client list, then I find another, and another. Unsure which one to go with, I print them all out. It seems to take forever for the printer to click on and for the pages to churn out. After they do, I close out the files, shut the laptop, and run up to my room. There are over fifty names on each list. It's going to take me a while to figure out who these women are.

I ride my bike across town to the library, the cool autumn air hissing against my face as I pedal. I made the excuse that I needed to concentrate on my homework, to get some quiet. The subtext that I expected them to fight was clear when I told my mother where I was going. But thankfully, she cares so little about where I am most of the time, she told me to shut up and get out.

Once inside, I relish the quiet, the way my nerves seem to unwind here. I only realize how tense I am at home once I leave. My body is always wound tight, like I'm expecting to fight off a punch from my mother, or to brace myself for the screaming.

But here, this is a safe zone. Somewhere that no one will touch me, no one will scream. I toss my backpack on the floor next to a computer terminal. Thankfully no one is in the computer room, so I can research all by myself.

I wait for the browser to load, then navigate to a search engine. Next to me I've got a stack of papers and highlighters so I can mark each of the patients off as I research them. Blue for the ones who are dead, green for the ones who are missing, yellow for the ones I can't find at all. The first three names I type into the search engine bring up nothing. My guts twist as I type in the next name, and the uncertainty hits me. What if the names not coming up in the searches means their body hasn't been found yet?

I stop myself. I can't think that way. I need to focus on getting through the list, not second-guessing myself. The next name brings up a news story. This woman is dead. I highlight her name in blue. Then another. And another.

By the time I'm done going through the lists, there are at least thirty women who are dead, fifteen who are missing, and the rest don't appear at all. I look closer at the lists and realize these aren't all my father's patients. Some of these women are assigned to other doctors in his practice. Is that how he hasn't been caught yet? He's not just killing women who are connected to him?

Guilt seizes me again. With one call I could stop all this. I could tell the police and no other women would die. But what would happen to me? Sealing my father's fate means that my life is forfeited. It means that I'm up on the chopping block. What will my mother do to me once he's gone? What kind of life would I even have left?

Tears burn my eyes as I shove the lists back in my bag. It's not fair that I have this hanging over my head, that I have to choose between a mother who hates me and a father who kills.

What kind of choice is that? I don't ride my bike home; instead I push it beside me, my feet dragging against the sidewalk as the night darkens around me. A few cars pass me and I stop, looking out at the city beyond.

What if I didn't go back?

36

I'm so tired, I feel like I'm dragging sandpaper across my eyeballs. For hours, I've been combing through the data that we got back from our record request for the pawnshop. Instead of just sending us the records we requested, Max sent us everything. I think he's trying to muddy the waters, to make it too difficult for us to glean anything from all the data. But thus far, I can tell for certain that all of our victims did business with Max, and all of them ended up selling him counterfeit goods. We've also dug through social media accounts for Gavin, our victims, and a few of the gossips in town. Thus far, I know the connection between Gavin and these women—but I need real evidence.

All of our victims were friends on Facebook, which could mean everything or absolutely nothing in a town this small. With all of them selling fake jewelry, I really question if they were working on this together. For Gavin and Max at least, right now, while this looks bad for them, everything we have is circumstantial. Though I've looked for more regarding Grover, I haven't found anything else pointing to him. I've learned nothing from social media, and if I have to look at another

THE GIRLS IN THE FIRE

picture of someone's lunch today, I may gouge my eyes out. As I pack my things up and trudge through the bullpen to get out of the office, I overhear Matthew on the phone.

"Are you sure that's what you heard?" he asks. There's a pause and I'm sure the person on the other end of the line is talking. Then he adds, "Okay, I'll send someone out there to check."

I approach his desk as he hangs up the phone. "What's up?" I ask, still feeling a bit like I'm intruding and kicking the sand in their sandbox. Working with the state police rather than a local team, most of the time it's very much an us-versus-them mentality. They want to keep their cases to themselves, and they want us to stay out of their business. I get it, we could complicate things. But at the end of the day we're all working in law enforcement, fighting for the same victims.

"A woman calling about hearing a scream in her neighborhood," he says as he shakes his head. "She calls every single day talking about gunshots, or screams—it's always something."

"Does she live anywhere near the logging road?" I ask. If a resident heard a woman screaming, we should take that report seriously, especially with everything that's been going on in town.

He shakes his head. "No, she's on the completely opposite side of town."

"It's still probably worth checking out," I say. If he doesn't want to send someone over, I'll swing by on my way back to the motel.

"I'll have a unit that's out patrolling go by to see if they hear anything. We've already got someone in the area," he says. "Thanks for your concern though."

I nod. "Call me if you need anything," I say, understanding the clear dismissal in his tone. Lucas left early today. It's his father's birthday, so he had planned to drive to see him tonight and head back before six tomorrow morning. I tried to get him to take a day off to spend with his dad, but he's nearly as bad as I am with taking time off—despite how much he likes to tell me that I need to balance work and time off.

When I walk outside, there's a chill in the air. It's not quite cold yet, but I know that by midnight I'd need a jacket to spend more than a few minutes outside. Soft clouds dot the inky sky, illuminated by the full moon shining above me. My phone vibrates in my pocket, and I check it as I walk toward my Jeep, which is at the far edge of the parking lot. The scuff of feet behind me draws my attention and I whip around to find a woman in a blazer with sleek hair and thick makeup. I've seen her before in the line of reporters cataloging each scene. She's local, not from one of the big stations near Manhattan or anything, and thankfully right now she's not being followed by a cameraman.

"Excuse me, Detective. Sorry, I didn't mean to startle you," she says, holding her hands up like she's surrendering to me. "I'm Cassie Curtis from the Saranac Lake News, and I was hoping that I could interview you," she explains.

I shake my head. "Sorry, but I can't comment on an ongoing investigation." I start to turn away from her, back to my car, but she starts speaking again.

"No, I don't want to ask you about the case. I was hoping to ask about *you*."

"Let me be a little more clear. I'm not interested in doing any interviews, whether it's about me or about the cases that I'm working on." My words are a bit more clipped than I mean for them to be, but it's hard to keep up pretenses and stay *nice* when I'm being ambushed by reporters.

"I saw a recent report that stated that children of violent offenders are far more likely to be violent themselves. And based on some digging that we've done, it seems several suspects that you've arrested have been beaten or injured while in your custody. Do you think that's due to DNA markers that may also be present in your father? The ones that led him to become a serial killer?" She speaks with an upward inflection that makes every single statement sound like a question. It comes off as more valley girl than it does journalist, and I wonder if this is some sort of tactic that she's developed so that people don't get angry with her about her line of questioning.

"No comment," I say before grinding my teeth together. At this rate, I'm going to grind my molars to dust. I stalk to my car, painfully aware that she's steps behind me, following me.

"You have no comment about beating suspects that were placed in your care? Do you not take police violence toward suspects seriously?" She jabs at me with her words.

Anger rises inside me like a tide, and I want to shove this woman, to slam her to the pavement if only to get her to shut up. Maybe she's right, maybe there is a violent streak that runs through me because I'm the product of two violent parents. My mother beat me, and my father killed women. How exactly was I supposed to turn out? It's not like I got the best start for being an even-tempered, productive member of society.

"Back off, lady," I say as I whip around to face her again. "You don't know anything about me. This is all assumption. Just because I brought someone in and they faced some kind of violence within the justice system while they were in custody does not mean that I'm the person who did that. Unfortunately there are many inmates who are attacked when they're thrown into gen pop. There's nothing I can do about that and I have no control over it. My job is to find killers, to collect evidence, and to help the DA build a case."

"So it's not your job to keep suspects safe? That's what you're saying?"

"No, it's not," I snap at her. "There have been zero complaints filed with IA about my treatment of anyone who was in my custody. So before you come at me with what you think are facts, I'd do a bit more digging so that you're fully prepared."

"I just find it a little troubling that someone with your sort of history is working in a town where there are two serial killers active. Doesn't that seem a little suspicious to you?" she asks as she raises a brow and appraises me.

"Suspicious how, exactly? I'm not sure I understand what you're getting at." Whatever she's trying to imply, it's lost on me. Why would it be suspicious that a homicide detective is in a town investigating a homicide? "Is it suspicious that Chad is in town investigating some of the crimes? Or that the rest of the team is here investigating? Or is it just me who's the problem?"

"Well, given the findings that have come out about violent parents having violent children, I'm wondering what the chances are that you yourself have a dark history. One that includes homicide."

"Are you implying that I'm killing women in this town?" I ask as I stalk toward her. I can't believe that this woman is walking down this path. This isn't journalism, this is slander.

"I'm not implying anything, I'm asking you." She crosses her arms and widens her stance, like she expects me to try and throw her off balance. Maybe she expects me to punch her.

"Okay, well let me make it very clear for you, Cassie." I say her name like a curse. "I'm not killing anyone. I'm a homicide detective here investigating homicides. For you to imply that I'm hurting anyone, let alone killing women in this town—when the homicides started before I got here—is absolutely ridiculous. I suggest that you back the fuck off or I will find out who sent you here and give you all hell."

A hand wraps around my arm, and I turn to find my mother. "Let's go, Harlow," she says, her voice low as she tugs on my arm. Her eyes are pleading. And I do not have the energy to fight her and this reporter at the same time. I knew she'd find me eventually. She always does. I guess I should have taken her emails and calls for the warnings they were.

I look back to Cassie, the warning clear in my eyes, I'm sure. "Do not come near me again."

I stalk toward my Jeep and my mother climbs in the passenger side. Being this close to her again makes my skin crawl, but I won't give Cassie anything else to talk about when it comes to my life.

"You're lucky she wasn't recording you," my mother says as I drive. I really look at her for the first time, and really take her in. She's dressed like she should be in a J.Crew catalog, not like the woman I remember. She always wore jeans, ratty T-shirts, back when I lived with her. It looks like over the years she's gained enough wealth to dress herself better. Large diamonds wink in her earlobes in the light.

"You're the last person I need advice from. I know you'd sell my story to the first person to offer you a half-eaten box of Tic Tacs. So don't even start with me. I am not in the fucking mood." I growl the words at her as I peel out of the parking lot. Maybe I should just run Cassie down with my car. Show her exactly how violent I am.

"I'm not your enemy. I'm trying to help," she says. "That's all I've been trying to do. But you've been ignoring my calls, my emails. I even stopped by the station. You left me with no choice but to chase you down again, to show up here."

"Why were you at the station?" I ask, as I realize how hard I'm gripping the steering wheel, how tense my body is. I should let it go, take a deep breath, and lower my heart rate. But I can't yet.

"I was going to try to talk to you. I wanted to check on you. I know how much pressure you must be under with this case."

"Why do you care?" This shift is throwing me off guard. Her attitude has completely changed since the last time I saw her and I don't understand why.

"Because you're my daughter. I'm always going to care about what happens to you," she says.

I glance at her out of the corner of my eye. Has she forgotten what she did? How she abandoned me? "You can't be serious right now," I say.

"There's a lot that you don't understand about what happened to my life when your father went to jail. I put you into foster care because I was being investigated. I was afraid I was going to go to jail as well," she says.

I don't believe her. Not even a little. She's trying to make herself feel better and to rewrite our past. I called her so many times from foster care. I begged her to take me back, despite how I knew she'd abuse me too. Because sadly, the abuse I'd become accustomed to was far better than what I faced in care.

"Investigated for what, exactly?" I ask.

"They thought that I helped your father. That I knew about the murders, that I helped him cover them up. There were a few murders that they were sure that he couldn't have committed alone. They were convinced that I knew all about it and I helped him get away with killing the entire time that we were married."

"But you told me that it was all my fault that my father became a killer, and that you were putting me in foster care because you couldn't bear to look at me since I was the reason your life had fallen apart." I remember that conversation so clearly, as if it were carved into my flesh. Things like that, you never forget, especially when your own mother says them to you.

"Harley, I was hurting. You have to understand that my life had fallen apart, I was lashing out. I shouldn't have, and I am so sorry for the way I treated you. But I wasn't in the right frame of mind. I was a very unhappy person. And I've worked a lot on myself and how I treat people. That's why I'm here to make amends."

Even being in this car with her right now, it's draining. Some part of me wants to give up, to let go of this anger, because it's so exhausting to hold on to it. And at my core, I can't deny that some part of me wants her to be genuine. I want my mother to be sorry, to atone for what she did. But that could be clouding my decision-making.

"So how exactly do you expect to make amends?" I ask, as I maneuver my Jeep through the streets of Saranac Lake. We're the only ones out, except for a patrol car that's rolling slowly down Main Street.

"However you'll let me. I'll just be here if you need me to be, I'll show you that I'll really be here for you. I won't abandon you again," she says.

"I'm an adult. You can't abandon me because I'm self-sufficient," I say. I wonder if she even thought this far, about how she'd really try to repair our relationship. My mother has never been one to plan ahead.

"Okay, well then, what would you like me to do?" she asks.

I shake my head. "No, you need to come up with a plan. You're not going to put the work on me to figure out how *you* can fix our relationship."

A vein pulses in her neck, but she nods. "Fine. I'll put some thought into it."

"Want me to drop you at your motel?" I ask, as I look down the empty street.

"Sure, that would be nice," she says, then tells me where she's staying.

I take a turn to the left, choosing to curve through the part of town where the call came from about a woman screaming. I'm not incredibly familiar with Saranac Lake yet, so I want to see what's over here. Where the scream may have come from. After that first scream, and finding Tazia's body, I can't let this go.

Though I do take Matthew's opinion about the woman who

calls a little too frequently to report strange sounds seriously, while there are two serial killers haunting this town, we can't let it slide that a woman may have been heard screaming. This could lead us to another victim. It shocks me that they disregard screams so easily. They may as well be gunshots if you ask me.

"What are we doing over here?" my mother asks.

"Checking something out real quick before I drop you off," I explain. I keep my eyes peeled as I drive, and a dark shape on the ground catches my eye. I throw the Jeep into park, grab an evidence bag from my glove compartment, and slide out of my car. In the darkness, the shape becomes clearer—a hammer. I pick it up gingerly with the bag, careful not to taint the evidence. My heart races as I hold the bag up; the inside of the plastic is smeared with red. Blood.

I glance down the street. No signs of a pickup truck, no signs of fire. The streets are abandoned in a way that's almost eerie. Our killer left this here, and its placement, knowing the blood was here—it almost feels like it was left on purpose. Like I'm being taunted. I climb back into my Jeep and stash the hammer. Though my mother asks about it, I wave her off. This isn't her business.

Silence builds between my mother and me as I drive through the city back to her motel. There's a tension in the air that's almost electric, like the static that builds before a lightning storm. All the words we should say, all the anger I've held inside all these years, they form a cloud around us. I want to say something, anything. To get this poison out of my mind and out of my veins. But I can't. There's nothing I can say to fix this, to turn this wreckage into some kind of bridge. Some relationships can't be saved, and I need to accept that.

My mother opens the door hesitantly as we pull up to the front of the motel. The lights are too bright under the awning, stretching the shadow beneath her nose all the way down her face, like a sundial. In the harsh light, I can see the years that have worn on her face, her history, her sadness. But then again, my mother was always pained. Grief was wound into every fiber of her being—in a way that I'm not sure she could ever let go of it. After she exits my Jeep, she turns around, her hand on the door like she wants to say something. But she doesn't. Instead she shakes her head, slams the door, and disappears inside the motel.

After she's gone, I turn back around and head to the neighborhood where the scream originated. Something tells me not to let this go. That call, the information that Matthew relayed, it's fresh in my mind and I can't pretend it never happened. No one in this town is safe, and I won't pretend that nothing is happening here, like the members of Saranac Lake PD seem to want to do.

I drive through the streets with purpose. My heart pounds as I look for something, anything, out of place. But nothing sticks out to me. No blood, no tire tracks, *nothing*.

As I turn down the last street in the neighborhood, I find a pickup truck that's pulled over to the side. The lights are off, the engine looks cold. It doesn't look like the truck has moved at all. I keep rolling, my eyes scanning the street. The road in front of me stretches on, curving into the woods. On either side, the large houses climb as the landscape slopes upward. Behind me, the flash of lights catches my attention as the headlights of the pickup truck flash in my rearview mirror.

My chest tightens as the truck revs its engine and speeds toward me. I hit the gas. I never should have passed the damn truck. I should have checked the cab. My Jeep lurches forward, the engine protesting as I push the RPM higher than I normally do. The truck slams hard into the back of my car, and I tighten my hold on the steering wheel as I fight to maintain control. I look in the rearview mirror, trying to see who's driving, but with the high beams on, I can't make out anything inside the cab. My heart pounds. I've never had a suspect slam into my car before. I was trained for this, but my thoughts and guts have turned to water.

I press the gas, trying to escape the truck. The road curves upward, leading me toward the trees, and I have no choice but to follow. The growl of the engine behind me warns of another impact before it hits. I grind my jaw and my whole body tenses as I brace for the impact. My Jeep skids, and I turn the wheel in the opposite direction of the skid, fighting against it. For a moment, I think it'll work, that I'll keep going and escape this. But another impact on the side of my Jeep sends my stomach into my throat. Darkness engulfs me as I hear a crunch; lights explode in my vision. I'm flying, spinning, before the world goes black.

37

Smoke curls into my nostrils as heat presses in on me from all sides. I sputter as my head throbs. The world strobes in and out, as I try to shake off a weird dream. Memories, thoughts, visions coalesce in my mind all at once, and vomit rises in my throat. I fight against it, against the acid burning my esophagus. My eyes open, but the world is blurry. Too bright and too dark at the same time. I try to make sense of it. More smoke floods my lungs, and my mind screams.

Fire.

Panic and dread fill me, and a cold sweat prickles at my skin. It all snaps into place, awareness hitting me at the same time adrenaline hits my blood. I'm in my Jeep. It's on its side, the forest rising around me. Flames dance from the hood, flickering in and out as they chase away the darkness. My hands feel stiff while I fight with the seat belt. A cough rips through my lungs. Smoke clouds the windshield. I finally free myself, then wedge myself between the door and seat so I can stand and climb my way out of the passenger door.

I tumble from the passenger door, and land hard on the soft floor of the forest. Adrenaline fades from my blood, and my body aches—from the impact, the crash, where the seat belt dug into my neck for hours. My Jeep is overturned, resting against a tree, flames dancing across the crumpled metal. The pickup that toppled me is nowhere to be found. Whoever the hell hit me, they left me for dead. I know what their intentions were here. They didn't want me to walk away from this. My heart pounds as I fish in my pocket for my phone, only to realize it's still in the car. It takes me a few minutes to extricate it, then I call Sergeant Dirby.

"Durant, is everything okay?" he asks, his words slowed as he shakes off the daze of sleep.

Night is still thick around me; the early morning is filled with the sounds of crickets and the croaks of frogs. I glance at my phone again, realizing it's nearly 2 a.m. I was out for an hour, at least. As I try to calm my nerves, I explain to Lucas what happened.

"Oh my God," he says, and I hear the rustling of fabric in the background. He was clearly still in bed. "I'll have someone there in five minutes. How are you feeling? Are you okay?"

"Yeah, I'm fine," I say, though I still feel woozy and disoriented. If I'm honest, I know he'll force me to go to the hospital or something. I'm not willing to do that. Our killer tried to kill me tonight, which means we're getting close. An image of the hammer flashes through my mind, and I head back to the Jeep. Smoke hangs in the air around me, clawing against my throat. Heat sears my hands, my cheeks, warning of the danger that's looming in my overturned vehicle. But I push past it. I need that evidence. After searching for a few minutes, I realize that it's gone. Did it fall out as I crashed? Or did the killer come to claim it?

38

Thick clouds shroud Saranac Lake as I emerge from my motel room. My head still aches from the collision last night. I came back to the motel and managed to get a few hours of sleep after refusing to go to the hospital. While I know Lucas hasn't had much sleep, I need his help this morning—and I can't stand back anymore. He should be back from seeing his dad. The more I thought about it last night, the more I wanted to stop by Mariska's to check on her. After her date with Gavin, I haven't seen her in town, so I would feel better if we check in on her— and got some questions answered about how her date with Gavin went. Once an abuser, always an abuser, so I want to be sure that he hasn't started turning his aggression toward other women in this town.

I've already called to see if my Jeep can be extricated from the woods, and possibly salvaged. That vehicle has been through so many moves, so many years with me—I hope it can be saved. By this afternoon, I'll have a rental car. I knock on Lucas's door, hoping that he's already awake. But a sound behind me sends my heart rate rocketing. I spin around and find

Lucas standing on the walkway with two coffee cups in his hands.

"You scared the shit out of me," I say as I grasp my chest.

"When did you get so jumpy?" he asks as he thrusts a coffee toward me. "Oh God, your head looks horrible," he says as he leans in and squints while appraising my forehead.

Last night, I must have hit it against the window during the accident. A bruise is spreading across the side of my head, with a gash about three inches across at the crest of it. It's not bad enough that I need stitches, but it looks like I lost a fight.

I take the cup and test a sip. The flavor of caramel melts across my tongue and I groan. "I'm not jumpy," I say, as I glare at him.

"Yeah, okay. Sure. Why were you looming outside of my door?"

"I'm not looming. I was trying to see if you were awake," I say, taking another sip of my coffee. "Thanks for this."

He nods. "I couldn't sleep after I got back, so I decided to grab some coffee and get on with the day. You already trying to head into the office?" he asks.

I tell him about the hammer I found, its disappearance, followed by my plan to check on Mariska, and he pushes back, thinking I need to get my head checked out again. But I brush him off.

"You think that Gavin did something to her?" he asks.

"You think he didn't? He's got connections to all the other victims. He's dated every single one of them. Grover's dead, so we know he wasn't responsible." I'm trying to find solid evidence that points to Gavin—that's what we really need here —but thus far, circumstantially, it's not looking good for him. While Max is still on my list too, his connection to the other women is financial, at best. Scorned lovers are far more likely to be the killing type.

"To give him the benefit of the doubt, he's dated nearly

everyone else in this town, and those women aren't dead," he says. And I know that he's covering all the bases. In police work, we need to challenge each other on ideas, on points that could be brought up during a trial. If I want to proceed with looking at Gavin, I need good reasons to do so, and more importantly, I need evidence.

"Yeah, I know that. But right now, he's the only connection we've got between these women who's still alive. We need to at least do our due diligence and look into that," I explain.

"All right, as long as you're willing to defend that when Gavin lawyers up and they track every single move that you made."

"I'm ready for it," I say.

"Then let's go."

Lucas and I climb into his rental car and drive over to Mariska's small house. This morning I called Matthew and got her address, and something stuck out to me about it immediately. Mariska's house is a block from where the woman called last night reporting hearing a scream, where I found the disappearing hammer. That in itself was enough to raise my hackles. There's something going on and I need to find out what it is.

We pull in front of Mariska's house. Her Toyota is parked in the driveway, but there are no signs of life in the house. The lights are all off, the blinds all closed. It is still early, so that could be the reason. We approach the door and knock. We wait in silence, straining to hear any movement inside the house. As each moment drags on without an answer or a noise inside, the louder my heart pounds in my ears. A bad feeling brews inside me, warning me that something is wrong.

"I'm going to check the windows," I say, motioning for Lucas to stay put in case Mariska answers the door.

He nods, though there's hesitation in his gaze. It's clear he doesn't want me creeping around by myself, but someone has to stay at the door. I follow a path around the front flowerbed, toward the side of the house. Out front, all of the drapes are sealed up tight. I wouldn't be able to look in even if I tried. On the right side of the house, I find a window with the drapes open, and I get a view into the living room.

A plush blue velvet couch sits along one wall; ornate golden tables flank the sofa. Throw pillows encrusted with sequins adorn the couch. Along the floor there's a large rug that's so fluffy it could very well be a Persian cat. Near the front door, glass glitters along the floor, the remnants of what looks like a vase or maybe a lamp. Several other decorations are thrown to the floor next to an overturned coffee table.

Even from my position at the window, I can tell there was some kind of struggle here. I jog back to the front of the house.

"We need to get inside, it looks like there was a fight in there," I say as I grab my phone and radio in what I see.

My training kicks in and my body moves of its own accord. I know what I have to do and how to do it. Though technically I could break down the door to gain access to the residence based on what we've seen, I'd rather try to find a way into the house without breaking anything—if at all possible. Though, typically, the goal would be to get a warrant. But with Mariska being in danger, we have to move fast. We can't sit on this and wait for Mariska's body to just turn up.

"Let's look to see if there's a key out here," I say to Lucas as I start to look under large rocks near the front porch.

Lucas pulls up the welcome mat, finding nothing but dirt and leaves beneath. I run along the side of the house, scouring every single thing that's out of place that could conceal a key. On the back porch, under a small birdhouse, I finally find one.

"Got it!" I shout to Lucas as I shove the key into the back door. It takes two tries, but I yank the door open.

I test the air inside, smelling for any hint of a body. But thankfully thus far, there's no stench.

"Mariska, it's the police," I call out, hoping that she's here, that she's got enough wits about her to call back to me. But there's nothing, the house is dead silent. My feet echo on the wood floors as I creep into the house. There's a hallway straight from the front door to the back, like a shotgun-style house. In the gauzy light cast by the front door I can see the glittering shards, and something more pooled on the floor—blood.

Lucas's footsteps on the porch behind me cause me to throw my arm out. I fish in my pocket for booties and latex gloves, pulling them both on before signaling for him to do the same. I try to piece together what could have happened, the chain of events. Was she attacked here and taken from the home? Maybe her attacker dropped the hammer on the way out as he struggled with the body and the weapon?

"There's blood near the front door," I explain.

He nods and pulls on his own protective gear so that our presence doesn't disturb the scene. Behind me, he pulls out his phone and dials the number for the forensics team. We're going to need them over here as soon as possible. I walk into the house, turn right, and survey the kitchen. No body, nothing out of place. She's not here. Next, I sweep two small bedrooms, the larger of which is clearly the main bedroom. In the main bedroom, I find what looks like the beginning of the blood. It starts here and trails to the front door. The end tables are overturned, a lamp broken on the floor next to one of the tables. The covers are askew, half off the bed, like Mariska was awakened. At my feet, there's a pool of red, a knife beside it, and droplets that shimmer around the corner.

As far as I can tell from what I've seen of the house, there's no sign of forced entry. So whoever did this to Mariska, she must have known them. Did Mariska let them inside? There's always the chance they found the key, but I doubt they would have put it back.

"Any body?" Lucas asks, as he pops his head in the door.

"The blood trail starts here, but no body," I explain. "But I did think I saw blood last night in the street," I say, the memory of what I saw surfacing.

"There's no blood from the front or back steps, and no blood on the driveway," Lucas says.

"Maybe Gavin bandaged the wound to move the body?" I offer. "He clearly didn't kill her here, there isn't enough blood for that. But it looks like she was injured during a struggle. Then taken through the front door, since there's more blood there." That's what we saw at Chloe's apartment too though. There was blood, but not enough that she died there. Is he hurting them as a warning to get the women to come with him?

"There's also blood in the living room on the carpet," he offers.

"Maybe he grabbed something in the living room to stanch the bleeding? A blanket?" There has to be some reason for that trajectory. There's a clear path out of the house from the back bedroom to the front door. It actually would have been faster and safer for him to take Mariska out the back door. So why did he choose that path? In the bedroom I find a lamp broken on the floor, an overturned night table, clothes and the duvet littering the ground.

"Any signs that there was another car in the driveway behind Mariska's? Any oil that's dripped on the driveway or anything?" I ask.

"I'll go take some pictures."

"Please also ask the neighbors if they saw anyone here last night with Mariska, or if they heard anything," I say. One of us has to stay at the scene to make sure no one enters the residence and tampers with evidence. I trust Lucas to handle his portion of this. Though I count myself lucky that he's working with me on this and not someone else.

He nods. "On it." He's out the door before he even finishes the words.

I take pictures of the scene while I wait for Racquel and her team to arrive. At the very least, I want to catalog what's here already, so I can try to piece together what happened myself. We need to figure out where Mariska is. She may not be dead yet. I grab my phone and put in a call to Sergeant Dirby. I need to get his help on this so we can track down Mariska.

"Durant," he says as soon as the call connects.

"I need an emergency trace on a phone. Can you reach out to the DA to coordinate that for me?" I ask, then explain to him the extenuating circumstances. It can be difficult to get some cellphone providers to assist when it comes to cases like this. They want to protect their users and their privacy. But at the same time, some of them understand that if they don't provide the data we're looking for, a life hanging in the balance could be lost.

"I'll see what I can do. Do you have a suspect?" he asks.

I catch him up on my thoughts on Gavin, and how he's the person I'm really targeting for this. I saw Gavin with Mariska with my own eyes yesterday.

"Sounds like a good direction. Get some evidence," he says.

"That's what I'm trying to do. We've got a knife. That's a start at least," I say.

"It better have some prints on it," he grumbles before ending the call.

Racquel's team shows up about thirty minutes after we called them in. As Racquel strolls through the back door, she looks frazzled, stressed. She's got a clipboard clutched in her hands as she approaches, and offers me a very forced smile.

"Everything okay?" I ask.

"Long day already and it's not even 10 a.m.," she says with a humorless laugh. "There was another body over in the woods last night, so we were up most of the night cataloging that scene, and here we are now just a few hours later to go over this one. This town is wearing me ragged," she says as she shakes her head.

"I'm doing everything I can to catch this guy. Then at least you can keep your attention on one serial killer, instead of being split between two," I say as I wave her over to the bedroom. "This is where it looks like the altercation started. Then there's a blood trail," I say as I motion toward the droplets leading from the room.

She nods. "First time we've had blood."

"First time we've found proof that this killer might be taking the victims and holding them before killing them." This is huge for our case. But, it still doesn't answer all the questions. Because this is the first time there's been evidence in a victim's home. This is the first time there was clearly a struggle. So what's changed? Why was this victim different? Did Mariska fight while the others didn't? Did Gavin figure out some way to subdue the others but it didn't work this time? These are the pieces I need to sort out.

"Hey, got a minute?" Lucas asks as he pops his head back in the bedroom.

I follow him out the back door as the forensics team starts to stream into the house. Four of them are suited up, holding cameras, bags of gear, and other instruments. It'll take them at least an hour to catalog the scene, so we need to give them the space.

"What's up?" I ask him as we stroll into the backyard.

"There's a couple drops of blood in the driveway. No signs of oil or any other liquids on the pavement. But the woman who lives to the left, Mrs. Stevenson, she said that she saw a pickup truck pull into the driveway pretty late last night. The headlights lit up her living room, so she got up to check if someone was pulling into her own driveway."

"Did she recognize the vehicle?"

He shakes his head. "No. She said she'd never seen a truck at Mariska's house before."

I try to remember. Does Gavin own a truck? He's got quite a

bit of wealth, so chances are that he owns more than his Hellcat, but I'm not sure that I'd peg him as a pickup truck guy. We'll have to check what vehicles are registered to him.

"Did she see any struggle or hear anything last night?" I ask.

"She said that she thought she heard something not long after the truck pulled up. But she didn't have her hearing aid in, so she doesn't know exactly what it was."

"Approximately what time?" I ask.

"She thinks that it was between 10:30 p.m. and midnight."

"That's helpful," I say as I jot down a few notes about that. Now we need to connect the dots directly to Gavin so we can bring him in on this. I have half a mind to go over to his house right now and ask him about Mariska. She could be in his house right now, being tortured, her hours left ticking to an end. I know that Lucas won't stand by and allow me to do that, so I may have to sneak away at some point today and approach him by myself. I don't care that he tried to lawyer up. There's a time to step back and a time to push forward—and now I can't let Gavin get away with this.

My phone rings and I grab it. Sergeant Dirby's name flashes on the screen and my stomach clenches. This might be the call about Mariska's phone trace.

"Sergeant," I say as I accept the call.

"We already got the details back on the trace for Mariska's phone. Her phone is currently off, but it last pinged at the end of her street at around 1 a.m. It looks like she opened an app, then the phone was immediately turned off."

Unfortunately, once the phone is off, there's no way for us to trace it.

"Can we get a search warrant for Gavin's house? We know he had something to do with this. He has connections to all the victims," I say.

Sergeant Dirby clears his throat. "The Croswells have a lot of connections in the town. They know the judge I asked. Our

request for the warrant was denied because this is all circumstantial."

"But he was out with all of them. He dated all of our
victims." There's an edge to my voice, and I can hear just how
shrill my tone is, even though I try to keep it even.

"Believe me, if I could push this through, I would. But for
now, we need hard evidence to push this forward," he says
before ending the call. I have so much more fight left in me, but
I deflate.

But I won't let Gavin get away with this.

39

HIM

There was something about passion that was contagious. That's what he thought as he wove through the town again. For hours, he'd done this loop, in his beige sedan with out-of-state plates. Camouflaged like this, he looked like a tourist, allowing him to blend in and disappear. He circled back toward the station, his heart racing a little with anticipation. He'd been watching Harlow for what felt like years, though it hadn't really been that long. She was usually too hard to track down after all.

The front door to the station finally cracked open and she walked into the parking lot. His headlights dimmed as he turned into the lot adjoining the station. Her long dark hair spilled across her back, part of it hung over her face, covering the bruises there.

Though Harlow didn't know it, he watched while she was trapped in her Jeep, and woke her when the flames began to tickle the warped metal. He'd disappeared into the forest when she truly awoke, as if he were never there at all.

It was hard to keep this distance, to not creep closer.

Harlow climbed into her rental, pulled out of the station lot.

But her turn surprised him. She wasn't heading in the direction of her motel.

"Harlow, darling, where are you headed?"

40

I'm getting myself worked up, but I know in my bones that Gavin has something to do with this. Years of training and my instincts can't be wrong. I've put in a request for a warrant on Gavin's place—but I'm not holding my breath. I know if I try to bring him in for questioning, Gavin won't talk at the station, and I know if I bring Lucas to speak to Gavin, he's even less likely to talk. But if I went over there—maybe Gavin would talk to me.

An inky sky presses down on Saranac Lake as I bound down the stairs of the motel toward my rental car. I waited to leave until Lucas was distracted, combing over the evidence again, so he won't even notice I've left. I climb in the car, slam the door, and turn the key. It rumbles beneath me, and I press the gas, my actions fully propelled by my frustration and the rage boiling beneath the surface. I need to make some real movement in this case; I can't keep spinning my wheels.

Every minute I do nothing, Mariska's life hangs in the balance. She could be in that house right now, being tortured, dying. If I can stop him, I have to try.

None of the lights are on in Gavin's house when I pull up.

And I wonder if he's out on another date. With another woman. Someone else who he'll eventually kill. I pull in alongside the house, waiting in the street as I watch. In one of the upper windows, a light flickers softly. A TV most likely. So, he is home.

I kill my engine and climb out of the car. My whole body feels rigid, wound tight with rage. At my sides, my fists are clenched as I walk, and I can't seem to unclench them. I don't approach the front door because I know that's where he's got the video doorbell. I can't afford for there to be any obvious evidence that I was here. Whatever is said between us, that's my word against his, unless there's a video. I stalk around the back of the house, and sure enough, there are no cameras and no monitoring devices on the back of the house. He could have easily gone in and out of this door to avoid detection from the video feed.

I knock on the door, hard. And it takes a long time for Gavin to come to the door. When he answers it, he's shirtless, with silk pajama pants hanging off his sharp hip bones. I will give it to Gavin: though he's a narcissistic prick, at least he's got a good body to go along with it. He is chiseled from head to toe. He leans against the doorframe and flashes me a sly grin, as if he's not the least bit surprised to see me here.

"You know, Durant, I knew that you couldn't stay away forever." He points from his chest to me. "This thing between us, this spark, the electricity, I knew that you felt it too." He reaches out, like he's going to brush his hand against my neck, and I take a step back. His gaze sharpens on me. And I wonder if it was smart for me to come here alone.

"Can I come in?" I ask, hoping if I get inside, with his permission, I can look around. If I get through the door, maybe I can find Mariska, or find clues that she was here.

"As tempting as that is... I'm going to have to decline," he says, his smile faltering. He crosses his arms, taking up as much space as possible in the doorway, I guess, so I can't find some way to sneak through.

Anger rises inside me, and I can't stifle it. It has its claws in me, and even if I wanted to control it, I don't think I'd be able to. "Where's Mariska, Gavin?" I ask, an edge to my words.

He raises a brow at that. "How should I know?"

"She was last seen with you. You know this. Stop acting like you don't know." I grind out the words.

"You need to chill."

I take a step toward him. "We found blood in her apartment. I know that you have some kind of connection to this, so tell me what the fuck is going on, Gavin." There's a ferocity to my words that takes me aback, but I hold on to it. That is exactly what I need right now. I need to show him how serious I am.

He sighs. "Come inside for a minute. I need to tell you about something."

I raise a brow to that. I didn't expect him to shift so quickly. But before he can change his mind, I step inside.

"Put on a shirt, please," I say as I follow him through a grand kitchen with sage-green cabinets and marble countertops, then through a sparse modern living room with a large flat-screen and a sleek sofa.

"Why? Is this too distracting? Not sure that you can focus on questioning me about a murder I didn't commit if I'm shirtless?" There's a levity to his voice, so I know he's joking. And he pulls on a shirt anyway.

I ignore his comment and sit on a modern couch that looks completely uncomfortable. The crisp straight lines are nice on the eye, but it feels like sitting on a park bench.

He takes a seat, buttoning the silk shirt, which matches his pajama pants. "I need you to listen to me carefully, because I know you probably won't believe me. But I did not kill Mariska or hurt her in any way. I didn't hurt any of the other victims. But I think I know why they're being hurt," he explains calmly, looking at the coffee table between us, not me.

I raise a brow, not believing a single word he's saying. "And why is that, exactly?"

"I'm being stalked by my ex, Christine Parsons. She and I dated for probably eight months, which I'm sure you've heard is a long stretch for me." He rolls his eyes. "She started pressing me about marriage about six weeks in, and by three months, she never stopped talking about it. It was always, when am I going to get a ring, why don't you want to settle down with me, and so on and so on. She never dropped it, and it really grated on me. So I broke it off with her. I'm not the marrying type, and I make that clear anytime I start dating anyone. Though most of the time it's ignored, no one has ever been quite as intense about it as Christine."

"That doesn't sound like stalking," I say, watching his body language carefully.

He looks back up at me. "I'm getting to that part. We broke up about four months ago, and since then, every time I take anyone out on a date, she's in whatever restaurant we're in. She follows my car; she'll walk down the street behind us. It's always something. She's always lurking in the shadows watching my every move. About a month ago, she threatened me and said that if I didn't take her back, she'd make me pay." He grabs his phone and unlocks it, taps twice on the screen and hands it to me. On the screen I find a thread of text messages. The name saved is Christine.

None of these sluts are anything compared to me. Are you just trying to make me jealous?

I'm sorry, I love you. I just don't understand why you can't see it. What do I have to do? I'll do anything to prove to you that we're meant to be together. I'm the one for you. Why don't you see that?

If you don't get rid of this bitch, I will.

I ran some bitch off the road. She deserved it.

So, it was her. She's the one who hit my Jeep. It goes on and on, pages upon pages of texts that are similar in message and intent. None specifically say that she's going to hurt or kill anyone, but the veiled threats are quite clear.

"So, you think that Christine is kidnapping these women and killing them because you dated them?" I ask. "Why didn't you tell us about this before?"

He nods slowly. "That's all that I can put together. Because I didn't do this." He shakes his head and sighs. "I didn't say anything because Christine has some information about me that I wouldn't want to get out, so I was hesitant to talk about it."

"What kind of information?"

"I really don't want to say."

Frustration needles me. "There's only so much I can do to help if I don't have all the information."

He sighs. "Believe me, I know."

"Gavin, you have a history of domestic violence. You have to understand that doesn't look good for you," I explain.

"Look, I was young and stupid. I have done my best to atone for what I did. I've never hurt any of the other women I've been with since then. I've gone to therapy and anger management. I know when I've reached my limits and when to walk away now. I really do my best. I've tried. I don't want to become like my father, and I'm going to do everything in my power to walk a different path."

I hate to admit it, but his words do seem genuine. This is not a side of Gavin that I even knew existed. He always seemed so filled with bluster and a bit of a sociopath. This person, he's hurting. I can see it in his eyes.

"Can you send me all the texts between you and Christine?" I ask.

He nods.

"Can you walk me down to your garage and show me the cars that you own?" I ask. While I had Matthew run through the database to see what vehicles were registered in Gavin's name, it's always possible he has an unregistered vehicle in his possession. So I need to cover all my bases here. I can't just believe him point-blank on this. For all I know, he could have bought a truck from someone online and never registered it.

"Sure," he says as he motions to a door. "We've got to go downstairs. The basement is the garage," he explains.

I follow him down into the bowels of the house, the weapon at my side feeling heavy as I walk. He flips the switch at the base of the stairs and illuminates a large space filled with cars. The first thing I can tell when I look through the garage is that he's a sports car guy. I don't see any pickup trucks. He's got probably a million dollars' worth of cars down here. Porsches and Ferraris, a Lambo, you name it, it's here. On the far side, there's a Porsche SUV. I'm guessing so he has a way to get around in the snow. None of these sports cars are going to go anywhere in the winter.

"Nice collection," I say.

"You like cars?" he asks.

"I'd never own one of these, but I do appreciate the artistry." And it's the truth; the colors, the lines, the speed, it does appeal to me. But the price tag and the risk are ridiculous.

"Does Christine own a pickup truck?" I ask as we climb the stairs back to the living room.

"No, she drives a Honda. But her brother has an F-150."

"Would she have access to that vehicle if she wanted it?" I ask.

He nods. "She and her brother share a house, so she can definitely use it if she wants to."

I walk toward the back door. I've got to call Lucas and update him on what I've found out from Gavin, and start looking into Christine. But I turn back to Gavin before I reach the door.

"If you're punting this to Christine because you want to pin this on someone else, I will make you suffer," I say.

A sly grin creeps across his face. But he shakes his head rather than fire back a comment. "Look, I'm not trying to make you chase your tails here. But it occurred to me a few days ago that Christine might really be doing this. I didn't think she was capable, not until I got the text that she'd get rid of one of the girls I was seeing. That's when I started to wonder what she was really capable of, and what kind of turn her obsession with me was taking."

"Did you tell anyone at the police station?"

He lets out a humorless laugh, his eyes far off. "Law enforcement does not take it seriously when a man says that he feels threatened by a woman. I could probably show up with a fresh stab wound that she gave me, and the boys in blue would laugh it off and say that I should *man up*."

I hate that he's right. But I know very well it's true. It's rarely taken seriously when men are the victims of domestic abuse, or when they're sexually assaulted. And while Gavin may be a victim when it comes to Christine, my empathy only goes so far, because he himself was an abuser.

"If you see Christine, let me know. I'm going to go talk to my team about how we proceed from here," I say.

He nods. "Thank you for taking me seriously," he says, his voice filled with sincerity.

I say my goodbyes to Gavin and head out the door. Seconds after leaving, I've already pulled up Lucas's contact on my phone, and I'm secretly praying he's not asleep, so he'll answer. He grabs the call on the second ring.

"I was almost asleep, this better be good—"

"Gavin told me that he's being stalked by an ex. He thinks that she might be the one murdering the women that he's gone out with on dates," I explain.

Lucas is silent for a long moment. "Okay, there's a lot to unpack here. You went to Gavin's house by yourself?" he asks, his voice rising with each word.

"Yes, I'm not a child. I know how to question a suspect on my own," I snap reflexively. The way that Lucas is talking to me right now, it's like he's chastising a child. I cannot tolerate being spoken to like that.

"He specifically said that he didn't want to speak to the police again without a lawyer present," he says, an edge to his voice. Technically speaking, Lucas is a lawyer. He passed the bar and considered going into prosecution because law enforcement didn't take it seriously when his mother and grandmother went missing during his childhood. But he ended up keeping his license active and pursuing work with missing persons instead. So, right now, I know I've stuck a needle in the paw of the lawyer side of Lucas. Law enforcement toes the line constantly of what's legally allowable when it comes to tracking down suspects in homicide investigations. I'm not doing anything strictly illegal. I wasn't questioning Lucas. I just wanted to talk to him.

"I wasn't interrogating him. But I wanted to make sure that Mariska wasn't at his house."

"If you had found *anything* there, it wouldn't have been admissible."

"But if she had been alive and on premises, I would have saved her life. I don't care about anything else. I don't care about building a case. I don't care about what can be used in the courtroom. I care about saving a woman who could be dying *right now*," I say, my voice rising as I slam the door of my rental car. My adrenaline is peaking as I start my car, and I fight back the urge to scream at him more. He just cannot understand what this feels like, how much I need to save Mariska. I can't let any more women die on my watch. I have to save her.

"But if she had been alive and on premises," he starts, mocking my tone, "then what? What exactly would you have done by yourself?"

I throw my car into drive, switch the call to Bluetooth, and turn right toward the motel. "Stop talking to me like I am incapable of doing things by myself. I'm not a child, Lucas."

"No one is calling you a child. Jesus Christ, stop throwing that in my face." He huffs.

"You're acting like I'm completely unable to do anything unless you're present. Guess what, I worked homicide just fine before I met you. And you need to have a bit more trust that maybe I know what I'm doing. Gavin wouldn't have said any of the things that he told me today in front of you. Because he thinks that men in law enforcement don't take stalking seriously when the perpetrators are women."

"The fact that you just blindly believe—"

"I'm not blindly believing anything," I snap. "He showed me the threads of text messages on his phone. He didn't have time to create fake message threads. He didn't even know I was going over there. There was no time for him to lay groundwork for this lie." If I had hauled Gavin into the station for questioning and given him days to prepare, then I'd believe that he could have concocted some of this. But based on the situation at hand, that doesn't make sense. "I also checked out the vehicles on his premises. He doesn't own a truck. So it couldn't have been him at Mariska's house unless he borrowed someone's truck. He informed me that Christine has access to a pickup truck whenever she'd like to use it. Her brother owns one," I explain, trying to calm myself down.

"Oh" is all Lucas can manage to say. "Look," he says after a long silence. "I'm sorry, it's just after losing my last partner, and me not trusting Gavin, that seems like a really risky move to me. It's not that I think you're incapable—quite the opposite actually. I really don't want to lose you."

I take a deep breath, letting some of my anger out with it. My death grip on the steering wheel lightens and I turn into the motel parking lot.

"Meet me downstairs," I say, and hang up the phone. I climb out of the rental, slam the door, and lean against it. The cold of the metal bites into my shoulder blades, and I relish the chill.

I watch the stairs, waiting for Lucas, and after a couple minutes he walks down, his hand a little too tight on the railing. His eyes meet mine when his feet crunch against the pavement. He's got on a black motorcycle jacket, though it's not quite cold enough to need one. His slim-fitted distressed jeans are something I only ever see him in outside the office. While we're working, he dresses in nothing but slacks and button-ups, but otherwise he's incredibly stylish.

"Are you going to yell at me in the parking lot now?" he asks as he raises a brow, then looks up to the walkways that overlook the parking lot.

"No, but I think it's easier to finish hashing this out in person, not over the phone." Things escalate in ways they don't need to on the phone. In person, it feels more real, and I know it's harder for me to lose my temper with someone I'm looking at.

He purses his lips, then chews the inside of his cheek. "Look, I'm sorry. I shouldn't have reacted that way. You are fully capable of handling yourself. I just worry. You know that," he explains as he tucks his hands into his pockets.

"I know. And I'm sorry I yelled. But my whole life I've been treated like I'm not capable of anything, especially not by myself. I have this drive inside me to prove everyone wrong."

"I'm not someone who you need to prove wrong, you know, and you don't have to prove anything to me. I already believe in you."

I grind my teeth and let out a guttural sound. "I know. Stop being mushy, that's not why I wanted to talk to you. I want to make sure we're on the same page and that you know I don't hate you."

He rocks back and forth on his heels. "Oh, I know you don't hate me. I'm the best partner you've ever had."

I roll my eyes at him. "Don't press your luck."

"So, you want to look at Gavin's ex for this?" he asks, his tone very skeptical.

"I want to keep an eye on Gavin for it as well, because I still don't trust him. There's something about him that's off. But based on the text messages he showed me from Christine, there are some huge red flags there. She didn't outright threaten the life of anyone in explicit detail, but she got pretty close to saying it. She admitted that she ran my Jeep off the road," I explain. "He's going to send over the text threads between the two of them so that we can go into it in further detail."

"She's that realtor on all the billboards, right?" he asks.

I nod. "Yep, that's the one." I give him a rundown of everything that Gavin said about her. Maybe she thought that Gavin could help her expand her real estate career.

"So what's our move?" he asks.

"Well, if the pickup truck is outside, and she used that to carry bodies, we can check that for blood if it's accessible, right?" I ask, looking for his legal expertise. I know it's legal to dig into garbage or collect anything that's discarded, so we should be able to test the truck bed for blood.

He shakes his head. "No, unless the vehicle has been abandoned, we need a warrant. Otherwise the evidence will be thrown out of court," he says.

"I don't care about court. I care about saving Mariska," I say as I grind my teeth.

"You will care if we find out the killer and we can't prosecute because you fumbled the collection of the evidence. Do you want a killer to walk free because you were impatient?"

"The warrant for Gavin's place was denied. What if the one for Christine's place is denied too?" I fire right back.

"Then we cross that bridge when we come to it. We can't assume it'll be denied. Gavin has a lot of connections in this town. Christine isn't anywhere near as popular. We can't assume she has the same pull."

I hate that he's right.

"Fine, call it in and see if Dirby can get us a warrant, but if we don't have one in twelve hours, I'm collecting the evidence regardless. The clock is ticking, and every moment that we waste, Mariska could be dying," I say.

He nods slowly. "I know, I want to save her too. But we have to do this the right way. Can we say that we think there was blood in the truck bed and it was washed out?"

"The bed has a black liner, so I'm not sure we can say that we saw blood in it. But we could say that it looks like it was recently washed. We need to check it for residue," I explain.

He nods and grabs his phone and calls the sergeant. This, at least, heads us in the right direction.

41

It took two hours to get the warrant approved. Two hours that I paced the station, adrenaline pouring into my veins, wondering if we were too late. After having the warrant for Gavin's denied, I was anxious that this one would fall through as well. I kept questioning if Mariska was already dead. This is the hardest part of the job, doing nothing, waiting while a life hangs in the balance. The truck would tell us everything that we need to know, but the judge gave us a full warrant for the entire property, citing that there could be evidence held inside the home pointing to the disposal of the bodies or the cleanup of blood.

We've rounded everyone up, and unfortunately everyone includes Chad. He's standing outside Christine's house with the rest of the team. She lives in a two-story farmhouse that, according to my sources, has been in her family for no less than a hundred years. Christine is in one of the squad cars, handcuffed; her brother is out of town, so thankfully we didn't have to remove him from the premises. It's always tenuous when two people live in the same home and we have to execute a warrant.

To execute the warrant, we need the forensics team to go in first, to look for any areas of particular concern where there may be blood or other evidence that needs to be collected. So that we lower the chances of contaminating the crime scene, we limit the number of agents who are able to enter the premises. Lucas and I stand outside with the rest of the team.

We wait, anxiously, until Racquel waves Lucas and me over. Her mouth is a grim line, and I spend too much time as I walk over trying to decipher the look on her face. Is it bad, is it good? I don't know her well enough to tell. My stomach is in knots as I approach and a nerve kicks at the base of my neck.

"We found a body in the basement, disfigured like Dr. Pagan believes the other victims were before they were burned. It looks to me like she'd planned to move the body tonight to burn it. She had a tarp laid out. The body was on it."

My heart sinks. "How long ago did she die?" I ask.

"It looks like it's been at least eight hours, possibly up to twelve."

"So she's been keeping her here, alive..." Did she do that with all the victims? Were we misled to believe the first two victims walked on their own to the scene? Maybe she staged it all.

"It's clear that she was being tortured for a while. It's graphic, but her face was disfigured so badly it's nearly impossible to tell her identity. We were only able to identify her because her purse was in the basement. I guess Christine hadn't had a chance to get rid of that piece of evidence yet."

A sick feeling swims in my stomach, and it's like guilt has punched me. We didn't save her. I didn't save her. Maybe if we had worked faster, if I had spoken to Gavin two days ago instead of last night...

Lucas reaches out and squeezes my shoulder, as if he can hear my internal monologue.

"Based on the amount of evidence we need to collect and how the crime scene currently looks, I'd prefer if no one other than the two techs I have in there right now walk the scene.

Once we've collected everything, you're welcome to come in. But considering the evidence collected here will be paramount in a case that locks up a serial killer, I need to be absolutely certain that there's no chance to have this evidence thrown out."

I nod, knowing that we have to do this by the book. We can't risk any of the evidence being tainted. While they're busy cataloging the scene, I head back to the station with Matthew and Lucas. They're moving Christine to the station, and we need to question her.

"We need to question Christine's brother, Jackson," Matthew says.

I raise a brow to that and glance at Lucas, who's in the passenger seat of the rental car.

"Why her brother?" Lucas asks.

"Christine's brother has lived with her for years. If she's really the one behind this, he'll know something about it," he says.

"Call and see if you can get a hold of him," I say.

42

While I drive, Matthew hooks his phone up to the Bluetooth and gets Jackson on the phone. The connection is tinny, echoing in a way that makes me think that Jackson is well out of the range of typical cellphone signals, like he's gone even farther upstate than we are. Though I know he was born and raised in Saranac Lake, his accent sounds slightly southern.

"What is it that you need?" There's an edge to his voice, and I can tell that he doesn't want to talk to us at all. I've got to make this quick and to get as much information out of him as I can.

I introduce myself and Lucas. Jackson already knows Matthew. I'm sure they went to high school together or something in a town of this size. Matthew already let Jackson know that we've got his sister in custody, so now I need to get down to the gritty details. Did he know his sister was killing? If he was in the house, I don't know how she could have hid it with the way she was torturing these women.

"Look, Jackson, I don't want to waste your time. And I hope that you'll show me the same respect. You know the trouble that your sister is likely in, so we need to know what you know," I explain.

"Could I be in trouble here?" he asks before he clears his throat.

"That would really depend," I say, carefully. I know how to play this. What promises I can and can't make. There's an easy path to lead him down to get these answers. I need to make sure that he follows me. "If you're honest about what you know, and it lines up with the evidence that we've collected, I'll make sure that we cut you a plea deal when it comes time to testify."

"Wait, I'm going to have to testify against my sister?"

"Very likely, yes. She committed murders in the home you shared. Chances are, you knew something about it. If you did and you didn't go to the police, that means we could charge you as an accessory to murder. But I know you don't want to get into any trouble here. So if you can tell us what you know, that'll help us clear all this up so you don't get into any trouble," I explain. Lucas eyes me, his gaze a warning that I need to tread carefully.

"Look, I didn't help her," he says, his words louder than they need to be. I can almost hear the panic.

"That may be, but she used your truck. You have to see how that looks to us..."

"She asked to borrow it, but I didn't know what for. I assumed it was for some real estate shit. She borrows it to stage houses all the time." The more he speaks, the higher and higher his octave goes. Full-on panic.

I note that down. Every single thing he says to us, I plan to keep it on record. Just in case he changes his story later—which I anticipate he will. Especially after he speaks to his sister.

"When did you leave town?" I ask.

"A few weeks ago," he says.

"Why did you decide to leave? It seems like you have a pretty good setup here." By all accounts, his sister pays all the bills, lets him live rent-free in a very nice house.

"Christine has gotten—strange since she and Gavin split up.

To say she's become obsessive would be an understatement. She stopped working so much because she was tracking his every move. She was using her connections in real estate and within the government to track what he was doing financially, his business. She'd follow him during dates. It was getting out of hand. I tried talking to her about it."

"And how did she react to that?" I ask, listening intently. The tension is thick in the car. I can practically feel how badly Lucas and Matthew also want these answers.

"Not well. She screamed at me. She said I didn't ever want to see her happy. I told her how ridiculous that was... And then she kidnapped Ellie. She had her in the basement for weeks. But I left. I didn't want to be involved. I thought about calling, I really did. I should have. But Christine is my sister, you know?" The panic starts to fade from his voice, the edge replaced by sadness. I can hear the regret hanging heavy on his words.

"So, you didn't know that Christine was torturing and murdering women, then?" I ask, the question probably a bit more blunt than it needs to be.

"I was afraid she would snap at some point. I was afraid she'd go after Gavin. But no, I didn't know she'd gone that far. I'd like to think if I did, that I would have called the police. But Christine held my life hostage. She didn't want me to leave. She made sure I couldn't get a good job in this town. There was nothing I could do."

"Then how did you leave?"

"I called our other brother, Steven, and begged for him to let me come stay with him. I promise, I didn't tell him about the situation. I just told him I needed out for a little while. He bought me a bus ticket, and I got out in the middle of the night, walked to the station."

"So, you're where now?" I ask, making note of Steven's name on my notepad.

"I'm in Vermont."

"And will you be remaining in Vermont?" I ask. If we decide to charge him, I'll need to know what office to coordinate with. At the very least, he'll have to come here for the trial.

"Yes, for the foreseeable future. It's not like I can go back to that house after what she did. How many women did she kill?"

"Four who we know of," I explain.

"I'm so sorry, Detective, if I had known, I—" His voice dies, along with any promise. We both know that he's not being honest. So at least he stopped himself.

When we finally pull back into the station, I've finished up my call with Jackson. I know that we'll probably have to bring him in, to question him more, but for now, we've got what we need. Lucas and I head into the station and carve our way through the back to the holding cells. In a small room next to the cells, they've got Christine waiting for us. As I open the door, her wild eyes survey me. This bitch tried to kill me.

She's cuffed to the table, still in an oversized sweatshirt and leggings. Her bleached-blonde hair is as wild as her eyes, her dark roots prominent. Bags hang heavy under her eyes, like she hasn't slept in weeks.

"That looks like it hurts," she says as she motions toward the side of her face. She's pointing out my bruise, the gash that she created.

"Yeah, I guess I have you to thank for that."

A cruel smile splits her overly filled lips. They puff out, and I know that she probably visits a plastic surgeon to get them plumped up at least twice a month. She looks like a fish. "My intention wasn't to hurt you."

"Yeah, it was to kill me," I say. She doesn't have to finish the thought. I know exactly what her game plan was.

"Oh, come on, Detective. I wasn't trying to *kill* you," she says in a way that's too playful for an interrogation room.

"Look, Christine," I say as I take a seat at the metal table across from her. She plays with her cuffs, and the jingle of metal fills the room.

Lucas sits down beside me, glancing between Christine and me. "We need you to tell us what happened," Lucas says, finishing my sentence.

She shrugs. "Nothing happened."

"Really? With all that blood in your house. The shoes that match the same dirt as the logging road—" I add in a little white lie about the dirt. I'm sure it'll match, but we don't have the data back quite yet. "You killed them, drove them out there in the pickup truck, rolled them out onto the ground, and then made it look like they walked willingly, didn't you?" That's what I've pieced together in my mind. At first, I wasn't sure how she got the bodies into the truck in the first place, but we found a wheelbarrow with blood on it. She must have used that to transport them.

She smiles again. "I want a lawyer. I've got nothing else to say," she says simply.

43

The wound on my head throbs. But I don't have the time or the motivation to get it checked out. So, I ignore it, like I always do. Living with the static hum of pain in the background is just par for the course. My motel room is silent around me, the calm after the storm I suppose. Tension still tightens my muscles, as if my body is waiting for something more.

On my nightstand, my phone vibrates. A text notification from my mother waits on the screen. She must have heard about Christine's arrest, so now I have to hold up my end of the bargain. I sigh, debating if I should answer it or not.

Finally, I scoop up the phone, and when it vibrates again against my fingers, I unlock the screen.

Three texts wait for me, sent one after another.

A pin drop with a location.

A picture of a tree, a half wall made from rocks, boulders circling it, the roots tangled in the wall.

And one word.

Help.

My heart pounds as I look at the message. Is she fucking with me? Trying desperately to get my attention? I'm not sure this is the route she'd decide to go. Why would she do this now? I call her, caging the phone between my shoulder and ear as I pull on my boots. The call goes straight to voicemail. I stare at the screen, debating if I should call Lucas or the sergeant. But if this is some stunt by my mother, God, that'd be embarrassing. I can't involve them in this.

I shove my phone in my pocket, grab my service weapon and leather jacket before bounding down the stairs. Night crowds around me as I jog to my rental. The streetlights seem dimmer, the clouds lower. The air is heavy with fog and moisture. Cold seeps into my thighs as I slide into the car. I press the start button, throw the car in gear, and follow the GPS to my mother's dropped pin.

An asphalt road curves through town, giving way as it's swallowed by a rocky dirt path. Trees thicken on either side of me, and my stomach flip-flops. I don't know whether to be pissed at my mother or worried. I still don't know if I trust her or if this is all some kind of stunt.

I turn off the main logging road when the route to the pin veers into the trees. Though I don't want to get out of the SUV, it's my only path forward.

The cool night air tousles my hair and rustles the foliage around me. When the breeze dies down, the shrill cries of crickets rise and the low croaks of frogs add to the symphony of the night. My stomach is in my throat as I search the trees for signs of my mother. I'm tempted to call out, to make it easier to find her. But on the off chance... if something really did happen to her... My training and my distrust with my mother are at war right now. My father would have a field day with this. Too bad he isn't here.

A sound, the snap of branches, draws my attention. I grab my phone, check the pin, and palm my service weapon. My pulse kicks against the grip as I hold it a little too tight. I creep forward quietly, toward the noise. Shadowed trunks stretch forward in front of me. They're huddled, the branches weaving together into a canopy above me. The limbs coiling together blot out the little moonlight I'd expect to see.

I continue forward, and the scene starts to look familiar. A half wall of boulders rings a tree in front of me. Then my mind sparks with recognition. The picture my mother sent me.

A scream cuts the night, followed by a wet thud. My heart skips and I force myself forward, toward the noise. A thousand questions clot my mind. There are too many variables, possibilities. Instead of focusing on them, I let my training take over, and force myself forward, over the rock wall.

On the other side, there's a drop-off, a tangle of tree roots. Then movement catches my eye. In the darkness, it takes several moments for me to make sense of it. A body on the ground. Someone standing over them, stabbing the body.

My mind screams. The McKenzie Mauler. Is it my mother? Is she the killer?

I run toward the attacker as I raise my gun.

"Stop!" I shout to the attacker, proud that my voice holds power, not the fear that I'm feeling.

The attacker stands up straight, their hand falling to their side. A blade, with blood dripping from the tip. The attacker turns, glances at me, then turns their attention back to the body.

As they raise the knife again, I know I have no choice. I raise my gun, press my finger to the trigger, and squeeze.

The bullet cuts through the night, but he doesn't fall. I fire another, then another, until finally he collapses. I pull out my phone, call for a bus, notify my team, as I'm seeing the attacker. Next, my attention turns to the victim, their wounds.

My mother.

I stare at the gaping wounds longer than I should. Shock grips me and slows my movements. My thoughts feel so far.

Like none of this real. Because it can't be, can it? So many times, I hate to admit it, but I prayed for this. I wished she would die.

But now, her wounded body is crumpled in front of me as she bleeds on the forest floor. Somehow, it all feels different. I press my hand to the wound in her chest, trying to stanch the bleeding.

"You're going to be okay." I force the words out, trying to separate myself from my emotions. I try to imagine what I'd say to someone else. A victim.

"I deserve this," she says, a dry laugh slipping out with her words. I want to agree with her. But I can't. Because what if this is the last chance to unburden my soul with everything she did to me? I bite back all the words I want to say because I know now isn't the time.

Sirens rise in the distance and my phone rings. They need to know how to get to us. I explain our location and set my phone down again. I've got to apply proper pressure to my mother's wounds.

"Harlow, I'm so sorry," she says, before letting out a rattling cough. Blood blooms on her lips and I know this isn't good. "If I don't make it…"

"Just stop talking, save your strength."

"You're the best thing your father and I did," she says before another cough wracks her body. "We failed you."

Lights and bodies swarm the clearing. All at once, the scene somehow slows and speeds up at the same time. Lucas detains the attacker, a man in his fifties who I didn't really recognize. My mother is loaded up, then they cart him off to be treated for his wounds.

When they put her on the stretcher, her heart stops, and part of me knows that my chance to move on died with her.

44

Afternoon light streams in through the windows of my motel. I spent most of the night in the hospital watching my mother. They were able to revive my mother and stabilize her. So early this morning, I came back here. Unsure what to do, where to be.

In this lighting, the orange carpet almost glows. There's a lightness now that we have our killer, now that Christine has been arrested. As I'm packing my bags back at the motel, my cellphone rings. I glance at the screen, surprised to see Chad's number on the screen. My pulse quickens and I debate whether or not to pick it up. Why the hell is *he* of all people calling me? Unfortunately my curiosity gets the best of me and I accept the call. I bet he's pissed I got his killer.

"Yes?" I ask as I throw the call on speaker so I can continue to pack.

"Durant?"

"Did you think you were calling Burger King?" I snap at him, though it's probably not necessary. I don't feel bad.

"You think you're so—" He stops himself and clears his throat. "This isn't a social call. And I'm not going to be the punching bag for your sarcasm."

"Why? Can't handle it?"

"I need you at the station," he says.

"Why, exactly? We already got everything we need from Christine," I explain.

"The McKenzie Mauler is still in surgery. We can't talk to him yet. And our main witness won't talk to us. He'll only talk to you," he says, frustration dripping on his words.

"Who's your witness?" I drop the shirt I'm folding. Why would anyone in this town insist on me questioning them? No one here even knows me. I'm still not certain of the identity of the guy we brought in. To be honest, I was too wrapped up with my mother.

"Gavin Croswell."

"What?" I'm completely thrown off guard.

"Just get to the station and I'll explain everything," he says.

I hate taking orders, especially from a douche like Chad. But I need to know why exactly Gavin asked for me, and how he's connected to the killings in McKenzie. Were my instincts right? Was he killing someone, but it wasn't the victims I thought? I grab a cup of coffee on my way to the station, and pull into the lot. When I reach the third floor, Chad is waiting impatiently, his arms crossed, leaning against a desk.

"Had time to stop for coffee?" he asks, glaring at my cup.

"Eat my dick, Chad."

A vein bulges at the side of his forehead and his fists clench at his sides. I know he'd love to punch me, but he can't, not with the rest of the team here watching our interaction.

"We need to call a truce, at least for a little while," he says.

I cross my arms. "Fine, if you can stop being a jerk."

"Anyway"—he practically growls the word—"we brought in Gavin because we've arrested his father. We have evidence that he was killing in McKenzie, but we need his son to verify some of the details that we have. We pulled Gavin in, and he said that he wouldn't talk to anyone but you."

"Is Gavin under arrest?" I ask.

"For now, we don't think he had any direct knowledge of the killings, but we're not sure."

"If he did know, do you intend to charge him with accessory?"

He shakes his head. "We'll cut him a deal if he talks. We need to get this wrapped up, so as long as he wasn't hands-on with any of the murders, he can walk."

"Even if he, I don't know, disposed of a body?" I offer it up because it's a very real possibility. There have been father-son teams before in serial killing.

"Yes, if it comes to that. Will you talk to him?" he asks.

"He didn't ask for a lawyer?"

"No, he asked for you."

"In a room with no two-way mirror and no recording devices, yes," I say. I want to be sure that I can talk to Gavin unfiltered. If his father was killing, if he *knew* his father was killing, that puts him in a unique situation—one very similar to mine.

"Are you serious?" He balks.

I nod. "Dead serious. I'm not interrogating him for you. I'll talk to him, get information out of him, if you like. But I won't be monitored while doing so," I explain.

"Were you fucking him?" he asks as he raises a brow.

I lunge at Chad, but another officer grabs me and holds me back. I shake off the grip, and glare at Officer Moody before turning my attention back to Chad. "If you ever disrespect me like that again, it'll be the last thing you ever do." Heat rises to my cheeks, and I try to tamp it down. But I can't believe the fucking audacity he has.

It takes a few minutes for Chad to move Gavin to a private room, during which time he huffs and complains. But I won't give in. Based on his behavior, I'm sure Chad makes many people bend to his will, but I'm not that kind of person. He will not win. Once Gavin is situated in a room, I grab a bottle of water for him and stroll in. I place the water on the table, and take a seat before taking a slow sip of my coffee.

I raise a brow as I look at him, but I say nothing.

"Why did you have them move me?" he asks.

"So that I know our conversation will be private," I say simply, raising one shoulder to shrug.

"Why do you care if our conversation is private?"

"Because there are things that I may say to you that I will not say in front of the rest of the team, because it's none of their business."

He leans forward in his chair. His usual façade is gone, all of his swagger, the narcissistic air. There's something about being held by the police that deflates you. I've seen it happen time and time again.

"Why exact—"

I shake my head. "Why are you here, Gavin?"

He leans back and sighs. He looks down at the table, his face grim, pale. "Because they arrested my dad and... They think that I know something about his murders," he says.

"And do you?"

He crosses his arms and leans farther back in his chair, making it rock slightly. "I'm not entirely sure how to answer that, because what I say could land me in jail."

"Well, if you weren't involved in the killings directly, then it sounds like they're going to give you immunity to testify." I try to keep my words vague. I don't want to promise him immunity for him to then find out that his involvement disqualifies him. I sigh and wait for his gaze to meet my eyes. "Look, I'm sure you've probably heard in the media, but I have some experience with this myself."

He nods slowly. "What did you do?" he asks.

"For a long time, I kept quiet. Because I didn't want to lose my dad. I knew what it would do to my family if he went away.

And I couldn't lose him. But I was also twelve years old when I found out. If I were an adult when I found out, things would have been different."

"What would you have done differently?" he asks as he raises a brow.

"I would have told someone the first time I saw him kill someone," I say simply. If I were talking to anyone else, I'd never say this aloud. I've never told anyone that I witnessed my father kill. In fact, I said the opposite. I told everyone that I had no idea that he'd done it. If I admitted to anyone that I saw my father kill, my life would be over—well, more so than it already is.

"You saw—"

"Yes. I did. I watched through the window. He strangled a woman in front of me." I don't tell him about the next time. I don't say that it was just the first time. Because then it sounds so much worse, then I teeter on the edge of becoming a villain. There must be something wrong with me that I let it keep happening, that I saw it with my own eyes and did nothing.

"I'm sorry," he says. And I hate the pity. That's not what I want. That's not why I'm here.

"So tell me, Gavin. What do you know and when did you know it? If you're anything like me, you need to unburden your soul. You'll feel better once you say it out loud." I'm absolutely bullshitting. He won't feel better. Saying the words aloud actually makes it feel more real. You really understand what you did, what you allowed to happen.

"My father killed a woman when I was in my twenties, that I know of," he says, his eyes on the table. "Recently, he started burning the bodies in the forest, rather than dumping them into the river. I'm not sure why it changed. I didn't ask. When I found out, I threatened to go to the police. But he said it was a one-time thing. He had a good reason for it: the woman he killed had threatened my mother's life—or so he claimed. I was able to rationalize it. Because I loved my mother, of course I wanted her to be protected. My dad made me feel like, by letting it slide, by not telling anyone, I was being a good son." He lets out a humorless laugh, and looks at me with pain in his eyes.

"I should have said something, and it's eaten at me since then that I didn't do anything. That I didn't say a word to anyone. I took on this persona. I became an asshole so that no one would dig too far. That's what broke Lucy and me up. She thought that I'd hurt her, that I'd attacked her in the middle of the night, but I think it was my father. I think he attacked her and she thought it was me. She'd been taking sleeping pills. I'd fallen asleep on the couch. I took the hit on my record. I let her go. I did it all to cover for him."

I don't buy any of it. Lucy told us about all the emotional manipulation, the time Gavin nearly broke her finger. It couldn't have all been Gavin's father. "You let him get away with attacking your girlfriend?"

"She was about to be my fiancée, actually. I wanted to marry her. I loved her more than I've loved anyone in my entire life. But I chose my father over her. He convinced me that he was sleepwalking, that he had a night terror and must have attacked her in his sleep. I was too dumb, too young, to really look into the story more. Because I didn't want it to be true. I didn't want to think that my father could attack a woman I loved."

"Gavin," I say, false empathy tethered to my words. He wants to get an emotional response out of me, so I'll give him one, if it gets us the info that we need.

"I should have done something. I should have told someone what I knew. But I've paid for it." There are tears in his eyes now, threatening to spill down his cheeks.

"Are you willing to testify against your father? To tell the court what he's done?" I ask.

He nods. "It will help me atone, right? It'll help me move on from this. To show that this isn't the person that I really am."

"It's a good start," I say.

"I have text messages from my father where he admitted in text that he killed the women."

"I'll need you to send those to me. And we may need your help getting your father to detail all of the victims. From what I understand, he's not being incredibly cooperative," I say.

"I'll do what I can, but I've never had much pull with my father. He doesn't respect me, he doesn't think that I'm a man. But I will try," he says, warning hanging on his words.

"Do you know the identities of any of the victims?" I ask.

"Two of them. Most of the women he got from out of town, from what I understand."

That makes sense, because there hasn't been a huge number of missing persons reports filed in Saranac Lake.

"Where do I go from here?" he asks, his face falling as he looks at me. "How do I make this right?"

"There are some things you can never make right. But you have to fight, to find your path forward, to find some way to feel whole again."

"Do you feel whole again?" he asks me.

I shake my head. "No, I'm a lost cause. Nothing I do will ever make me feel whole again, because I was there. I watched death firsthand. There's no coming back from that. The look on that woman's face as she died, it's burned into my memory and I will see it every day for the rest of my life." There's an honesty I don't expect to my words. But there's nothing I can do about it. They flow out of me unbidden.

"You're not a lost cause," he says, and he reaches across the table like he wants to hold my hand. But I shake my head at it. I'm not here for comfort. I'm just telling him the truth. I hate the offer of sympathy.

"Is there anything else? I need to get back to Monroe," I say.

"You're leaving town?" he asks, his brow furrowing.

"Yep, I was only here for my case. Now that it's over, I'll be heading out, unless I need to come back for the trial. But that's unlikely," I explain.

"Can I call you?"

I raise a brow at that.

"Not for like, dating or anything. But if I need to talk."

"You can email me," I say. Because I need to have boundaries. The last thing I want is Gavin calling me to talk about our serial killer fathers. It's like we could start some kind of support group.

I finish up with Gavin and turn him back over to Chad. I leave the station without another word, and I slip back into the world. For now, I'm leaving Saranac Lake behind me, the case, the deaths—the women I couldn't save. I'll put their souls to rest, hoping that they know that I'll keep fighting. I'll keep searching, and I will not rest as long as there are killers like my father still out there.

I grab my cellphone and step outside as I call Sergeant Dirby. For a few minutes, I update him on the cases, the McKenzie Mauler, Christine. He's silent for a long time. Honestly, I'm surprised no one else called him already.

"How's everything with the Green investigation?" I ask, my nerves gnawing at the pit of my stomach. I figure if they'd tied it to me, they would have brought me in for this already, but I need to know for sure.

He clears his throat. "We're still not sure who we caught on the security footage, but the investigation is still open. I've got to run. Update me if anything else comes up. But start packing and get back to Monroe."

"Yes, sir," I say, looking forward to putting this town and the carnage here behind me.

45

I got the worst news this morning. After the accident, my Jeep can't be saved. I shouldn't be surprised—it was consumed by fire and hit a tree—but still, we went through a lot together. I stalk a used-car lot in a small town halfway between Saranac Lake and Monroe. The afternoon sun warms my shoulders as I walk between the options. None of these Jeeps have the same feel, the soul that mine had. All our years together, I want to cling to those memories. I don't want to move on. But all good things must come to an end, I guess. Maybe it's time for a new chapter.

A shiny teal model is what finally forces me to make a decision. In a few hours, I've got the keys. As I drive off the lot, trying to get the feel for my new baby, my cellphone rings. It takes me a bit too long to figure out the Bluetooth, but finally, Lucas's voice filters through the speakers.

"All done?" he asks, a weird lilt to his words. Something's up, I can hear it.

"Yeah, finally. It's criminal how long it takes to buy a car," I say as I turn left on the road toward Monroe. "Headed home?" I ask. We were going to ride together, but I didn't want him to sacrifice his afternoon too.

"Not sure yet. I just got a call..." He trails off, and I wait for him to continue. But he doesn't.

"Why?" I try to coax the answer out of him.

He sighs, as if he's trying to be dramatic. "They found another body in McKenzie Wilderness this morning right after you left."

My mind turns the information over, the possibilities. What does that mean? That there was an old body there? Or did we bring in the wrong guy... or was there someone else? What did we miss?

"Harlow, Chad's dead. They found his body in the same clearing where your mother was attacked."

46

NINETEEN YEARS AGO

My father's cold hands are clamped over my eyes. A soft blindfold is tethered over my eyes, beneath his callused fingers. My heart has crept into my throat, and it pounds there, like a warning drum. What is it trying to tell me? A bad feeling has bloomed inside me all day, and I know that something is coming. My mom is out of town, visiting my grandma in Arizona. They think she's only got a few months to live, so my mom may stay with her until she passes. I know I should feel sad, but I barely know her. I've probably spent an hour of my life with the woman.

"Are you ready?" my dad asks, his fingers wriggling against my eyes.

"Ready for what?" I ask uneasily.

"Oh, you'll see. Step down," he urges me. And my body stiffens.

The basement. We must be walking into the basement. The musty smell of mold and earth hits my nostrils and anxiety tightens around my chest. I hate the basement. I can't spend more than two minutes down here without feeling like my skin is crawling. My breath catches in my throat and sticks there, threatening to strangle me. It's like all the musty air has gone out of the room. Sweat traces a path down my spine, propelled by fear.

"Please." I manage to croak the word out, but the rest of my words are lodged in my windpipe. I just want out of here. I need out of here.

Instead of releasing me, his hands tighten on my shoulders. They feel like claws, digging into my flesh, trapping me. Panic coils up my legs and my knees tremble. Why is he doing this?

My feet hit the floor, the dirt and rocks crunching under my feet. The sharp edges of the rocks dig into my bare soles; somehow, the pain comforts me, because it's the one thing I know is real. A sound, like the low moaning of a trapped animal, filters around me. But I can't place the source of the noise. I exist in this limbo of darkness, of panic, until finally he releases me. The blindfold slips off my face, and I wince against the light. On either side of the basement, single light bulbs dangle from the ceiling, swaying slightly, casting shifting shadows over the dirt floor.

In front of me, shapes take form, and my body goes rigid. A woman with greasy blonde hair is tied to an old chair. The paint is peeling, flecks of it littering the ground around the woman. Gashes in the dirt around her mark her movements. She's tried to move the chair, to escape. But my father has her tied to the chair, and the chair chained to a pillar in the center of the basement. My mouth goes bone dry as it all clicks into place in my mind.

My father's hot breath mists against my ear as he leans down. "You're going to save her, Harley."

A LETTER FROM DEA

Thank you so much for reading *The Girls in the Fire*. I hope that you enjoyed the second book in the series. There's much more coming for Harlow and Lucas, so I hope you'll continue to read the series!

If you did enjoy it and want to keep up to date with all my latest releases, just sign up at the following link. Your email address will never be shared and you can unsubscribe at any time.

www.bookouture.com/dea-poirier

This second book in Harlow's story was so much easier for me to write than the first book, and I cannot wait to tell more of her story in the books to come! Not only is there danger ahead for Harlow and Lucas... but there are many more secrets waiting to be revealed.

If you loved the characters in this story, please consider leaving a review. If you have a few minutes to drop a short review on Amazon, it would be very much appreciated.

Thank you for reading.
Dea Poirier

HEAR MORE FROM DEA

dhpoirier.com

 facebook.com/dhpoirier
twitter.com/DeaPoirierBooks

ACKNOWLEDGMENTS

I am so thankful for my incredible editor, Laura Deacon, and my incredible support team at Bookouture (thank you all so much for everything!), and my wonderful agent Jill Marsal.

To my critique partner, and the best friend, Elesha Halbert-Teskey, as always, I appreciate all the support, advice, and your ability to help me shape a first draft into something that isn't a dumpster fire. You're the best <3.

To my readers, thank you so much for joining me for another book. Your support, kind words, and reviews are wonderful. I appreciate every one of you.

To my family—thank you for everything. Kiss noise.

CPSIA information can be obtained
at www.ICGtesting.com
Printed in the USA
LVHW031028120322
713168LV00001B/149